DAUGHTERS OF THE PRIMALS

DAUGHTERS OF THE PRIMALS

THE PROGENY WARS™ BOOK 4

G.Z. RODRIGUEZ
D.J. VARGAS

DISRUPTIVE IMAGINATION

This book is a work of fiction. All of the characters, organizations, and events portrayed in this novel are either products of the author's imagination or are used fictitiously. Sometimes both.

Copyright © G.Z. Rodriguez and D.J. Vargas
Cover by Mihaela Voicu http://www.mihaelavoicu.com/
Cover copyright © LMBPN Publishing

LMBPN Publishing supports the right to free expression and the value of copyright. The purpose of copyright is to encourage writers and artists to produce the creative works that enrich our culture.

The distribution of this book without permission is a theft of the author's intellectual property. If you would like permission to use material from the book (other than for review purposes), please contact support@lmbpn.com. Thank you for your support of the author's rights.

LMBPN Publishing
PMB 196, 2540 South Maryland Pkwy
Las Vegas, NV 89109

Version 1.00, October 2022
ebook ISBN: 979-8-88541-301-5
Print ISBN: 979-8-88541-941-3

THE DAUGHTERS OF THE PRIMALS TEAM

Thanks to our Beta Readers
Kelly O'Donnell, David Laughlin, Mary Morris, Rachel Beckford

Thanks to our JIT Readers

Dorothy Lloyd
Diane L. Smith
Jackey Hankard-Brodie
Jan Hunnicutt

Editor
SkyFyre Editing Team

GLOSSARY

Factions

Watchers—A group of Angels who took pity on mankind. Diabolos took advantage of their vulnerability and deceived them. Thus, they abandoned their heavenly abode and were the first to cohabit with the women of Earth.

The Fallen—The first group of Angels who committed treason against the Sovereign One and were cast out of the Heavenly Realms along with Diablos.

Daimons—Collectively Demons and Watchers, set to undo the Sovereign One's ways and establish a New World Order. Daimons cohabited with the women of Earth who gave birth to hybrid children.

Hybrids—A Daimon offspring, male or female, typically not associated with Daughters of the Watchers or Nephilim.

Daughters of the Watchers—AKA DoW, A global group of female hybrids with special gifts destined to stop Nephilim and their Daimon fathers in their conquest. The Five Pillars of the Daughters of the Watchers are Emissary, Seers, Scouts, Guardians, and Influencers.

Nephilim—Sealed male hybrids with supernatural abilities and indestructible bodies set to do their Daimon fathers' bidding. Nephilim are made up of seven types: Principalites, Warlockites, Anomalites, Maladities, Elementalites, Temptationites, and Nephilites.

Star of Nimrod—An organized faction, all humans, set to rid the Earth of all hybrids.

Tektonites—A religious organization made of humans and hybrids that follow the way of the Tekton. They dedicate their time and effort to help all those in need.

The Furies—A group of female hybrids who branched off the traditional ways of the DoW. They hunt and kill all male hybrids, sealed and not sealed.

Sons of the Lords—Six of the elite Nephilim, all Principalites, under the leadership of Therion. Their names are Therion, Leon, Aetos, Aner, Pytho, and Katastrofi.

Angels—Celestial beings still serving the ways of the Sovereign One.

Primals—Superior types of Angels.

Priests & Priestesses—A group of humans that work for the order of the Daimons.

Characters

Female Hybrids
    Angelica Gabriella Santos—AKA Angel and the Daimon

Killer, a female hybrid part of the DoW Tristate Area. She is part of the scout team and has the gift of service.

<u>Latisha Brown</u>—AKA Pretzel, one of Angel's closest friends and also part of the DoW Tristate Area. She is one of the team leaders of the scouts and has the gifts of comfort and understanding and interpreting other languages.

<u>Chrissy Davis-Navarro</u>—AKA Reina, one of Angel's best friends and also part of the DoW Tristate Area. She is part of the scout team and has the gift of comfort.

<u>Abigail Chen Sun</u>—AKA Tassel, one of Angel's best friends and also part of the DoW Tristate Area. She is part of the seers and has the gift to predict the future.

<u>Jessie Johnson</u>—AKA Kitty, one of Angel's best friends and also part of the DoW Tristate Area. She is part of the scout team and has the gift of discernment.

<u>Caroline Boswell</u>—AKA Gypsy, second in command of the Tristate group. She is part of the emissaries and guardians and also one of the Tristate's twelve council members. She has the gift of leadership and is also one of the team's best fighters.

<u>Amelia Isabella Evans</u>—AKA Joan, team leader of the DoW Tristate Area. She is an emissary and a member of Tristate council. She has the gift of leadership.

<u>Charlotte Hannah Adams</u>—AKA Mist, team leader of the Lancaster group. Mist is an emissary with the gifts of leadership and comfort.

<u>Briana and Erika Patel</u>—AKA Cookie and Dough (twin sisters), Second commanders of the Lancaster DoW and friends of Angel's. They have the gift of service, which includes supernatural strength.

Grayson Aiden Thomas—AKA Mrs. Mozart, the curator of the Tristate Area and part of the influencers group. She has the gift of wisdom and understanding and is a member of the council.

Ruth Williamson—AKA Grace, chief of the Tristate DoW and one of the group's influencers. She has the gift of love and is a member of the council.

Dr. Jane Lillian Russo—AKA May, the caretaker of the Tristate DoW and one of the team's guardians. She has the gift of healing and is a member of the council.

Jewels—AKA Villainous, she was once the second in command of the Lancaster DoW until she betrayed the group and became known as Villainous. Real name, Laurie Marilyn Davidson.

Penny Stockton—AKA Erinys, is the leader of the Furies.

Athena—leader of the DoW London.

Cherry—second in command and curator of the DoW London.

Nyala—part of the DoW London team and assistant curator. She has the gift of understanding languages.

Crimson—AKA Candle. A member of the Furies and one of Erinys' closest confidants. She is a member of the council.

Crystal—the lead warrior coordinator for the DoW Tristate group.

Olivia—young hybrid and part of the DoW Tristate group.

Sparkles—part of the DoW Tristate group. She runs a company with Reina.

Libitinia Smierc—AKA Libby. The daughter of Mara and of El-Samar Seper. She is Therion's twin sister.

Sefani—a former fighter in the Mesopotamian Games, rescued by the DoW. She, along with Margaret and Leo, is working to end the games worldwide and find her siblings.

Horizon—once a member of the DoW Tristate, leader of the scouts, and one of the council members. She is now a member of the Furies.

Glory & Robin—former members of the DoW and part of the leadership council. Now members of the Furies.

Male Hybrids

Alexander Thomas Miller—AKA Therion and the Son of Destruction, was a Principalite and the son of Diablos. He was also the leader of the Sons of the Lords. His power was to induce fear.

D'Angelo Lewis—part of the Tektonites. He is a friend of the DoW Tristate group.

Pytho—Principalite and the son of Legion. He's a member of the Sons of the Lords and has the power of mind control.

Katastrofi—Principalite and the son of Hades. He's a member of the Sons of the Lords and has the power of Telekinesis.

Leo Archie—the son of Apollyon and also Angel's young brother.

Aner—Principalite and the son of Gadreel the Watcher. He's a member of the Sons of the Lords and has supernatural intelligence.

Leon—Principalite and the son of Arakiel the Watcher.

He's a member of the Sons of the Lords and has lion-like features and abilities.

Aetos—Principalite and the son of Semyaza the Watcher. He has bird-like features and abilities, including flight.

Peccable—Maladitie who worked for Apollyon and Diablos. He was responsible for Eva Santos' death.

Humans

Margaret Boswell—Gypsy's twin sister, once part of the Star of Nimrod. She is the daughter of Grand Luminary Tammuz.

Lash Boswell—AKA Grand Luminary Tammuz, the leader of the Star of Nimrod.

Maria Santos—Angel's grandmother (*abuela* in Spanish).

Eva Santos—Angel's biological mother.

Daniel Javier Ortega—former FBI agent and one of the few Tristate DoW's closest confidants.

Awilda Ortega—Agent Ortega's wife and leader of the Tektonite group located in New York City.

Theresa—priestess of the Daimons. She is also the biological mother of Therion and Libitinia.

Dr. Patrick Ostero—AKA Luminary Masmasu, a scientist who worked for the Star of Nimrod.

Mia and Timothy—siblings and members of the Tektonites.

Adrian—a geeky guy and conspiracy nut who uses mythological goddesses' names as pick-up lines.

Enoch—Prophet who cast the first judgment on the Watchers and their offspring.

. . .

Celestial Beings

Sovereign One—the Supreme Being, the creator of the Heavens and the Earth.

Carpenter's Son—AKA the Tekton, is the eternal son of the Sovereign One through whom all things were created.

El-Samar Seper—AKA Diablos & Mr. Sam'mael. The King of the Daimons and the Lord of the Watchers.

Apollyon—AKA Leonard Archie, was one of Diablos' three top generals and the Lord of North and South America. He was Angel's father.

Legion—one of Diablos' generals and the Lord of Europe and Africa.

Hades—one of Diablos' generals and the Lord of Asia, Australia, and Antarctica.

Mara—the Angel of Death and the mother of Libitinia. She is one of the Primals.

Haniel—a celestial being, the Primal of Balance.

Gabriel—a celestial being, the Messenger of the Sovereign One.

Michael—a celestial being, the Warrior Angel of the Sovereign One

PREVIOUSLY ON THE PROGENY WARS

Therion, the Son of Destruction, is dead, killed while battling the Daughters of the Watchers. Though a great loss for the Nephilim and the Sons of the Lords, through his death, Diablos has gained a great ally, Mara the Primal of Death. The King of the Abyss also discovered that he has a daughter, Therion's twin sister, Libitinia, who also has the Veil of Deception.

The Daughters of the Watchers won a great victory, though it came with a great cost—the loss of several of their own and their home, to the Furies. In addition, the NY group uncovered many deceptions in this war which has led them to question their place in the global organization. The Tristate DoW have settled with their new friends, the Tektonites, hoping to end the conflict between the hybrids.

Luminary Tammuz has become the grand luminary, the sole leader of the Star of Nimrod, after he publicly revealed the impious acts of the other Luminaries and had them executed. He now searches for the last remaining luminary, Masmasu, and for his daughter, Margret, whom he believes was swayed from the organization by her hybrid twin sister, Gypsy.

With the Son of Destruction now gone, Angel, Pretzel, and Reina have a sense of a better and brighter future in the hopes of living a normal life.

PROLOGUE

Shadows danced on the walls of a small, dank room wherein a light bulb dangled precariously from the ceiling. A muscular woman stood near the center, her brawny forearms tensing as she gripped quartz blades in her hands. The weapons were stained crimson, and blood dripped from the tips. Each drop joined a sizable pool on the floor.

The warrior wore a pained expression, but it dissolved when she heard footsteps near the room's sole entrance.

"Damn, Horizon! You don't mess around," announced a lean young woman with tawny hair as she entered the room.

"We came to do a job, and I get things done," Horizon responded. "Did you clear the other rooms, Buitre?"

"Yea, all clear."

Buitre approached the corner of the room closest to her and bent down. Several slumped bodies were laid out before her, all males no older than early teens. She quickly rummaged through their pockets, beaming as she discovered some money. Finally, the woman straightened and approached another set of bodies at the far end of the room.

Horizon glowered. "What are you doing?"

"We don't have little heiresses to fund our operations," Buitre answered without interrupting her task. "I usually wait until after you softies are done, but this place gives me the creeps. I don't want to spend one more second than I need to here."

Horizon's brow furrowed.

Satisfied with her findings, Buitre stood and finally looked at Horizon. She shook her head and sighed. "You can take it up with Erinys if you don't like it. Maybe if you changed your Memento Vivere and fully committed as a Fury, you'd be more aware of what's going on." The petite woman glided toward the exit without glancing back. "When you're done judging me, you can meet us outside. I think we're all done here."

Horizon glared at Buitre as the other woman left the room, then noticed the soreness in her hands. The adrenaline had finally subsided, and she realized she hadn't released her grip on the blades. She took turns shaking out her hands to alleviate the discomfort. Then, Horizon started toward the door, but not before taking one last look at the bodies and sighing.

The work is necessary, she thought. *It's either them or us.* The sadness on her face deepened. She exited the room and stared curiously down the corridor in front of her. The hall was much darker than she'd expected.

How long was I in that room? She started to shiver, and the hairs on the back of her neck stood on end. She pressed her arms against her chest as her lip quivered from the unexpected drop in temperature. Before she'd had a chance to process the change, out of the corner of her eye, she noticed a shadowy figure darting into a room.

"Buitre, is that you?" Horizon cried. There was no response. She heard a crash come from the room the figure had disappeared into. *Damn, that Buitre. All clear, my rear end. I only wish she was as vigilant as she was concerned with corpse robbing.*

The warrior steeled herself, shrugged off the cold, and slowly approached the room's entrance. Beads of cold sweat formed near her temples. The corridor seemed to get darker and chillier with each step, and the battle-hardened fighter got knots in her stomach.

Get hold of yourself, Horizon, she instructed as she inched closer to the room. She drew a deep breath to calm herself and thought of her mission to kill Nephilim. No amount of creepiness would deter her from that task.

Rusty old wheelchairs and rollable bedframes adorned the hall between the woman and her target. She quietly moved some out of the way to clear her approach. Her footsteps were nearly silent as she inched forward. She reached the door, tightened the grip on her blades, and pressed her back against the wall. Then, the experienced warrior crouched and extended the weapon in her left hand at an angle to try to catch a glimpse inside the room. She was focused intently on the blade, looking for signs of movement, when she felt something cold and hard press against her side. The color left her face and she lurched forward, then whirled and scrambled to her feet.

"You've got to be kidding me!" she blurted as she stared at the source of her fright. One of the wheelchairs she'd disturbed as she'd crossed the hallway had rolled toward her. Horizon let her heart settle from its full gallop back to a trot and approached the room's entrance to look inside. It was empty.

"I'm so done with this freaking place!" she exclaimed, relieved.

She turned to leave and saw a strange purple smoke in front of her. Before she could make sense of it, a figure materialized from within and struck her savagely in the throat. The warrior dropped one of her blades and slammed against the wall. Her breathing was ragged and labored as she tried to cry for help. She could barely get enough air to stay conscious, much less form sounds.

Her only chance of survival was to get to Buitre and the others, so she darted away from her assailant and toward the exit. She stumbled near the room where she had met Buitre. Her lungs burned as she caught her balance, and somehow, the resilient warrior mustered her strength, but not before getting one last look at her handiwork inside the bloody room.

Horizon then looked back and saw the smoke rapidly approaching her. Terror filled her face, and a shriek carved through the fog in her mind. *Move!* she cried to herself. She caught a second wind and scurried away from the mystery attacker. Every muscle in her body screamed in pain, and her airways felt like they could close up at any moment, but she would not be deterred.

She scampered through the empty halls to the entrance corridor, the light at the end of this horror in the distance. Horizon made out voices outside of the building and tried to yell for help, but she still couldn't produce any sounds.

Finally, she marshaled what little strength she had left and made one last push. Her sight blurred, and her heart threatened to burst out of her chest with each step toward the exit. Then the world turned upside down, and her face hit the floor hard. Despair filled her mind as she struggled to get up, to no avail.

A body slumped down next to her as she tried to understand what was happening. It looked familiar, but oddly, it was missing its head, and blood was gushing from its neck. Her brows rose in realization as the light began to leave her eyes.

"Justice is paid," was the last thing Horizon heard as the world went dark.

PART I

REVELATION

1

INSANE REVELATION

After the Death of Therion
    The full-bodied Mozambican, who was five foot five, solemnly walked alone into the two-millennia-old temple. In her left hand, she gripped the Spear of Longinus, and she felt the connection the spear had to the sacred sanctuary.
    The first time Nyala had been here, there had not been time to explore or marvel at the four fifty-foot-tall weather-worn stone pillars or the inscriptions and carvings on the massive stone walls of the single-room temple. She gazed at the small opening in the center of the ceiling that served as an inferior light source to the one from the entrance. Though the temperature outside was above one hundred degrees Fahrenheit and extremely humid, the vast tomb was much cooler and had the pleasing flowery scent of roses.
    By sheer instinct, the Mozambican quickly removed the boots from her feet. The place felt too sacred to be trampled by her secular boots. She strode toward the stone

pedestal in the center of the room where the spear had rested for thousands of years. Stopping at the empty podium, she reached into her right pocket and extracted her cell phone. She quickly opened the notes app and read the prayer given to her by the Tektonite.

"May this spear return to its resting place and be sealed away until the Spirit of the Tektonite way is restored. Let no mortal take claim of it unless it is done with a heart of harmony." The Mozambican gently placed the spear on the pedestal.

No sooner had she removed her hand than a bright light encompassed the Tekton relic. After a few seconds, the light faded, leaving only the majestic spear.

Her first visit had been made in haste, but on this day, she had all the time in the world. This temple was a treasure trove for a linguistics and history major. She studied the inscriptions and carvings on the walls, some dating back to the first century. Her gift of languages made it easy to read the writings, which were mainly Hebrew and Greek, with a few in Latin. She scrupulously studied each and took photographs with her smartphone, not for sharing but for personal use.

In a corner of the tomb, concealed by dusty cobwebs and column-cast shadows, was an inscription on the top and the bottom of the wall. She carefully removed the webs and noticed this carving looked much older than the rest. By her estimation, it had been carved between the sixteenth and thirteenth century BCE.

Her greatest surprise was that she couldn't read it. For the first time in her life, she had found writing she could not read or understand. There was something special about it. Deep in her heart, Nyala sensed this ancient text had meaning and served a significant purpose. The wonder of its implications made the Mozambican slump as she studied the characters.

The lack of reception made it impossible to google the inscription, so Nyala took photos in the hopes of studying the carving when internet service was available. Something bizarre and unexpected occurred: the photos on her phone showed only a blank stone wall. Perplexed, she took more photos and got the same result.

She wondered if her camera was malfunctioning and took test photos of other inscriptions. She was stunned when each showed the exact image on the walls. She returned to the ancient carvings but again, it only displayed blank stone.

"How can this be?" she asked. She walked toward the inscription, placed her hand on the cold stone wall, and traced the strange carving with her fingertips. "Sovereign One, I'm able to understand the tongues of men and Angels, so why not this one?"

"Because this is not the tongue of men or Angels but the language of the Primals," came the response.

Startled by the unexpected voice, Nyala turned to its source. Before her stood a very tall female figure dressed in a fawn-hued robe. Her midnight-black hair was bound in a braid that crowned her head. She had the same dark complexion as the Mozambican but had sparkling cerulean eyes. The stranger was attractive, and though she looked young, Nyala could sense she was older than she looked.

"Who are you?" Nyala questioned, quivering.

"My name is Apocalypse. I am the Primal of revelation, wisdom and knowledge." Her thin lips quirked a warm smile. "You are highly favored, daughter of Tenzi, servant of Legion. The Sovereign One has sent me to show you the things that were, are and are to come."

Troubled by the stranger's sudden appearance and words, Nyala questioned, "How do you know my name, and where did you come from?"

"Be not afraid, Nyala. It was imperative that I appear at this appointed time. Though you will suffer much for what will be shown to you, you will be a source of help to your friends across the oceans as plans are set in motion for their destruction and that of the rest of the world."

The Mozambican tilted her head quizzically with a frown etched on her brow. "I have so many questions. What's a Primal, and why are you reaching out to me?"

"Time is of the essence." Apocalypse extended her hand. "Come. I will show you."

Nyala stared at the hand with hesitation, but an inner prompting nudged her to trust the stranger. She took a few steps forward, and the moment she touched the Primal's hand, she disappeared.

It felt like hours for the young woman in Earth time, but it was only seconds. Nyala reappeared alone on her knees with tears of wonder coursing down her ebony features. She was panting, and she placed her hand over her heart to keep it from breaking free.

After several minutes, she shook her head and with a hard swallow, stood. "I must warn Angel, Joan and the others of what is to come," she murmured. As she rushed to the exit, she dropped her cell phone and quickly picked it up. Accidentally, she turned on video recording and placed the device in her pocket.

The Mozambican stopped when she saw a familiar face—a white-haired woman. "Cherry? What are you doing here?" She tilted her head quizzically.

"Greetings, Nyala. I was surprised as well."

"I'm confused, Cherry." Nyala's voice strained. "What are you doing here?"

The older woman ignored her question. "I have to confess that we underestimated Joan and her group of women."

Nyala frowned. "Wait, how did you know about and find this place?

"We knew all along about this place and the relic." Cherry pointed at the spear. "Many times, we attempted to but had little success in retrieving it. It was a shock to hear that Joan's group was able to retrieve and use the spear on the Son of Destruction."

She took a step forward, glancing at the inscriptions around the room. "We hoped her quest would take her on a wild goose chase, or at minimum, detain her as it did us many times in the past."

"So, you knew about this location and said nothing when she requested your assistance?"

"Hush now, child. Don't look so surprised. You saw the scripts when you were snooping around with Mrs. Mozart." The London curator sneered at Nyala. "We're no different than our counterparts. We act the part, but in the end, we're all the same."

Nyala's dark complexion paled. "So, it *is* true, what the

book of *The Annals of the First Daughters* stated? About the Daughters agreeing to stay at war with their brothers?" She led out a frightened sigh. "But why?"

"It was the only way to keep our kind alive. Our Daughterhood was almost extinct, so to ensure our survival, the Daughters of long ago agreed to keep this war going, and we have."

Nyala wiped an errant tear from her cheek. "This is wrong, and you are wrong. Our survival was not in the hands of Diablos but in the one who existed before all time."

"Don't preach to me, young one." She waved her hands at Nyala. "I've been on this planet long enough to understand such complex matters. While others might consider working with the enemy as evil, I viewed it as essential." She took a deep breath. "Who knows if this is the manner the Sovereign One chose to maintain our survival?"

"There is a distinction between light and darkness, truth and deception, good and evil." The Mozambican raised her voice to her mentor and long-time teacher. "You can't mix the two."

Cherry squeezed the bridge of her nose. "I hoped you'd be different. You seemed intelligent, but I can see more than ever that only the strong can accept such facts." She intently gazed at the relic. "I see you've returned the relic. How good of you."

"If you think I can retrieve for you, you can forget about it. I cannot. Only in the Spirit of the Tektonite it can be obtained—"

"Yes, yes," Cherry interrupted her. "I'm aware of such babble. The one who sent me wanted to ensure it was returned to its rightful place." The curator's eyes turned to the ancient Primal inscription. "Though he was more concerned about this thing. After hearing that you had linguistic abilities, he was gravely concerned."

She turned back to Nyala. "I'm curious if you were able to understand it."

The Mozambican looked terrified. "Who sent you here?"

"Question for question," responded Cherry. "I'll tell you who sent me if you tell me what that inscription says."

"You're delusional, Cherry. I can't believe I ever trusted you."

"No, my child, it is you who is delusional. The instructions were to have you killed, but we're not in the business of killing our own. We convinced our superiors to keep you alive until you came to your senses."

"Cherry, what are you saying?" No sooner Nyala finished her utterance, she sensed that all too familiar prickle in her spine.

Right behind Cherry walked a Nephilim who was seven feet five inches tall. He was dressed in dark attire, and his long and wet black looking hair covered much of his face, so it was impossible to make out his expression.

"His name is Psychosi or, as you might interpret it, Psychosis. His ability is quite extraordinary. With a blow of his breath, you go from sane to demented." Cherry gestured at the Nephilim to apprehend Nyala. "Please don't take this personally, child, but we must ensure the survival of our kind."

"Please, Cherry, don't do this," Nyala desperately requested as she watched her assailant approach. "I have a special message to convey regarding the survival of all of us."

Psychosi swiftly approached the Mozambican, who attempted to run but was no match for his speed. He gripped her arms, and Nyala struggled to get loose to no avail. He stared at her, then blew a white substance into her frightened face. She let out a blood-curdling scream and collapsed.

The Nephilim turned to Cherry. "What should I do with her?"

The curator sighed. "She will return with me. We'll take care of her going forward."

2

A NORMAL LIFE

Present Time

Not a single bleacher seat was available in the vast auditorium. Guests leaned against the surrounding walls attentively, gleefully watching the main stage in the lecture hall. Another round of applause reverberated, as did a few cheers, as the Dean of Academics announced the next graduating student.

The five-foot-four young lady with shoulder-length ebony hair, who was wearing light-blue academic regalia, stood from her seat and filed out of her row toward the stage. No sooner had she stood than a high-pitched voice from the crowd yelled her name.

"Go, Angel! We're so proud of you!"

Through the celebratory commotion of the crowd, Angel heard a familiar voice tell the high-pitched female to take a seat since she had not yet received her diploma. Though her nerves always got the best of her in these situations, her girlfriend's cheer brought a smile to her face.

After waiting for a few minutes, she went up on the stage and waited to be called.

"For excellence in educational studies, Angelica Gabriella Santos, I confer this diploma," announced the dean.

Angel took a deep breath and proceeded forward. She shook the hands of the deans and several professors and grasped her hard-earned diploma—a Bachelor of Arts in Education. The high-pitched girl yelled her name again, along with other familiar voices. She proudly lifted her diploma and waved at her friends and her grandmother from the stage.

No sooner had the graduation ceremony concluded than she was greeted by a joyous and rambunctious Reina, followed by Kitty and Tassel. Shortly after came Pretzel, who was assisting Angel's beloved grandmother Maria Santos.

"*Mi angel*, I'm so proud of you," said Maria as she embraced her granddaughter, then wiped the tears from her eyes. "I've always believed you could do this."

Seeing her grandmother with tears always gave her waterworks too. "Thank you, *abuela*. I would've not made it this far without you." She glanced at the group and called gleefully, "Without you guys as well!" They gathered in a huddle and hugged the graduate affectionately.

Angel then turned to her closest friend. "Thank you so much for your help on the last paper. You know how much I hate writing, but you made it possible, Pretzel. Or should I now call you 'Professor Brown?'"

"Who told you?" Pretzel asked with a deep frown. "I

was gonna tell you after your graduation celebration. This is your day, and I didn't want to spoil your party."

Pointing at the woman on her right, who by now had a sheepish grin, Angel uttered, "Reina."

"Technically, I'm an adjunct professor for a small college on the upper east side of the city. It's something until I finish my doctorate in Philosophy."

"Regardless, congrats. I am so happy for you."

"Thanks. Back to your celebration. Since you didn't want a graduation party but requested something more intimate with your friends, Tassel made reservations at that Columbian restaurant you like."

In Reina's high-pitched voice, Angel exclaimed, *"Yea!"*

After the restaurant and dropping off her sweet grandmother at her Bronx apartment, Angel and her friends set out for Battery Park, and as customary, got themselves pretzels and took seats to gaze at the sunset. It was May, so green leaves and flowers had begun to sprout, perfuming the area with the scent of spring. The air was also warmer, designating the end of the cold months and the beginning of a new season. A gentle yet warm wind engulfed them, perfect for their catch-up conversation.

Munching her pretzel, Angel turned to Kitty. "So, no college for you?"

"Not for now, at least. My online business has really picked up." Breaking off a piece of the dough and eating it, she continued, muffled, "Thanks, Tassel."

"Absolutely," Tassel responded.

"What type of online business is it?" asked Pretzel.

"It's like an online seller market. I buy products at

wholesale and use seller platforms like eBuy, Windfall, Ketsy or FaceTwit Marketplace to sell them."

"What do you sell?"

"Just about anything. This was where Tassel was extremely helpful." She took a slurp of her lemonade and continued, "Based on the season, area, and geographical conditions, she created a computer algorithm that surfs the internet for these highly anticipated items. I then use that information to track best wholesale vendors, buy in bulk, and sell it forward."

"Wow!" exclaimed Pretzel. "You go, girl!"

"Thanks," said Kitty with a smirk. "But the real business guru is this girl over here." She pointed at Reina.

"What is she talking about?" asked Angel with a curious expression.

Tilting her head from side to side, Reina uttered, "I wasn't going to say anything since it was your graduation and all. I wanted to wait until afterwards."

That made Pretzel give her a mischievous sneer.

Reina excitedly extracted her cell phone and opened one of her emails and then the attached PDF file. "Look," she said, showing her friends an image on her phone.

Shocked, Angel was the first to express, "Oh, my God! You and Sparkles are on Fortune Magazine?" She snatched the phone from her friend's hand and gazed at the image intently. Reina and Spark stood side by side, wearing gray business suits. The front cover read *Sunrises Service Inc. is on the rise*. On the left corner had the words *Meet the Sunrise Leaders*.

"I know! Isn't that awesome sauce?" the blue-eyed girl exclaimed while clapping her hands.

"Reina, I'm so proud of you," Pretzel expressed, her eyebrows furrowing and then relaxing. "Though, I'm surprised you didn't mention it when you first heard the news." Her eyes were on the image on the cell phone.

"I know," said Reina with a large smile. "I wanted to surprise you both. Sunrises Service is now expanding beyond the New York location to Chicago and Los Angeles. Next week, we're planning to meet with investors in the Orlando, Florida area."

"That is *great* news," expressed Angel. "I'm proud of you both."

"There is something else," disclosed Reina as she ostentatiously raised her hand and tapped her third finger on her face.

Everyone's eyes popped wide at the ring around the finger.

"You got engaged!" yelled Angel.

The girls encircled Reina with celebratory hugs and tears of joy.

After they all took their seats again, Pretzel asked, "When did this happen?"

"Yesterday morning."

"C'mon, Reina. Spill the beans. We want details."

"Well, before he left on his flight yesterday, we met for breakfast. Then he took me to my favorite spot, The Wall Climbing Complex. When we reached the top, he mentioned how much he loved me and that he wanted to spend his entire life with me. He proposed on top of the wall."

Angel was fanning her face with her hand. "Oh, my

God! That truly sounds like a Reina proposal." She hugged the perky girl again.

"Yes! He knows me so well."

"Any wedding dates?" inquired Kitty.

"Not yet. We'll discuss those details when he gets back next week." Reina turned to face Angel. "Hey, I wanted to ask you a question."

"Yes, I want to be a bridesmaid!"

Reina chuckled. "No, silly. It wasn't that."

"Oh," Angel expressed with a dejected face.

"Of course, you're gonna be a bridesmaid. You all are." She glanced at the group. "I wanted to ask if you would come work for us. We're looking for a manager to lead our training department. There'll be some traveling to the different facilities, but it pays well. You've the degree for it." Reina winked at her.

"I would love to, Reina, but I've already got something lined up." Angel turned to the entire group. "You guys know that I've been a part-time substitute teacher for the last six months."

"Affirmative. At South Bronx Academy," responded Tassel.

"The principal of that school really likes the way I teach, so she offered me a job as a first-grade teacher, and I accepted."

"That's super!" exclaimed Reina.

"I know," stated Angel. "And my first priority is getting my grandmother out of the apartment."

"Amen to that," chimed in Pretzel.

"Next week, I'm taking a look at several apartments in the Morris Park area."

"Nice," said Kitty. "The Bronx Zoo is around there, and they have great pizza. But how can you afford an apartment by yourself in the city?"

"Rent control, girl. If anyone ever asks, I'm ninety years old." Angel snickered. Seconds later, she let out a sigh of relief and joy. "Is this what normal is supposed to feel like?"

Tassel responded, "If you mean normal in the sense of not being engaged in battle with superhuman beings and their overlord Fathers, then I would agree." She pushed back her glasses. "These last three years, since the death of Therion, I've never seen our group so stale."

She looked around the group. "Don't misunderstand me. It's a good thing. We haven't had any major events or engagements with Nephilim in quite a while. Many of the full-time women spend most of their time either assisting the Tektonites or dealing with day-to-day operations. Even May is volunteering half her time at the Red Cross.

"The most exciting event recently was getting an email from Nyala last week." Tassel shrugged.

"Nyala? Wow!" stated Pretzel. "We haven't seen or heard from her since she left to return the spear."

"Mrs. Mozart made a few attempts to get in contact with her, but the London group insisted she was involved in a special operation."

"What did the email say?"

"It was...awkward." Tassel scratched her head. "The first few sentences didn't make any sense, but from what I could make out, she seemed to be asking for help." The geeky tech gazed at Angel. "She mentioned you and Joan by name and said something about a war with the rising damned."

"The rising damned? What's that supposed to mean?" Angel asked, followed by a hard swallow.

"We don't know. I've shared the information with Joan, and she is sending Mrs. Mozart and Gypsy to England posthaste."

"Why not just call her?" inquired Kitty.

"That's the other weird thing. Every time Mrs. Mozart calls Nyala, it goes directly to her voicemail. When she asks the leadership about her whereabouts, she gets the same line about a special operation."

"What type of mission lasts for three years?" asked Pretzel.

"Exactly!" responded Tassel. "It's the reason Joan saw it fit to send Mrs. Mozart and Gypsy to investigate the matter further." Seeing all the concerned faces, the seer cleared her throat. "Look, it's probably nothing to be overly concerned about, and tonight is a night of celebration. Right?" She raised her Styrofoam lemonade cup and made a toasting gesture. "To normal."

The rest did the same and exclaimed, "To normal!"

3

BETWEEN TWO EXTREMES

A warm breeze blew gently over the dense foliage in the lush tropical jungle. Small critters darted across open areas to cover to avoid the watchful eyes of voracious airborne predators. Bubbling brooks flowing from rich mountain springs teeming with all manner of fish. The place was a paradise of natural beauty and splendor, yet one sight stood out: a lone human woman.

She was blond and middle-aged and had a toned physique. She was standing on a precariously balanced log on top of a large boulder. Her hands were clasped together in a praying pose, and one of her feet was suspended in mid-air. Sweat poured down her face as the midday sun beat mercilessly on her skin. The serene scene was interrupted by a loud roar.

The woman opened her eyes, revealing piercing dark-green orbs. She glanced toward the disruption and sighed as she jumped off the log, causing it to keel over and crash on the ground behind her.

"Do we really need to go through this again?" she inquired, staring at a hulking primate ten yards from her.

The creature huffed and waved its arms in a display of dominance. It rushed forward several yards and brushed its hand against the ground, then blew dust and debris in the woman's direction.

"I really don't have time for this today. I need to catch my dinner. Honestly, I think we just got on the wrong foot. My name is Theresa. Let's be friends, ok? How about I call you Lucy?"

The primate pounded on its chest with its fists and bellowed.

"Yea, I didn't think that would work, but it was worth a try," Theresa told it. Then, she placed her left hand in front of her with an open palm and positioned her right foot back. "Well, come on, then. I don't have all day."

From the corner of her eye, Theresa saw an even more massive primate jump out of the bushes nearby and dart toward her.

"Clever monkey, but not clever enough."

The second primate attempted to pounce on her. However, the woman deftly repositioned her body and used the second primate's momentum against it, causing it to hurtle into the boulder behind her. While Theresa's back was turned, the Lucy-primate dashed forward and raised both arms, intending to bring them crashing down on the woman. However, Theresa swung her body around and rebuffed the incoming blow with the back of her hand.

Lucy lurched back, confused. If she'd been human, she would have been wondering how such a small creature could so easily deflect a blow from a much larger opponent. Instead, the primate roared, creased its brow, and dashed forward again. Theresa dropped to the ground to the right of the incoming attacker and used her leg to trip the primate, sending it careening toward the other one.

"I wish I could make you understand that I wish you no harm," Theresa uttered. "We could be one big happy family, Theresa, Lucy, and…" she glanced at the second creature's nether region, "…Abel."

The two creatures were now back on their feet, grunting and huffing at each other and Theresa. The second primate grabbed the log Theresa had balanced on earlier and hurled it at the woman. It tore through the air, and Theresa stretched out her hand instead of dodging. On impact, the log's forward momentum was negated, and it fell harmlessly to the ground.

The primate roared in frustration, then it motioned at its partner, and both creatures slowly approached the woman from opposite sides. When they were several feet away from their target, they grunted, huffed, and rushed her simultaneously. Lucy approached from the right and swung her muscular arm at Theresa's head, but the latter stopped it with her hand. Abel reached Theresa's location, retrieved the fallen log, and raised it above his head.

Theresa stepped toward him and kicked at him to make him lose his balance. The creature lurched forward and crashed into Lucy.

"Had enough yet?"

Lucy threw Abel off her. Both scrambled to their feet and lunged at Theresa in synchrony. However, the woman used her arms to redirect the blows, so the pair struck each other instead.

Frustration was written all over the primates' faces as they recovered. This time, Abel rushed at Theresa first, and Lucy took off after him. The first primate attempted to hit her with a wide swing of his arm. Instead, he ended up turning around when she ducked the blow. While this happened, Lucy tried to stop but ended up crashing into Abel.

He turned to his smaller companion and brought his fists down on her, murderous rage visible in his eyes. Lucy crashed to the ground from the impact and braced herself for another assault, but further attacks did not come. Instead, she looked up and saw Theresa standing between her and Abel. The woman was blocking and parrying a flurry of blows from the other primate.

"Now, now. There's no need for that," exclaimed Theresa as she stared intently into Abel's eyes as he tired himself from the onslaught.

The creature slumped back, then his shoulders drooped, he grunted several times, and turned away from the woman. Abel disappeared back into the bushes as quickly as he had first appeared. Theresa swiveled her body toward Lucy, who was still on the ground. The primate looked deeply into her eyes, then turned her face away and exposed her belly in submission. The woman sighed and walked away from the creature, who silently crept away moments later.

"I hope they finally get the point," Theresa grumbled.

"You've come a long way, child," a voice said behind the woman.

Theresa's lips thinned, and she craned her neck to look at the speaker.

"Haniel!" she exclaimed, exasperated. "It's been months! I've barely survived out here."

Haniel studied her. "But you did survive. More, you've thrived. You have truly made my gift your own."

"Yet I'm no closer to understanding what beating on monkeys and balancing on logs has to do with stopping Diablos."

"All in due time, my child. Remember, I'm the embodiment of balance and order. When I first found you, you were an unbalanced mess."

Theresa shot him a sour look. "Well, I'd just lost my son, so forgive me for being a grieving mother."

Haniel shook his head. "It was not your grief. Grief is the properly ordered response to great loss. Your long servitude to Diablo was the cause of your unbalance. That and what was done to you before."

"I don't remember anything before I joined the order. They always told me it was retrograde amnesia. Do you know about my past?"

"I do, and I will reveal all to you once our task is done. Now come. It is time for your first mission."

The Primal stretched out his hand, and a portal opened several feet from him. The opening was large and glowed yellow-red. Its edges were not well-defined, so it seemed more like a tear in space than a typical Daimonic portal. Theresa drew a deep breath, looked at her benefactor, and stepped through the gateway.

Several hours later

Theresa and Haniel stood on a hill overlooking a

wooded area with a large clearing in the middle. There was a small stone building surrounded by a metal chain link fence inside the clearing. Armed guards patrolled the perimeter and the sole entrance.

"There are scrolls vital to our cause inside that place," announced Haniel. "You will go and retrieve them."

Theresa's face dropped. "Monkeys in a jungle are one thing, but these are armed soldiers. How am I supposed to sneak past them?"

"I never suggested you should sneak."

The woman's jaw dropped.

The Primal stared at her intently. "It seems you did not learn as much as I had hoped during your training. Your abilities extend beyond merely avoiding blows. As my agent in this world, you channel the forces of balance. No physical or supernatural attack can harm you as long as you remain in balance within yourself."

"So, you're trying to tell me I can survive being shot?"

"No. If you trust in my power, no bullet will touch you."

"How will I know I have the right scrolls?" Theresa inquired.

"Whenever you find yourself uncertain of how to act, seek the mean in the situation."

"The mean?"

"The average between the extremes," Haniel clarified. "A good example is bravery. It is the mean between rashness and cowardice. Throughout our mission, you will need to act without my input. See with more than physical sight to find the action that brings balance."

Theresa sighed and muttered, "I just love the riddles."

Two burly men stood talking in front of the entrance. In his peripheral vision, one of the guards noticed a blonde woman approaching them at a casual pace. He motioned to his colleague and pointed at the unwelcome guest.

"*Nu te apropia!*" one of the men yelled and held up his hand, palm out.

The woman continued to approach, undeterred.

"*Nu te apropia!*" yelled the other guard. He raised his gun and pointed it at her.

A woman's voice exclaimed from their radios, "*Impusc-o, Impusc-o!*"

The men opened fire in short bursts, but their shots seemed to miss. They switched the settings on their rifles to full-auto and emptied their magazines. By this point, the other guards in the facility had come running to investigate the commotion and joined in shooting at the intruder.

The woman was unfazed and drew even closer. She dashed toward them and engaged them in close quarters. A few of the men attempted to grapple her and others to strike her with the butts of their rifles, but she rebuffed their attempts. One by one, she knocked them unconscious. Finally, she was the only one standing.

"Holy crap! That was scary," Theresa exclaimed.

The woman headed toward the building and opened the door. As soon as she stepped inside, a muscular woman with jet-black hair and full tattoo sleeves on both arms lunged at her with a knife. The blade's tip made contact with the center of Theresa's chest, but it stopped abruptly, which perplexed the attacker.

"I'll take this," Theresa announced as she twisted the woman's wrist with one hand and disarmed her with the other. Then she struck her hard on her temple, knocking her out.

Theresa finally took a good look inside the building. She saw numerous shelves and overstuffed drawers replete with all manner of books and scrolls.

"You have got to be kidding me." She remembered Haniel's words. She drew a deep breath, closed her eyes, and centered herself. When she opened her eyes, she could see something else. In front of certain shelves were ethereal sets of scales. Some of the scales were tilted to one side, but she noticed a perfectly balanced pair. Theresa approached the shelf and grabbed the scrolls behind the scales.

Haniel's voice resounded behind her. "Well done!"

Theresa jumped. "Are you ever going to stop doing that?" She shook off her fright and stared at the Primal. "This was a test, wasn't it?"

"All of our actions are tests, and the results propel us on the path to chaos or equilibrium. But, yes, this was a trial run of how far you've come. It is finally time."

"Time for what?" inquired the woman, her dark-green eyes fixed on the towering Primal.

"To free my sister."

4

AXIS OF ADVERSARIES

Mara sauntered down a dark, winding corridor, arms stretched. Both sides of the hall were adorned with rows of shelves that held hourglasses of varying shapes, sizes, and sophistication. However, they all had one similarity: they were cracked and colorless.

As the Primal ambled through the passage, she ran her slim fingers through the broken pieces. Occasionally, she would stop to look at one or another hourglass and caress its fissure for several seconds before continuing her slow march. Rarely, she would break the deathly silence. "Sweet Justice!"

After several more minutes of walking, stopping, and pronouncing, Mara stopped before a collection of nearly identical hourglasses. The sand that had once filled the hourglasses had long since spilled from the cracked cylinders and littered the shelves and floor. The tall, elegant woman crouched and sifted through the scattered sand before scooping up a heaping handful and pressing it to her face. She allowed the sand to run down her body and reveled in a sensation no mortal creature could hope to describe or comprehend.

"Perfect retribution," she exclaimed shortly, then rose and continued.

Almost indiscernibly at first, the corridor had grown brighter the farther Mara progressed. The joy on her face waned the closer she came to the light source that cast its rays into the deathly passage. The Primal traversed one final turn before the hall opened into a massive central chamber. Along the room's perimeter were numerous corridors similar to the one Mara had just exited. Near the hall's center, an hourglass was suspended in mid-air.

Mara shielded her eyes. "Blasted light!"

The two glass bulbs were capped by wood adorned with gold leaf. The symmetrical ends were filled with equal amounts of white sand that flowed toward the center, maintaining a perpetual equilibrium. The timepiece shone like the sun, illuminating the room and piercing deep into the connected corridors.

Additionally, tendrils of energy protruded from the glass and extended into the corridors. Mara's beautiful visage cracked when she saw them.

"*Why?*" she screamed. A scythe materialized in her hand, and she dashed toward the hourglass, then swung the weapon and slammed its sharp point into the timepiece. It was undisturbed. Mara continued to swing the scythe, growing more irritated with each failed attempt to destroy her target. Finally, she slumped to the floor, defeated.

"Why is this injustice allowed to persist? Why can't I destroy it?" she cried. A necklace appeared around her neck. The chain hung loose on her chest and had a pendant attached in the shape of an hourglass with an infinity snake enveloping it.

The Primal remained on the floor for several minutes with her head down and her eyes glazed, then a familiar sensation disturbed her stupor. Her daughter beckoned her.

Mara materialized into a luxurious penthouse loft overlooking the East River. The apartment was decorated with artifacts from ancient cultures, Mesopotamian, Olmec, and Xian Dynasty Chinese. Four other individuals were already in the apartment.

"Lady Mara, thank you for joining us."

Mara glanced at the person who had spoken. "It's been some time, Diablos."

"Yes, it has. I called Libby here and asked her to contact you." Diablos spoke with a sly smile.

"And those two?" Mara inquired, pointing at the other two men in the room.

"Two of my most trusted generals, High Lords Hades and Legion."

Legion bowed his head slightly while Hades stared coldly, arms crossed.

Mara turned back to Diablos. "Have you made any progress on your designs?"

"Yes, my lady. I've incorporated your input, and we're finally ready to begin the next phase."

Legion and Hades looked at each other.

"Um, my lord, if I may be so bold as to interrupt. We don't understand. What does an Archangel, one of the Primals, have to do with our plans?" Legion inquired.

"And why is this human woman here?" growled Hades, pointing at Libby.

"My loyal friends," Diablos started. "My plans run deeper and are more ancient than you know. Only Apollyon knew some of them, but even he did not understand their full breadth. The next step in my grand design is finally upon us. We will bring this world to its knees and exploit it to continue our fight beyond."

The Daimon generals' eyes grew wide.

"It's best not to speak of such things aloud. The enemy has eyes and ears everywhere," Diablos explained. "As for this young lady? Well, I'll let her show you."

Libby dropped her Veil of Deception, and the Daimons sensed an amethyst aura coming from her.

"What? How?" Hades snarled.

"It's all thanks to Apollyon. The human scientist he employed to create Therion was also able to create an offspring for Lady Mara, one that had part of my essence and part of hers. Libby is Therion's twin sister, endowed with my powers and that of the eldest Primal."

"She is formidable indeed, my lord. I knew the loss of Therion would not be the end of your plans," Legion stated as he sized Libby up.

"His death was the beginning. We have need of the Sons of the Lords again."

"But my lord, our sons have been busy creating dissent among the Nephilim ranks," Hades complained. "Countless hybrids have abandoned their places and threaten to destabilize the influence we've gained through the centuries."

"Ignore the weaklings who fail to see the glory in our cause. They've done us a favor by weeding themselves out," announced Diablos. "Assemble the Sons of the Lords under Libby's leadership. There are time-sensitive tasks they need to perform. Before long, we will openly rule this world, and not even Michael and his horde will be able to stop our advance.

"Only one piece of my plan is missing, one I've been playing close to the vest but will yield unprecedented results soon. While I'm gone, all Daimons and Nephilim will report to Lady Mara and Libby."

Hades and Legion bowed their heads and placed a fist on the center of their chests. Portals appeared behind each of them, and they walked through.

Diablos turned back to Mara. "None of this would be possible without your aid, my lady."

"I'm not interested in your platitudes or gratitude."

"O mighty Primal, I have not forgotten what troubles you. Trust me. I seek to undo the thing that injures you," Diablos clarified. "Now, if you'll excuse me, I have some urgent matters to attend to."

A red swirl appeared next to the king of the Daimons, and he disappeared into it.

Mara took several steps toward her daughter and placed a hand on her shoulder. "What have you discovered of Diablos' plans?"

"His commands were to lead the other Nephilim in acquiring certain materials and manufacturing facilities necessary for his designs. Additionally, he's been working on a secret project. Unfortunately, it's almost impossible to track him once he engages his Veil of Deception."

"We'll go along with his schemes for now, but we'll bring his entire charade crumbling down around him at the first sign of treachery."

"Yes, my mistress," Libby responded. She opened her mouth to say something but changed her mind.

"Out with it, child," Mara commanded.

"You were visiting the Chronal Halls, were you not?"

Mara raised an eyebrow, then let out a chuckle. "You truly are my child."

"You've never told me what you see there, but for as long as I can remember, whenever you come from that place, your face is downcast, and your presence lessened."

Mara briefly touched her chest with her palm. Though nothing was visible, Libby sensed something unnatural coming from the spot her mistress touched.

Mara returned her hand to her side. "Yes, child, I was in the halls. That is why we're helping Diablos in his scheme. As powerful as I am, there are things I cannot do. However, he has been clever from the beginning. If there is any being in creation who can undo the Great Injustice, it is him."

Libby nodded. "As you say, my mistress."

"Now come, child. Let us see to the mess these men have left us."

5

UNEXPECTED VISIT

The traveling bags were placed outside the spacious and artistically decorated office. Two suits of silver knights' armor stood imperiously in opposite corners, and hanging on the wall behind the large mahogany desk were expensive paintings depicting several queens of England. In the middle was a portrait of Queen Elizabeth the first, who sat majestically and authoritatively gripping a scepter between her hands. To the left of the entrance, in front of the glass windows, four women sat around a small oak table with an antique vase in the middle.

"This is a surprise to have you both in London again, though I'm curious why this sudden visit," began the middle-aged woman. She pushed back her salt-and-pepper hair, revealing her high cheekbones and chiseled features. Her piercing dark-brown eyes stared at the two women across from her.

"Athena, I concur that it was unexpected, and I do apologize for not informing you beforehand, but we felt it was urgent and essential to come posthaste," said the gray-haired lady as she delicately placed her pale hands on the polished table.

"You two flew thousands of miles unexpectedly, so you have made Cherry and me curious, Mrs. Mozart. Why the visit and not a phone call?" Athena steepled her fingers in front of her thin lips.

Mrs. Mozart quirked a polite smile. "I will cut to the chase. The reason Miss Gypsy and I are here today is because of Miss Nyala."

Athena's eyes gravitated to the older woman sitting next to her.

"Athena and Cherry, we're gravely concerned for Miss Nyala. In the past three years, we have had no word from her, but we recently received an email communication. To put it bluntly, it was a bit disturbing."

The wise woman turned to her right and asked, "Miss Gypsy, would you please pass me my briefcase?" The warrior did, and Mrs. Mozart reached into her briefcase and extracted a copy of the printed message. "I hope this justifies our unplanned visit today."

Cherry took the note from Mrs. Mozart and read its contents. She took a deep breath and passed the message to Athena.

The local leader carefully read the email, then shook her head. She stood and walked to the windows and closed the shades. As she reseated herself on the leather-upholstered chair, the leader disclosed, "Nyala is not well, and she hasn't been for the last three years."

"What do you mean?" inquired Mrs. Mozart grimly.

"How can I put it…"

"To say it succinctly, she suffered a mental breakdown

after joining you and your companions on that chaotic excursion," interrupted Cherry. She was clearly agitated.

"What the hell?" asked Gypsy. "She was perfectly fine when she left us."

"I don't know what you mean, but when I discovered her, the poor girl could not even speak," revealed Cherry. That left Gypsy and Mrs. Mozart shaking their heads.

Athena added, "I won't dive into the details, but suffice it to say that Cherry found Nyala in Nampula's local hospital." She cleared her throat. "In their psychiatric unit."

"I am confused," stated Mrs. Mozart, her hand over her mouth. "What occurred, and why state she was on a special assignment?"

Athena gave Cherry a quick glance, then returned her attention to Mrs. Mozart. "We knew how special she was to you, and we hoped she would recover. On the contrary, her condition worsened, and a few days ago, she broke free from our care, hurting two of our caretakers, and wandered into the streets of London. We eventually located her and brought her back. I suspect that's when she wrote this email to you." The London leader pointed at the piece of paper on the table.

"Whatever excursion you sent her on affected her psychologically and physically. The first few months, she was incapable of grabbing a spoon, let alone using the loo on her own." Cherry's thin lips pressed tight into a grimace. "I have to say, Mrs. Mozart, I'm highly disappointed in how you and Joan governed those you oversee. I was hesitant to assign Nyala to you but seeing this poor girl's current condition proved what a grave mistake we made. It shows how incompetent you are to lead."

Gypsy jumped to her feet and slammed her hands on the table. "You listen to me, asswipe! I don't care who you are. You have no right to speak to her that way. Unless you have something nice to say, I would keep shut." She brandished her prosthetic fist at Cherry.

Mrs. Mozart gently chided Gypsy. "There, there. She has every right to express how she feels."

"So I do," mumbled Gypsy and took a seat.

"Please understand our confusion. Miss Nyala was in a perfect state prior to her New York departure. Do you know what transpired to have left her in such bad condition?" inquired Mrs. Mozart, looking directly at Athena.

"We don't know," responded the leader. "When she initially called, Nyala mentioned she was heading to Mozambique to some sacred temple before returning to London. We believe something happened to her there."

"Is it possible to see her?"

Athena sighed deeply. "Mrs. Mozart, we have a long history, so I'll be bloody honest with you. I'm gobsmacked to hear about the radical decisions and changes your group has undergone. Allowing male hybrids into your factions, engaging in civilian affairs, specifically with the group the Tektonites. Worst of all, losing Daughters and your warehouse to those fanatical women, the Furies."

The London leader shook her head in disappointment. "It is the responsibility of each group to run their affairs as best they can, but to move away from traditional core values is unacceptable."

"Athena, upholding traditional values for the sake of tradition does not make them true. We're to adjust our ways in view of the truth and not the reverse."

"Are not our traditions based on truth?"

Mrs. Mozart directed her gaze at Cherry. "Are they?"

The local curator turned her eyes away.

Athena cleared her throat. "This isn't time for an alethiological debate, but since you're both present, it's with great disappointment that, in light of the Tristate group's illicit actions, a recent order has been issued by the Global Daughter Community to have a committee further investigate these matters. If a vote of no confidence is confirmed, all those in leadership will be removed and replaced by others deemed to be trustworthy."

"What in hellfire?" howled Gypsy, her face red. "Such committees are put in place during the most severe situations. I don't think assisting the Tektonites and male hybrids who believe in our cause is justifiable."

Cherry chimed in, "We see it otherwise and feel it was long overdue."

"That's BS, and you both know it."

Athena stood from her chair. "I don't think there's anything else to discuss. I'll just say that I'm sorry but given the situation your group is in and Nyala's current condition, I cannot let you see her. Regarding your accommodations, you both can stay in our guest quarters."

"Don't bother." Gypsy scoffed and stood. "We can find our own accommodations."

"You misunderstand me, Gypsy. That wasn't a kind offer but an order. You are to remain on the premises until tomorrow morning, and thereafter, you are to fly back to the States."

Mrs. Mozart and Gypsy exchanged grave gazes.

"You are holding us prisoner?" inquired Gypsy.

Cherry, with a smirk, responded, "Simply under careful observation."

"Until the investigation is completed, we need to ensure the safety of our Daughters," added Athena.

"Father Mocker," muttered Gypsy.

The small guestroom was quiet save for the ticking wall clock. Both hands approached twelve, and all that could be heard was the occasional snoring of the fierce warrior who lay uncomfortably on one of the twin-sized beds. The glistening moon cast moving tree shadows through the unsheltered window, which caused Mrs. Mozart to cover her face with her forearm. Even though the sole door had been securely locked by Gypsy before bedtime, it opened, and along with it came cumbersome bright lights.

"What the hell?" blurted Gypsy. "Someone is gonna really get it."

"Rise quickly," said the female as she closed the door. She was about five foot two, with bright green eyes and curly red hair. "Your lives are in danger. You must leave this place now."

"Who are you?" questioned Gypsy with a frustrated expression.

"I'm a friend of Nyala's, and she waits for you by the garden."

"What do you mean our lives are in danger?"

"There's no time to explain. If you want to save your lives and hers, you need to leave now." The stranger walked to the minute closet and grabbed their bags.

Gypsy sat on the edge of the bed and squinted her eyes. "Why should we trust you? You could be leading us into a trap."

The stranger's eyes went to Gypsy's biomedical prosthetic arm. "Nyala mentioned she was researching the Residual Spiritual Projection phenomenon for you, correct?"

Gypsy frowned and nodded.

She turned to Mrs. Mozart. "I know about the first female hybrids making a deal with Diablos and slaughtering peaceful groups."

"That is right," answered Mrs. Mozart.

"If you want to learn more, you need to help Nyala. She has much to say, but you must first take her far from this place."

Trusting their instincts, both women grabbed their remaining belongings and stuffed them into their bags. They followed the short woman out the door and noticed the two guards on the floor, asleep.

Gypsy whispered to Mrs. Mozart, "Did you know they placed guards to watch us?"

Mrs. Mozart shook her head.

After walking through a long corridor, down a few staircases, and through some spacious rooms, they reached the garden of the London compound. There, under the glistening moon, stood Nyala.

The moment she saw her two friends, she raced forward and embraced them.

"My child," said Mrs. Mozart. "How great it is to see you."

"The pleasure, i-it's all mine," stammered Nyala. "I'm so happy you came for me."

Mrs. Mozart frowned at her manner of speech. "Miss Nyala, to put it more accurately, we came to see you. I was very concerned for you."

"Much has happened for sure, and there's much to tell. But I sense our lives are in danger, so we must leave quickly."

"What's going on?" asked Gypsy. "Why are you and your friend saying our lives are in danger?"

Nyala frowned. "What friend? It's unfortunate to say that after many years in this p-place, I've never had anyone I can call a friend."

"Yeah, she's right over…." Gypsy stopped when she turned and found no one else there. "Where did she go? She was standing right here. She led us to you."

"I haven't seen no one except you two."

Mrs. Mozart's eyes opened wide. "A visiting celestial," she whispered, though Nyala and Gypsy both caught the words.

"You mean an Angel?" asked Gypsy.

"Something of that nature," responded the wise woman.

"It could explain why one minute I was strapped to my bed, and the next I was here," added Nyala.

"Huh, you think?" Gypsy snickered.

A look of apprehension appeared on Mrs. Mozart's face. "We must leave these premises as speedily as possible. Whoever appeared to us tonight was not only here to free us but to warn us."

With those words, all three left the London compound.

6

INCOMPREHENSIBLE

Prayer and motivation posters hung around the walls of the Tektonite meditation room. Its only occupant was Mrs. Mozart, who was leaning her head on her clasped hands with her elbows resting on a large circular table. The once-hot cup of tea before her was cold and still untouched. The wise old curator sat contemplating the events of the past few hours. She was feeling the jet lag of the early morning flight, but there was no time to rest. She had to meet with the council members and deliberate on the recent news.

Her deep thoughts were interrupted by footsteps entering the conference room. She raised her head at the arriving leader. "Greetings, Joan." She barely raised her voice.

Joan's expression slid into a frown at the sight of Mrs. Mozart. "We could've waited until tomorrow to have this meeting. You could use the rest."

She managed a smile and articulated, "A sound advice. Unfortunately, recent events dictate that I relate my information urgently."

"I couldn't gather all twelve members in such a short time. Only Grace and May are present, and, well, Gypsy. I had to wake her once I had finished making all the phone calls. All three will be here shortly." Joan walked over to the curator and took a seat next to her, placing her coffee on the table.

"Were you able to reach Miss Angel?"

"Let me check." She reached into her pocket and pulled out her cell phone. "Per Tassel, she'll be here soon. As you might know by now, you call her, and the other three will show up too."

The curator let out a small chuckle. "I have come to call them semibreve." Seeing the leader's confused expression, she elaborated, "A musical term meaning four quarter notes."

Joan smiled. "They are inseparable, indeed." The leader stared into Mrs. Mozart's eyes. "But why the urgency? We haven't had one of these emergency meetings," she rolled her eyes up and sighed, "well, in the longest. And I wasn't aware you were bringing Nyala back with you. A bit daring for your tastes."

"I completely comprehend your astonishment. It was not in my plans to bring Miss Nyala along, yet Sovereignty was at work."

"Yeah, Gypsy informed me of the miraculous escape and about how Nyala unexpectedly found her passport and IDs in her pockets at the airport."

She took a deep breath before continuing. "She desires to speak to us all, including Miss Angel, but I will warn you, Joan, she is not the young woman we knew three years ago."

Joan frowned. "What do you mean?"

"She said very little on our flight over, and the few times she spoke, she either stammered or lost her train of thought. As you will recall, the young woman is one of the most intelligent people I have ever met."

"What happened to her?"

Mrs. Mozart shook her head. "I do not know, except that she experienced a psychological trauma after returning the Spear of Destiny. That is, according to the London leadership."

"So, she wasn't on some special mission?"

"They fabricated that to protect her image." She steepled her fingers and gazed out the window, where afternoon showers were beginning to pour.

"Do you believe that?" Joan pursed her lips while shaking her head in disbelief.

"I have heard some convincing falsification during my years." The wise curator turned to Joan. "That was not one of them."

"I figure, but did Nyala tell you anything about where she's been for the last three years?"

"Unfortunately, she cannot recollect much. I suspected she experienced some trauma and was held by the London team this entire time. The mystery is what caused it and why the London group withheld that information from us."

Joan grabbed her coffee and took a sip. "Do you think it's smart for us to have her speak to the group?"

The curator was quiet for a moment, glancing at the storm outside the window. "Joan, the London council issued a vote of no confidence in the Tristate group, and soon a panel will be assembled to look into this allegation." She stared at Joan's troubled expression. "I sensed Sovereignty is leading us to hear what Miss Nyala has to say."

Angel, Pretzel, Reina, and Kitty entered the networking space soaking wet. In one of the corners, by a small wooden table, sat Tassel, who was too preoccupied with her laptop to even notice the arrival of her companions.

"There she is," said Angel, shaking her head with an annoyed look on her face. "*Que chavienda*! I just had my hair done yesterday." She glanced at her three friends.

"Greetings!" said Tassel, standing and then stopping herself from embracing her girlfriends. "What's up with the wet looks?"

"It's raining cats and dogs out there," responded Pretzel.

"It was?" asked Reina, eyes open wide.

"It's an expression, Reina."

"I wasn't aware it was going to rain today," uttered Tassel, looking at her weather app on her phone. "I would suggest you change, but Joan wants to see you ASAP."

"What's this about?" inquired Angel as she continued to dry her hair.

Tassel glanced at the door and then gestured to Kitty to close it. She lowered her voice. "I'm not sure, but I suspect it has something to do with Nyala. She is here."

"But didn't Mrs. Mozart and Gypsy travel to London to see her?" asked Pretzel.

"Exactly!" Tassel pushed her glasses back. "Apparently,

they had a miraculous escape and brought Nyala along. They arrived this morning."

"Why an escape?" asked Kitty with a quizzical look.

"I don't know the reason, but they were being held by the London team, and something or someone helped them escape and warned them to leave ASAP. From what I'm hearing, Nyala wants to speak to the team."

"Does this have to do with that email she sent?" asked Angel.

Tassel pursed her lips. "Maybe."

Angel swallowed hard, walked toward a nearby chair and slumped into it.

"Angel, are you OK?" asked Reina.

She buried her face in her hands, then let out a deep sigh. Angel lifted her head and glanced at the group. "Guys, I, um…I have to be honest with you. These last few years have been the most normal time of my life. I finally graduated and have a job lined up, and later today, I was gonna show my grandmother the Morris Park apartment. Things seemed to be going so well, and I don't want that to change." She shook her head apprehensively as her eyes went from the friends to the floor. "I'm not sure if I wanna do this anymore."

"I completely understand," expressed Pretzel. "I think we all are experiencing the normalcy of life, and the thought of interrupting it is alarming." She walked toward her friend, knelt, and placed her hand on Angel's shoulder. "My advice is let's at least hear what they have to say. Who knows, it might be good news?"

Angel gave her a blank stare. "*Vamos a ver*. Yeah, let's go with that."

Pretzel laughed. "All right, a bit farfetched there. But whatever it is, we'll be there with you."

Angel managed a fake smile and nodded.

Unexpectedly, Tassel's laptop beeped, which made everyone's head turn to the source.

"My script!" yelped the seer as she rubbed her hands together. She strode to the table and sat on the wooden chair. After adjusting her glasses, she focused on her screen, and moments later, her jaw dropped.

"What is it, Tassel?" asked Reina.

"Guys, you might want to see this," declared the geeky seer.

The group huddled around the seer, attempting to fix their eyes on the small screen.

"What are we looking at?" inquired Pretzel, squinting.

"Before your arrival, I created a script to hack into the London team's main system. Primarily to obtain any information they had on Nyala. It states that for the last three years, she was kept locked up in their psychiatric ward."

"What?" exclaimed Angel, pushing forward to read what was on the screen.

"That sounds crazy…" Tassel stopped and cleared her throat. "Sorry, no pun intended." Her eyes were again on the screen. "It states here that she suffers from delusions, paranoia, and hallucinations." Her gaze switched to the phone when it rang. She swallowed, then continued, "Joan wants to meet now in the meditation room."

The five companions arrived at the Tektonite Prayer and Meditation room, which was occupied by Joan, Gypsy, Mrs. Mozart, Grace, May, and Nyala. The Mozambican plastered on a large smile at the sight of them. She waved, but it was reciprocated with awkward smiles and hand gestures.

Upon taking their seats, a flash of lightning hit close to the window, and shortly after, a loud thunderclap. Everyone in the room except Nyala was startled by the unexpected interruption.

"Thank you all for meeting us on such short notice," greeted Joan as she glanced at their damp clothes. "I do apologize for meeting under these conditions. I wasn't expecting this storm, and from what I can see, you had a time of it." She motioned to the seat across from her. "Team, I'm going to cut to the chase. You remember Nyala. She was instrumental in retrieving and returning the Spear of Destiny three years ago. While we won't dive into her whereabouts during these last few years, she has some pressing information she would like to share with us." She looked at the young woman. "Nyala?"

"Hello, everybody," began Nyala while the outside storm subsided. "Thank you s-so much for having me among you once again. I urgently needed to tell you about this vision... No, wait, it was a dream." Her eyes darted from left to right. "No, it was more than a vision. It was a visitation, a breathing-taking heavenly visitation. It was so beautiful."

She spoke as if she were talking to herself and then smiled, leaving everyone in the room with wondering eyes.

"Yes," she continued, "in that visit, I was shown things

of the past, the present, and the horror of a possible future to come. A future that you must stop." She pointed her finger at Angel. "That's correct." Once again, as if she were speaking to herself, "For she stopped death, and now justice demands payment. An atonement."

A deep frown crossed Mrs. Mozart's features. "Miss Nyala, do you need a moment to collect yourself?"

"Oh, I'm perfectly fine." The Mozambican smiled and then glanced at the ceiling. "That's right, but the woman from the other world is not fine. She works with the Keeper of Balance. Yes, yes, Therion, the Son who died but will rise again. The rise of the…the damned, and the Daimon Killer who is to stop them." Again, she pointed at Angel, and then at Kitty.

"Nyala, I'm so sorry, but you're not making any sense," Angel told the woman, her voice laced with agitation. "Can you explain yourself better?"

"Yes, that's right, but in time, you will understand and will teach others," divulged Nyala, looking around the room as if she were searching for someone. "Can you hear the voice too?"

"This is getting interesting," quipped Kitty.

"Ahem. Maybe we should take a break," interjected Joan. "May, can you escort Nyala outside for a moment?"

May nodded, stood, and walked to the Mozambican, but as she was walking her out, Nyala stared at Tassel and uttered, "So good to see you alive. You are precious. Yes, that's right, so precious."

"Team, I'm out of words," started Joan. "I will disclose that Nyala suffered a mental breakdown, but I wasn't aware of its extent. I'm sorry. I, um, I should have screened her beforehand."

"*Ella esta loca*, Joan!" exclaimed Angel. "I'm sorry to be blunt, but some of us are trying to move on with our lives. We don't need these shenanigans to get pulled back into this old life again if that is what you were attempting. Call me when you have some real news." She abruptly stood from her seat and stormed out of the room.

7

A LIVING NIGHTMARE

No light to depict the charcoal burn marks on the dilapidated building, once used for luxurious living in the early twenties, now a home for rats, cockroaches, and other pests that do their deeds in the darkness. The boarded-up first-floor windows and closed doors made the eight-story building look inaccessible. The ground was strewn with shards of broken glass and trash of every kind, and the walls were covered in graffiti.

Erinys and six of the Furies stood looking at the old edifice, trying to find a way in. Though it looked like it should be condemned, it could house several male hybrids. Nothing was stirring at this time of night, with the exception of a rat that scuttled between Crimson's feet and into the building. It made her leap in fright.

"C'mon, Crimson," mocked Buitre. She was five-seven in height and of a smooth olive complexion. "You can take on Nephilim twice your size, and you are afraid of a small rat?"

Crimson did not respond but simply flipped her middle

finger at her companion while continuing to look for a way in.

"Love you, too," responded Buitre with a hard laugh.

"Crimson, this place is a dump," stated Erinys. "I see no movement, no light emanating from the upper floors. Looks like no one has been here for years."

Crimson extracted her cell phone and reviewed the notes on the screen. "This is it, all right. Though I understand your doubt." The girl's eyes were now glued to a second-floor fire escape and near it, an open window. She pointed her finger and advised, "That could be a way in."

"What are you talking about? I see nothing," declared Buitre, squinting.

"You're as blind as a bat, Buitre." She pointed again with her index finger. "There!"

"It's the only entry I see." The leader turned to her team. "Let's split into pairs once we're in. Eris and Lex, inspect the upper floors while Buitre and Crimson take charge of the middle. Moirai, you're with me on the lower level."

The Fury trotted over and climbed the shaky but stable fire escape. Before entering through the window, each flicked on their flashlights and turned on their walkie-talkies, still tagged *Property of DW Tristate* on the back. The group split up, leaving Buitre and Crimson to their assigned floors.

The two Furies meticulously searched each apartment and room on their level. Each had its own form of debris, though each one had mold-infested walls along with rat feces littering the floor. The dank air was permeated with the stench of urine mixed with burned wood. The women had to cover their nostrils to continue their search.

"Crimson, you got this wrong. It's impossible for someone to live in such conditions. How did you find this place?" She coughed after inhaling some dust.

"Through a computer script I created."

"Are you freaking kidding me?" blurted Buitre. She stopped searching and illuminated Crimson with the flashlight. "You lead us out to this dumb site based on a computer program? Does Erinys know?"

"Get the light out of my face." The girl moved out of the light and continued her search. "She knows. The script is how I found the abandoned asylum with all those Nephilim creeps."

"You mean where Horizon killed herself?" She flashed the light at a nearby walk-in closet.

It was Crimson's turn to put the spotlight on Buitre. "Do you really think she killed herself? How could she manage to decapitate herself with a blade?" the girl asked, disturbed.

"I don't know." Buitre shrugged. "All I know is we cleared out the place. There was no one left in the building. Besides, I don't think she really wanted to be one of us." The Fury raised her hand to cover the light and started to walk out of the room.

Crimson grasped her arm before she could leave. "Why would you say that? You and Horizon were good friends, Robin."

Buitre forcefully freed herself from the woman's grip. "I'm not Robin no more, and maybe that's the reason Horizon is dead now. She couldn't commit!" The Fury glanced. "The bigger question is, are you Candle or Crimson?" She went to check the adjacent room.

Crimson froze for a moment, tightly gripping the blade at her side. She sighed, then walked out of the apartment into the fusty hallway. She called back to her partner, "There's nothing on this level. Let's check the floor below us. If nothing there, let's reconvene with one of the other groups."

The women descended and inspected the apartments on the lower floor. The air on this level didn't have the same stench as above but reeked of dead flesh. They covered their mouths and noses and began to cough.

"What's that stench?" Buitre managed to ask.

"I think it's a corpse."

As they moved on, they saw blood splattered on the walls and floor, and they heard a low buzzing sound. Their light finally identified the hum—an amputated arm surrounded by flies, mice, and rats. Buitre pulled her light away as she covered her mouth with her forearm to keep herself from vomiting.

Crimson inspected the limb and noticed a strange marking on the deltoid. She moved her light a few feet away and saw a body with a missing left arm. "C'mon," she called to her partner.

They moved closer to the dismembered body. The left side was stained with dried-up blood. Crimson moved her light to a shining object on the right, a red-stained quartz blade. On the corpse's right hand was a half-empty vial containing a yellowish liquid.

"What the hell?" asked Buitre as a deep frown crossed her brow. "Did he do this to himself?"

The girl nodded. "He must've bled out." Crimson saw

the vial, grabbed it, and took a sniff. "Kollourion?" she asked.

"What did you say?"

The girl handed the vial to her companion. "Take a whiff. It smells like Kollourion and something else too."

"Yeah, you're right," stated Buitre, pulling the vial away from her nose.

The woman quickly dropped the vial, and they turned their flashlights toward the end of the hallway when they heard a raucous laugh. Instinctively, the women gripped their blades.

"We were wondering how long it would take you witches to show up," said the masculine voice. He continued to laugh as he dragged his body along a mold-infested wall. He lifted a bottle to his lips and took a large gulp, he then used it to gesture at the corpse. "Poor Efiáltis. He went at it alone. If he'd waited, he would be alive like me." The man chuckled, then revealed his missing left arm. "I'm not the enemy anymore. You see? I'm not marked."

"What the fu..." Crimson was saying when a blade punctured his forehead.

The man released the bottle and hit the floor with a thump. Instantly, scrambling noises were heard down the hall.

Crimson flashed her light on Buitre. "Weren't you curious why he chopped his arm off like the other one?"

"No, and call Erinys. The rest of these scumbags are there. Hopefully, they are all drunk like the one I killed." The warrior's light flashed toward a door at the end of the hallway, and she rushed ahead.

The other warrior unclipped her walkie-talkie and called the others. "They're on the third floor. I repeat, third floor." Crimson dashed after Buitre. Along the way, she got an eerie feeling, an odd sense she had never felt before. She slowed and then stopped, dropping the knife and flashlight. The girl looked at her hands and realized she was shaking from the unexpected drop in temperature. The area around her was cold; she began to shiver, then dropped to her knees.

Crimson turned her head back, sensing or hearing—she wasn't sure which—footsteps emanating from the staircase she had come up early. It was dark since her flashlight was pointed in the opposite direction. Like a nightmare materializing, the woman saw purple smoke pass before her and stop at the source of the light—the door Buitre had gone through.

She gasped as the smoke took shape and formed a female figure, then entered the apartment Buitre had vanished into. Seconds later, she heard a loud scream. Then there was silence.

Crimson closed her eyes and remained on her knees. A hand grasped her shoulder, and she let out a shriek.

"Crimson, are you OK?"

The girl warily opened her eyes and gazed at her leader's face. She shook her head.

"Where's Buitre?"

"S-she, um...s-she went through that door," Crimson stammered.

Erinys turned to the three women behind her. "Go and check on Buitre." The leader gave her attention to Crimson again while the women rushed to the apartment. "Are you hurt?"

"Not physically."

The leader squatted to meet the woman's gaze. "What happened?"

"I don't know. Something just…just came out of nowhere. It or she passed me and then stopped at the end of the hall."

"What do you mean, it or she?"

Before Crimson could answer, the three women returned.

"Buitre's dead," disclosed the one named Moirai. "Her head was chopped off."

"What!" exclaimed Erinys, standing up straight.

"There are five dead bodies in that room. One was Buitre, and the rest were Nephilim with no left arms."

Erinys turned her flashlight toward Crimson, who was still on her knees. "Do you know who did this?"

The girl gulped and looked up at her leader with panicked eyes. "I don't know, Erinys. All I saw was a cloud of purple smoke that transformed into a woman, and I felt the entire fear of hell."

"Did it hurt you?" asked Moirai.

Crimson shook her head.

Moirai moved her flashlight to the door and back to Crimson. "Then why did it kill Buitre and not you?"

Crimson stood and grabbed the flashlight and her knife. "When you find out, let me know. I'm getting the hell out of here."

8

A FRESH COAT OF PAINT

Construction workers and equipment created a cacophony at the work site next to the Star of Nimrod headquarters. The ground had already been dug up and the foundation laid for a sizable building and an accompanying parking structure. An unassuming man stood at the edge of the construction site, watching the progress. He sported a graying beard and matching hair. His plain face was marred by scars that covered most of it. In addition, his blazer had accumulated a thin layer of pollen and debris during his time there.

"Grand Luminary Tammuz," a slender young man cried from behind.

Tammuz turned to face him. "Yes, Patrick?"

"Your eleven o'clock is here, Your Radiance."

Tammuz glanced at his Swiss watch. "My goodness, I completely lost track of time. Thank you for fetching me. Go on ahead and let her into my office."

The middle-aged man made his way from the construction site to the office building. He greeted the security guards and the office staff as he walked toward his office. When he reached his destination, he stopped several feet from the door, straightened his jacket, and took a deep breath before he entered the room. Waiting for him inside was a black-haired woman in a pantsuit studying the Sumerian and Akkadian decorations on the walls. She turned to face Tammuz when she heard him enter.

"Mr. Boswell, it is a pleasure to finally meet you in person," she exclaimed as she stepped toward him and stretched her hand.

Tammuz grabbed her hand, "The pleasure is all mine, Ms. Reddy."

"Please call me Rani. Is that a Yorkshire accent I'm detecting?" quizzed Rani.

"It certainly is. And you have a southern accent. London?"

"Guilty as charged."

"Well, I won't hold it against you." Tammuz joked. "Please sit." He motioned toward one of the chairs in the office and sat behind his desk. "The floor is yours. I'm excited to see what you have for me. You come highly recommended."

"Thank you, Mr. Boswell. As you know, I'm a faith organization image and branding consultant. I'm the person you call when a faith-based organization needs to recover its image after a scandal or when they want to rebrand to increase attendance, social media optics, and donations."

Tammuz's face lit up at the last words.

"I brought a packet of the mockups of materials and image rebranding strategies you requested in our email correspondence," Rani stated as she drew several folders from her leather briefcase. "I also took the liberty of going a step further and prepared a presentation of what we call our Hierarchical Creed Model or HCM for short."

"A Hierarchical Creed Model?" inquired Tammuz.

Rani placed the folders on Tammuz's desk and leaned back in her chair. "In your emails, you expressed interest in branding your organization in a way that would attract newcomers so you can spread your beliefs and increase your coffers."

Tammuz nodded.

"I read through the materials you sent me outlining your core beliefs and doctrines. In my experience, you fall into the category I call socially taboo."

The grand luminary's face grew dim.

"Wait, hear me out, Mr. Boswell. I'm not trying to insult your beliefs. On the contrary, my job as a consultant is to respect your deeply and sincerely held principles while telling you the truth about how the average person will perceive them," clarified Rani.

"So, you don't think my organization's belief in the light of man and the evil of the Utukkus and their spawn is strange?"

"No more strange than a belief in ancient aliens, horoscopes, or healing crystals. However, those things have already become part of our society's commonly accepted ideas. If you lead with Utukkus and half-breeds, you won't attract the type of people you want."

Tammuz sat back in his chair and squinted at the woman. "What kinds of people do we want?"

"You want the guppies and the whales."

"Explain."

Rani opened one of the folders and handed Tammuz a document with some charts. "Whales are the people who will fund your big projects and follow you to the depths of the abyss to see your vision come to fruition. Guppies are people who just want to feel good about themselves and be part of a social group that performs charitable actions so *they* don't have to.

"Individually, a guppy is not as useful as a whale, but there are many more of them. Having them in large quantities will legitimize your organization in the eyes of potential whales. If you look at the charts, you'll see what I consider to be the critical mass points for your type of organization for each kind."

Tammuz briefly looked at the charts, then placed them on the desk. "How do we attract them?"

"That's where the HCM comes in. You need a subset of more palatable beliefs for the masses that will attract all the cute little guppies. The other beliefs are gated behind a series of hierarchies that only people who prove themselves to be whales are allowed to climb."

"So, hook them in with a watered-down version of our beliefs, and only reveal the rest to those we deem worthy."

Rani's face lit up. "Exactly, and I have some suggestions on how you might do that." She produced several additional sheets of paper. "Here are some seeker-friendly advertising materials. Also, I suggest one major change."

Tammuz raised an eyebrow. "I'm almost afraid to ask."

"The name of your organization invokes the wrong first impression. For example, the name Nimrod has changed meanings over the years and is now associated with someone less than capable. You can keep the term for the highest levels of the HCM. However, for your public brand, I suggest Luminosity. We did some market research on the name and got favorable results."

"Luminosity, huh?" Tammuz mouthed.

"It rolls off the tongue and brings up the right type of imagery that aligns with your beliefs and brand."

"I can't say I *dis*like it."

"Excellent!" exclaimed the consultant. "Now, I have a question about your organization's leadership. Do you report to a board or council?"

"No, I'm the final authority on the Star of…Luminosity's direction," Tammuz responded.

"Wonderful. These transitions are much smoother when the leader doesn't have an oversight board hindering their vision. Now let's discuss the types of coffee you want to serve in your gathering hall and the merch that sells best. We'll make your organization the new faith group to be envied."

"I will press you to have these ads going by the end of the week. It's imperative we reach the masses sooner rather than later."

The young consultant gave him a pensive stare.

"Is that a problem, Rani?"

She offered him a polite smile. "Not a problem, sir."

The consultant and Tammuz shook hands after their meeting, and she left his office. Moments later, Tammuz's assistant Patrick knocked on the door.

"Come in, Patrick. What is it?"

"Your Radiance, I just received information on our facilities' most recent string of break-ins."

"Outstanding! What do you have for me?"

"Well, the camera footage shows a lone intruder. However, she must have had insider knowledge because she knew how to bypass our security protocols."

"What was taken?" the grand luminary inquired.

"She made her way into the archives and took a series of records—hard copies. Unfortunately, the records were mostly of the traitor's work."

"Masmasu!" Tammuz exclaimed and slammed his fist on his desk. "Of course, this would happen right when we're in the middle of rebranding ourselves. What do we know about this intruder?"

"Well, we ran her through facial recognition, Your Radiance. Her name is Laurie Marilyn Davidson. Her last known affiliation was with a shelter in the city, Saint Miriam's Shelter for Children and Women. It's a known front for a group of hybrid women."

"I know that place well. Contact Agent Owen. We need to find this mongrel fast."

Rani arrived at her office whistling a happy tune. She was always in a good mood when she landed a client with deep pockets.

"Lakshmi is in the house!" announced a tall, slim man with curly tawny hair from a swivel chair. He was wearing a shirt that read *Avoid the top of the bell curve. Everyone there is mean.*

"Ugh, Adrian! Can you dial the skeeve down to a two? Well, whatever. Not even you can ruin my good mood today."

Adrian furrowed his brow, "How am I being skeevy? I'm saying you are the goddess of beauty."

"You better get to work on the website for this new client before I channel Vishnu and fire you for sexual harassment in the workplace. Check the cloud for the files in the Luminosity folder." Rani warned as she ducked into her office.

"All right, all right! Jeez."

Adrian turned his chair to face his computer and pulled up the documents for the client. Then he sifted through the mockups.

"Meh, amateur hour."

He continued to navigate through the files until he ran across the archives for the Hierarchical Creed Model. His face turned beet-red as he read through the client's core beliefs.

"It's a whole religion based on the sightings!" he exclaimed loudly.

Rani stuck her head out her office door. "Did you say something?"

"This client believes in everything I've been investigating for the past few years. The Star of Nimrod thinks the superpowered people are a threat to humanity."

"Luminosity," corrected Rani.

"What?"

"The client's public brand is now called Luminosity."

"Who cares about their brand?" Adrian cried. "This proves everything I've been saying in my podcast. Haven't you been listening to it?"

"Uh, no. And I don't care if the client claims that lizard people run the world's governments. Cut the crap and get to work. We need to give them something by the end of the week," Rani announced before disappearing back into her office.

Adrian pouted and went back to staring at his screen. "I can't wait to discuss this in next week's episode. The guys on Reddit are going to flip!"

9

DRASTIC CONDITIONS

The navy-blue-suited man stood gazing at one of the three posters hanging from the conference room wall. All three posters depicted the Greek goddesses of vengeance. Arms behind his back, he remained motionless apart from rotating the loosely fitting gold ring on his right hand. The man turned his head at the sound of footsteps entering the doorway.

"Is it Agent Owens?"

"You can call me Kenneth or Kenny, whatever your preference," responded the man. "Is it Penelope Stockton?" A smile plastered on his face.

"You may take a seat, Agent Owens."

He chuckled and proceeded to sit on one of the conference table chairs. Before him lay a closed manila folder. "I'm not here on official FBI business if that's your concern, Penny."

"Ms. Stockton, please. And if you're not here on duty, why *are* you here?" inquired the Furies' leader as she sat across from the agent.

"I hear this is no longer a shelter, and that it's under new management," disclosed Agent Owens, gently tapping the folder on the table.

Erinys gave the man a hard stare. "What's the reason for your visit, Agent Owens?"

He smiled in return. "I'm here for personal reasons. Religious, to be frank, and just like this place, we're also under new management. My organization is expanding and becoming more public. Have you had the chance to look at the posters or TV spots for Luminosity? They came out this week."

"Agent Owens…"

"Kenneth would be fine," he interjected with a smile.

"Kenneth," she drawled. "I'm a busy woman and don't have time for these shenanigans. Can you please get to the point?"

The man pushed the envelope toward Erinys. "Luminosity is an organization that seeks peace for mankind. We hope our message of the new way reaches the masses, but we can't do so if we continue to be interrupted by the likes of your kind."

Erinys opened the folder and scanned its content, surveillance images of a woman dressed in black. She stopped at an enlarged facial picture.

"The woman in the photos is Laurie Marilyn Davidson, but she's known among your circle as Jewels. During the past couple of years, she's been responsible for vandalizing several of our facilities, costing the organization thousands. We're hoping for your cooperation in turning her in."

The leader closed the folder and slid it back to the man.

"You're an FBI agent. I'm pretty sure you have the resources to find her. Besides, I don't know the woman."

He let out a soft laugh. "My intel suggests otherwise, but regardless, I believe you know the women who do. Furthermore, the people I represent would like to keep this off the record."

"I'm sorry, but I can't help you." She abruptly stood from the chair.

The agent remained sitting and disclosed, "Ms. Stockton—or should I call you Erinys—I think I need to make myself clearer. It is my understanding that since coming under new management, this facility has incurred some significant debt which could look like tax evasion, thus defrauding the IRS. Furthermore, while my organization teaches peace and love, we don't offer them to your kind."

His expression turned dark. "I can either have Uncle Sam knocking at your door or my people breaking it down. You choose, but I think your option is clearly laid out." He went into the suit's inner pocket and tossed a business card on the table. "Call me when you've apprehended the woman. You can keep the folder in case you forget again what she looks like."

The man stood and walked out.

Erinys sat in her office, contemplating while stroking the mark on her face. On the desk was the manila folder Agent Owens had left behind, a half-empty whiskey bottle, and a glass. Grabbing the glass, she went to sip but realized it was empty. She needed to think about how to get herself and her team out of this jam, so she poured herself another glass. No sooner had she finished it than there was a hard knock on her door. She let out a long sigh. "Come on in," she said miserably.

The door rapidly opened, and through it came a panicked-looking young woman. "Erinys, we lost two more!"

"What do you mean we lost two more, Crimson?"

"Lexis and Vice are dead," the young woman elaborated.

"How and when?"

"Earlier this evening. They had just finished a hunt, along with Eris, when our mysterious attacker reappeared and killed them both."

"How do you know it was the same killer?"

"Eris witnessed the same thing I did, the room getting extremely cold and some dark purple smoke taking the shape of a woman before Lexis' and Vice's heads were chopped off." Crimson clasped her hands behind her head and paced in front of the desk. "This is getting out of control."

"And Eris?"

"She's shaken up, but she's fine." The woman swallowed in despair. "Who is doing this to us?"

Erinys remained quiet as her wide eyes shifted from Crimson to the folder. The leader pushed it toward the young woman. "It must be this witch. I should've killed her when I had the chance."

The young woman stopped pacing, picked up the folder, and scanned the images. "Villainous? How did you get this?"

Erinys took a gulp from the glass. "A story for a different time, but I hear that she's been stirring up trouble as of late."

"Why do you suspect it's her? I mean, it seems that whatever it is can appear out of nowhere in a cloud of smoke."

"She's known to work with demons. It must be some form of witchcraft those things gave her." The leader leaned back in her chair. "Haven't you noticed she's only targeting women who were once a part of Joan's group?"

"I was once part of Joan's group, so why not come after me when she killed Buitre?"

"Because you were not here when Villainous came to this facility. She must have a personal vendetta against those women, or she must be working for…." She shook her head to dismiss the thought.

"Or what?"

Erinys was quiet, but her desk phone rang. "Hello?"

"Greetings, Erinys. Do you have a moment to chat?" asked the person on the other end of the line. "This is Cherry, Daughters of the Watchers London."

The leader scoffed. "Yeah, I'm not interested in joining your boy band if that's what you are calling about."

"I promised to make it worth your while if you lend me your ear for a few."

The Furies' leader placed the phone on speaker and grabbed her glass. "You have two minutes," she stated, slugging the rest of the whiskey.

"We have it on good authority that you have had some run-ins with the former leader of the Daughters of the Watchers Tristate, Joan."

Erinys frowned. "Former? Isn't she still?"

"Not in our book." Cherry cleared her throat. "She was already in bad odor with the Global Daughterhood Committee but complicated the matter when she kidnapped one of our women—who is seriously ill, I must add—last week. We will only accept so much before taking drastic measures to rectify the matter, but we believe in giving people second chances."

"This sounds like an internal problem, so why are you calling me?"

"We misjudged you, Erinys, partly on the narrative of Joan and her followers. We believe it to be a Sovereign sign that you are now running the New York compound. Thus, the committee is deeming you the new Tristate Daughters of the Watchers' leader."

The Furies' leader laughed. "You've got to be freaking kidding me."

"Believe it. You have the leadership qualities Joan lacks, so to spare us taking those drastic measures and afford those fallen Daughters an olive branch, we hope you can intervene and provide them with a message."

"Sorry, but I'm no one's..." Erinys began, but she was interrupted by Cherry.

"Of course, you and your group will be generously financially compensated."

Erinys remained silent. She poured herself another glass and took a slurp.

"Are you still there, dear?"

The leader wiped her lips, then asked, "What's the message?"

"The Global Daughterhood Committee has laid out

certain conditions for Joan and her followers, and if they abide by them, we'll be more than glad to receive them back."

"I'm listening," uttered Erinys.

"First, give up any Nephilim they are harboring so they can be dealt with. They must remove themselves from those zealots called Tektonites and have no association with them. Lastly, Joan and the other council members must relinquish their authority and submit to yours."

"If they reject your proposition, will I still get the generous compensation, as you call it?"

"Expect half of it the moment you agree."

"One more question. What type of drastic measures are you talking about if they do not comply?"

Cherry breathed heavily over the line. "The answer is simple: eradication. I'll give you until tomorrow to consider the offer." The line went dead.

The leader shook her head in surprise. "I thought *I* ran a tight ship." She glanced at Crimson. "Do me a favor and get Joan on the line."

The young woman gave her a curious look. "Are you really considering that woman's offer?"

"If Joan has gone rogue, she could be behind these attacks. If so, I'll add condition number four, to turn in Villainous. Also, I suspect that Kollourion-like substance you found at the abandoned building might have been concocted by her if she's harboring Nephilim."

"What do you mean?"

"If she's protecting those killers, that's one sure way of doing it."

PART II

JUSTICE

10

A TIME BEFORE

Twenty-Eight Years Ago

A boisterous crowd lined the streets on either side of a luxurious high-rise hotel's entrance. The throng erupted in cheers each time a vehicle arrived and let its passengers out onto the purple carpet that adorned the path leading to the hotel. Media personalities and news reporters interviewed the arriving guests as their adoring fans hooted and hollered from the sidelines.

This parade continued for some time. Suddenly, the mob went silent. All eyes turned to the latest vehicle to arrive, a low-profile sports car painted bright orange with black stripes down the doors. It sat for a few moments before the passenger side door opened upward like the unfurling wings of a pegasus. An attendant hurried to the side of the vehicle and stretched out his hand, and out stepped a tall, stunning blonde woman with dark-green eyes. She wore a black plunging V-neck dress that perfectly accentuated her ample curves.

"It's her!" shrieked a voice from the crowd, breaking the silence and initiating an eruption of cheers and applause.

The woman waved at her fans and approached some of those nearest her. She shook several hands and posed for a few pictures before making her way toward the waiting reporters.

"Ms. Luna Topaz! I know you hear this all the time, but you are stunning," exclaimed an enthusiastic news personality as she rushed to meet the celebrity. "No one here can take their eyes off you."

"Oh, thank you, darling," replied Luna as she placed a hand on one cheek. "I'm overwhelmed by the love and support of my fans."

"Tell us about your outfit."

"Oh, I'm so glad you asked. I know my chest steals so much attention." The woman smirked playfully. "But you just have to get a good look at these."

Luna lifted her dress to reveal an elegant pair of stiletto heels with precious stones encrusting their laces.

"Wow, those are incredible!"

"Thank you, darling. They were custom-made, just like this exquisite dress," responded Luna as she twirled. "I always aim to please my fans."

"Well, you have certainly succeeded. Tell me, is there anyone special in your life right now? The people are dying to know," inquired the reporter.

The sophisticated woman winked and placed her index finger in front of her lips, "Tonight is about the work my charitable organizations have done and will continue to do with the funds raised at this event. We can talk juicy gossip another time."

With this last statement, Luna continued making her way toward the hotel. She had taken no more than a few steps when a short, dark-haired woman stood in her way.

"Hello, Ms. Topaz. Judy Glass with WWJD news. Congratulations on the reported success of your non-profits."

"Oh, thank you! I'm so proud—" Luna began before Judy cut her off.

"Could you comment on the record about the discrepancies in the financial reporting at several of the organizations you operate?"

The celebrity stared blankly at the reporter before giving her a half-smile. "I'm so sorry I can't stay and chat, but the event is about to start, and I need to be on my way." Luna hurried off and disappeared into the building.

Judy asked her cameraman, "Did you get all that, Max?"

Max grunted. "All what? She barely said anything."

"It's not what she said, it was the look on her face. We'll get another chance to confront her inside. This scandal is about to blow up, and I'm not letting anyone else scoop us."

"Whatever."

Judy and Max waited for the retinue of reporters and celebrities to make their way inside the hotel before approaching the entrance themselves. Two burly security guards stood menacingly in front of the doors.

"You aren't allowed inside," announced one of the guards.

"Oh, it's all right, we're with WWJD," explained Judy as she produced her press credentials.

"We've been instructed that neither you nor anyone else from your organization are to be allowed in."

"Oh, the boss isn't going to be happy about this," muttered Max.

Judy spun and grabbed her cameraman by the arm, "No, this is great. Don't you see? Censorship and media lockouts are the tools of the guilty. We're close, Max. I can feel it in my gut. Let's head back to the office."

"You're fired!" yelled a middle-aged man with a head full of gray hair and a twitch in his eye.

"What?" protested Judy, "You can't be serious, John."

"I'm as serious as cancer," John retorted. "You've gotten our entire organization blacklisted from every event Ms. Topaz is part of."

"That's proof that I'm on to something."

"The only thing you're on to is unemployment."

Judy crossed her arms and furrowed her brow, "Come on, John. Just calm down."

"I'm not sure what you aren't understanding. Do I need to spell it out for you? OK, here you go. F-I-R-E-D!" exclaimed John, moving his arms to form the shapes of letters.

The young reporter's mouth dropped, "You're really firing me?"

"What gave it away? Was it the half-dozen times I've yelled it at you?" snarked John. "Empty out your desk by day's end."

Judy stared at her now-ex-employer for a moment. "Fine. Great! Now I can crack this story and take it to a better news organization. Maybe one without cruddy coffee and toxic bosses."

John's eyes softened, "Listen, kid, I like you. I really do. For your own good, drop this. Lay low for a few months and find a job somewhere else. I'll even give you a recommendation when the time comes."

The young woman stormed out of the office without responding.

Judy sat in her car as hot tears streamed down her face.

"Come on, call me already," she yelled at her phone.

She tossed the mobile on the passenger seat, buried her face in her hands, and muffled a scream. Just then, a notification chirped. The woman fumbled for the device and looked at the screen.

Mr. B, the display read.

Judy drew a deep breath, calmed herself, and answered the call.

"Hello, Mr. B."

"Hi, Dame Judy. Sorry to hear about your job," said a deep, raspy voice. Judy was accustomed to the voice being altered during their conversations.

Judy paused. "How do you know about that?"

"It's my job to know things."

"Well, good. That makes this easier. You're my source, and we're in this together, but I need more. Something tangible I can use to break this story and get my job back. You owe me this."

Mr. B was silent for a few seconds. "I don't owe you a

thing. I provided you with information to break a major story, and you blew it. How is that my problem?"

Judy's lip quivered slightly. "Please, Mr. B. I'll…I'll be in your debt. I'll do anything."

A soft chuckle crackled through the phone's speaker. "I can work with that. Give me a few hours, and I'll send you some documents that link Ms. Topaz to the embezzlement and fraud at her non-profits. Also, a little bird told me she'll be at the Hoof & Claw Lounge tonight."

"Thank you, thank you. You won't regret this," exclaimed Judy.

"I know I won't."

Luna sat alone at her usual table at the Hoof & Claw. She sipped a cocktail as she scanned the room, taking inventory of the most attractive patrons in the establishment.

A lot of juicy prey tonight, she thought.

An intrusion into her personal space took her attention from a remarkably handsome young man.

"Ms. Topaz, you really need to talk to me," stated a vaguely familiar voice.

Luna glanced side-eyed the meddler.

"The noisy reporter." She huffed and took another sip of her drink. "Shouldn't you have lost your job already?"

"Yes, you are a formidable woman," Judy admitted. "But even you can't cover up this kind of evidence."

The young woman plopped a stack of papers on the table in front of Luna.

"You've been embezzling money from your charities to

maintain your lavish and decadent lifestyle. This is just the tip of the iceberg. Multiple payoffs to silence abuse accusations, expensive trips worldwide."

The celebrity's face started to crack, but she quickly composed herself. "You foolish mouse. You walk into the snake's den, thinking your little papers will protect you."

"Oh, I'm no fool. I've sent copies of all this evidence to the relevant government agencies. Every major news organization has also received it, except my former employers. They can read about it from everyone else."

Luna's brow furrowed, and her grip on her cocktail glass tightened. Her gaze grew increasingly wild and menacing.

"Ms. Topaz, it's over. I'm here to get your side of the story. What do you have to say about this mountain of evidence against you?"

The woman glared at the reporter with murder on her face. The pressure on the glass became too much and it shattered, leaving Luna's hand bloody and still gripping the stem and bottom of the glass.

"Oh, my God! Are you all right?" exclaimed Judy.

The elegance in Luna's face melted, leaving behind a turbulent expression more animal than human. Without warning, she jabbed the broken stem into the unsuspecting reporter's throat. Judy clutched her neck, fear marring her face.

Luna was not done exacting her punishment. The enraged woman lunged at her victim, dragged her from the table, and slammed her head against the floor until a pool of blood formed under the young woman.

"Oh, my God! She killed her!" shrieked another patron.

Luna came to her senses, standing over Judy's body.

The club's owner came running, with several bouncers, "Ms. Topaz, what have you done?"

"Get everybody out!" ordered Luna. "And barricade the doors. I need some time."

A red portal opened in the middle of the floor at the nightclub. The space around the portal had a series of circles and diagrams drawn in blood on the stone floor. Luna was kneeling several feet away from the crimson swirl, chanting in muffled tones. Moments later, a tall man with flaming red hair and piercing blue eyes stepped through.

"Belial!" Luna cried.

The man looked around the room and noticed the cold body on the floor.

"Well, you've made a mighty mess of things."

"My lord, I don't know what came over me. I've served you faithfully and supported your cause through the money I've collected through the companies you've blessed me with. Please help me."

Belial stroked his chin and approached the woman. "Even I can't make something like this go away easily."

"I'll pay any price. Give any amount."

"Well, there might be a way, but it will be...unorthodox."

"Whatever it is, I pledge myself to you," affirmed Luna.

"Well, that's just it. It is not allegiance to me but to

another master. One you would not meet for some time, but who would give you an incalculable honor."

"What honor would that be?"

"To become the mother of the most powerful man to have ever lived. To birth a Son of Destruction."

Luna hesitated for a moment, "What about my life here?"

"That life is gone. This is the only path that doesn't involve dying in a jail cell."

"OK, my lord. I'll do it."

Belial produced a trinket from his pocket, a wooden sigil depicting a hollow tree. He spoke some ancient words, then tossed the sigil across the room. A portal appeared at the spot where the charm hit the floor, one unlike any Luna had ever seen.

This portal swirled with a purple hue. Energy crackled around the edges of the circular opening and seemed to bend the space around it. Moments after it opened, a tall, elegant woman stepped through, and the temperature in the room dropped abruptly.

The newcomer looked at Luna, then at Belial. "Is this the one?"

He nodded.

"Let's go, child. We have a long way to travel and much to discuss about your new life."

Luna sheepishly approached the imposing woman. "What do I call you, mistress?"

"You may call me Mara. What do I call you?"

"Luna..." she started, then shook her head. "My birth name is Theresa."

11

DIGGING FOR CLUES

Present Time

A family of deer was grazing in a grassy field outside a dilapidated building. Unexpectedly, a blonde human woman and a majestic humanoid figure appeared in the field next to the animals. The creatures froze in fear for several seconds before rushing into the nearby woods.

"Jeez, what a dump. You'd think a Primal would have better taste," exclaimed the woman.

"I care not for its aesthetic properties, Theresa, but for the mark that past events have left on this place," Haniel clarified.

"This straight man act doesn't ever get old," Theresa quipped as she rolled her eyes.

Haniel glanced at her with a blank expression. The woman shook her head and started for the entrance to the building. "Let's just get this done."

The abandoned facility had seen better days. The wood on the front doors had partially rotted through, and one side was off its hinges. From the façade, Theresa could tell it must have been a care facility long ago. She reached the entrance and pulled on the door that looked to be sturdier. The knob came off, and then the door broke free from the frame and crashed to the ground.

"Well, we're off to an auspicious start," Theresa muttered as she stepped over the wood. A pungent odor assaulted her nostrils and caused her to gag involuntarily. "Something must have died in here."

"Not something, many someones," Haniel clarified from outside. He followed her inside, and they continued into the building in silence.

The pair made their way up a few floors and through several corridors until they came across a room whose walls and the floor were covered in dark gray patches of a dry mineral.

Theresa frowned. "This is dried blood, and a lot of it."

Haniel glanced at her with a raised eyebrow.

"When I was a priestess in Diablos' order, we made many sacrifices. You never forget some things; you just learn to live with them. Balance them, if you will."

The Archangel nodded at her. Then, he glanced around as if searching for something. Moments later, he narrowed his eyes and fixed his gaze farther down the corridor. "This is the spot."

"What spot?"

"The place my sister inadvertently marked with her power. Watch."

The Primal stretched out his hand, and a set of balanced scales appeared in front of it. He rotated his hand slightly, causing the scales to lean toward one side. Translucent images appeared like a hologram running in reverse.

"What is this?" Theresa asked.

"This is the record of those things that have transpired here. We will witness the events surrounding my sister's intervention."

The images showed a woman entering the room covered with dried blood and savagely attacking a group of young males. Moments later, another woman entered the room but quickly exited and headed toward the entrance. Then the first woman left the room, but she went farther into the building, hugging the wall. Suddenly, the woman was reeled back as if she had been attacked.

"Wait, what just happened there? Who attacked her?" Theresa inquired.

Haniel remained silent and continued watching the unfolding events. They saw the woman struggle to her feet and run in the opposite direction. When she was nearly at the entrance, a blade appeared behind the fleeing woman and decapitated her.

"Why can't we see the attacker? Was that your sister? Answer me!"

Haniel dropped his hand to his side, and the scales rebalanced and then disappeared. At that moment, the image of the beheaded woman on the floor faded. "No, it was not my sister. She is bound, as I am, not to directly affect or interfere with human affairs. The attacker is her agent; someone imbued with her essence and something else. She is a very dangerous individual whom you will undoubtedly confront soon."

Theresa opened her mouth to speak, but out of the corner of her eye, she saw a metallic object hurtling toward her. She barely had enough time to move out of the way.

When she recovered her footing, she glanced in the direction from which the object had come. At the end of the passageway were several young men with gaunt faces and sunken eyes.

"You here to try to finish us off? Well, it ain't gonna work, witch. Francis, hit her!"

One of the young men stepped forward, then breathed deep, and blew out, releasing a cloud of a noxious green gas that headed for Theresa. She took a horse stance and centered her body and mind. When the cloud reached her location, she waved her arms in a circular motion and guided the gas toward the exit, leaving her unharmed.

"What the crap!" cried the original speaker. "Johnny, blast her!"

A different boy took aim at Theresa this time. Arcs of electricity started dancing between his arms, then he yelled and stretched a hand toward the woman, firing a massive bolt of energy directly at her. The blast reached her before she had time to react and struck her dead-on. She winced as the electricity coursed through her body, then she gritted her teeth, regained her composure, and reached out. The energy collected and welled up inches from her arm.

"It can't be," muttered her stupefied attacker as beads of sweat flowed from his forehead. A few seconds later, his body began to shake, and the stream of electricity faltered and sputtered until it stopped. His arm dropped limply in front of him.

Theresa finished collecting the last of the torrent before guiding the ball of energy that had gathered near her fingertips into the floor. The electricity dissipated harmlessly.

The young men stared incredulously at the woman. "What do we do now?" asked one of the younger ones in the back.

Theresa caught her breath and yelled, "I'm not here to harm you."

"How can we believe that? You're crazy. You've been staring around and talking to yourself the whole time you've been here. We can't let you tell your murdering friends about us," replied the one called Johnny.

"Do I look like them?"

"Well, no, you don't have the same aura as them. Yours is weird. It's not like any hybrid we've ever seen."

"That's because I'm not a hybrid," Theresa clarified. "I have no quarrel with you. I simply needed to investigate something here." She paused for a second. "The…kids that were killed here. You knew them?"

Johnny's eyes grew misty. "They were our friends. Our brothers."

"For what it's worth, I'm sorry this happened to you. But why are you hiding here?"

Johnny wiped his eyes on his sleeve and sniffled. "Everything went to crap after the Son of the Destruction showed up. He was supposed to lead us to a glorious future or some crap. Instead, he worked us to the bone, then went and got himself killed like an idiot."

The young man's words cut Theresa's heart deeply and threatened to reopen the wounds of grief. Anger flashed in her eyes, but it quickly subsided and turned to sadness.

"I'm done here," she stated tersely, then walked out the door as she fought back tears.

For the first time since the attack commenced, she noticed that Haniel was no longer next to her. He was waiting in the grassy field where they had first appeared. She sauntered over to him, regaining her composure on the way. "So, other people can't see or hear you?"

"I'm only perceived by those I choose. I…" Haniel stopped in mid-sentence and stared into the distance.

Theresa followed his gaze to see what he was staring at. She waited a few moments before interrupting his contemplation. "What is it?"

"It's my sister."

"Is it another attack like this one?"

"No, my other sister." the Primal clarified.

"Other sister? There are more of you?" Theresa queried incredulously. "What's this one doing?"

"Apocalypse has always been a mystery, even to us Archangels."

"Is she against us or for us?"

Haniel narrowed his eyes and flared his nostrils. "I cannot say, though, I suspect that our goals might align. I sense she's also chosen a conduit to work through in this world, a female hybrid."

"Oh, goody! She, the psycho killer, and I can start a girl band." Theresa quipped. "So, what do we do?"

Haniel pondered that for a moment, then stared into Theresa's dark-green eyes. "I think you should go and introduce yourself."

12

NOT A WALK IN THE PARK

A woman of average height with ash-brown hair leaned on the rail between her and the water, using the dark waters of the Hudson River as her ashtray. Her large sunglasses not only offered coverage from the bright afternoon sun but hid much of the claw-sharped scar on her face. She took another puff from the cigarette and examined her watch.

Pursing her lips in annoyance again, she huffed. She was looking for the late arrival when her eyes fixed on a group of children on a nearby playground. An unexpected tear coursed down her scar as she watched two small girls gleefully play with each other. The woman removed the sunglasses to dry the tear.

"My apologies for my tardiness, Erinys. There were subway delays," said the approaching female.

The Furies' leader quickly replaced her shades, dropped her cigarette to the ground, and snuffed it with her foot. "Hello, Joan." She sniffled and cleared the hoarseness from her voice.

Hearing her dejection, Joan asked, "Are you OK?"

Erinys turned to the river. "I'm never OK. I guess that's the problem." The woman took a deep breath. "On to the real reason I called. Is it you?"

Joan joined Erinys by the rail. "Is it me what?"

The woman reached into her inner jacket pocket and pulled out a folded envelope. She gently slapped it on Joan's right arm.

The other woman looked inquisitive as she took hold of the envelope, then opened it and extracted its content. Her eyes darkened as she scanned the images. "Jewels?" she uttered in a barely audible tone.

"Apparently, she's been stirring up trouble with those fanatical zealots." Erinys met Joan's eyes. "And for me."

"What do you mean?"

The woman scoffed. "Don't play coy with me, Joan. Villainous has killed four of my women."

"What? Why?"

"What do you mean, why?" Erinys lowered her voice at the sight of passing pedestrians. "You know why."

A look of shock came over Joan. "Wait! Do you think I'm behind this?"

The Furies' leader bit her lip. "Don't act so surprised. The women she killed were once part of your team." She pointed her finger at Joan. "Horizon, Robin, Lucky, and Venus. I guess you didn't take it well when they didn't come along, so you sent that witch and had them killed."

A tear ran down Joan's face at the mention of those names. "Those were wonderful women who I worked with for years. I had no idea about their deaths, much less being part of it."

"Yeah, OK. Let's go with that." Erinys returned her eyes to the dark water.

Gazing at the side of the woman's face, Joan uttered, "Erinys, I'm serious. I know we have our differences, but I wouldn't stoop to that level."

Erinys reached into her pocket and pulled out a box of cigarettes and a lighter. Popping one into her mouth, she lit it. In a muffled voice, she disclosed, "That's not what I'm hearing." She replaced the cigarettes and lighter in her pocket as smoke spewed from the side of her mouth. She then clutched the cigarette between her fingers. "I'm hearing you and your group have gone rogue."

Joan let out a disappointed sigh. "Is that what they are calling it now? *Rogue?*" The woman shook her head.

"I heard more than that. How you broke away from most of the Daughterhood code of conduct and kidnapped one of their mentally ill women. I have to say I was surprised by that." Erinys turned around and glanced at the playground. She eyed the two girls, who were still playing. "What didn't come as a shocker was that you are harboring and rescuing male hybrids. You even have concocted a Kollourion to hide their aura. How pathetic."

"Erinys, please listen to me. There is more than what they are telling—"

"No! You listen to me." She turned and faced Joan. With the cigarette between her fingers, the Furies' leader poked the woman's chest. "I had huge respect for you, Joan, but you are now playing with fire. They are coming after you. Yes, that's right. Your beloved group is on the precipice of warring with you and your women. Those zealots are also after you unless you give up that wretched witch Villainous.

"And one more thing. I never fight my own, but if you stand in the way of my killing those Nephilim monsters, trust me, I won't hesitate to bring you down along with them."

The Furies' leader reached into the inner pocket, pulled out a folded piece of paper, and slammed it into Joan's chest. "These are the demands. You have a week to comply, or all hell will break loose." She took another puff, dropped her smoke, and walked away.

"Bye, Miss Santos," said the child, waving his hand. He had a big grin plastered on his face, although the two front teeth were missing.

"Bye-bye, Kalif. I'll see you tomorrow," Angel responded as she stood by the classroom door. She watched as the last of her students exited the school, then returned to her classroom.

She cleared the workbooks left on the first graders' desks, picked up pieces of construction paper and crayons off the floor, and lastly erased the whiteboard. She then sat at her desk and began grading the weekend homework. Angel looked up when she heard a knock on the open door.

"Can I come, Miss Santos?" Her visitor drawled the last name.

"Hey, Pretzel. Good to see you, girlfriend. Yes, come in and close the door if you don't mind."

After closing the door, Pretzel walked over to Angel and embraced her. Then the young woman took a seat at a small desk in front of Angel's.

"What's this pleasant surprise?"

"I haven't seen you for over a week, and you didn't come to the Sunday meeting yesterday," answered Pretzel, staring at her girlfriend.

Angel stacked the homework on the desk and continued grading them. "I've missed Sunday meetings in the past."

The young woman nodded. "Yeah, I know, but I tried calling you. No answer, and this particular Sunday was a few days after the meeting with Nyala."

Angel cleared her throat and pointedly engaged in grading. "I've been very busy this whole week. That's all."

"I have known you long enough to know when something is up with you. What's going on?"

Angel swallowed, then shook her head. "Nothing. You know. It's the end of the school year, and I need, um, to prepare for the end-of-year exams." Angel continued to avoid eye contact.

Pretzel pursed her lips, then remarked unconvincingly, "OK." After waiting a few minutes in silence, she stood. "If you wanna talk, you know how to reach me."

As the young woman reached for the door handle, Angel revealed, "I'm afraid, Pretzel."

Pretzel stopped and turned to her. "I figured as much."

The Latin woman covered her face, then gazed at her friend. "You heard what she said about Therion coming back to life. We didn't even stop him the first time; we got some mysterious help. How could we fight him now?" She shook her head. "I don't know if I can deal with that."

The other woman returned to her seat. "So, you don't think Nyala is out of her mind?"

Angel rubbed her arm, then looked around the classroom. "I don't know. Part of me doesn't believe it. I mean, she sounded and acted off, so there's plenty of reason to think she isn't all there. Besides, things have been great, and not just for me, for all of us. Think about it, Pretzel. We have lives now and haven't had to worry about hiding or being chased or hunted."

"I couldn't agree more," responded Pretzel. "You said those things out loud because you're the most impulsive of the bunch, but we were all thinking it," She smiled, and so did her friend. "To be honest, you are not the only one who's afraid."

That left Angel quiet and thinking. Her eyebrows drew together. "I'm so sorry, Pretzel. I guess I took it personally without factoring in how you and the others were feeling. Do you think she was telling us the truth?"

Pretzel pressed her lips together. "I'm as confused as you are, and just like you, I hope it's not true. She seemed psychotic, but you know me. I always apply reasonable doubt."

"I understand. Like, I'm trying to convince myself that she was out of her mind rather than simply accepting her words. Does that mean anything?"

Compassion appeared in Pretzel's expression. "Maybe it's that you believe her words were true."

Angel slouched in her chair and laid her head back, staring at the ceiling. "*Soberano, ayudame,*" she whispered.

"I believe the Sovereign will help you," responded her friend. "Hey, why don't we put this behind us for now and head over to *Somos Hispanos* Café?"

The girl gave Pretzel her attention. "Yes, please, and we'll talk about Adrian's latest SuperHuman podcast."

Her friend chuckled. "That's a good idea. I need a good laugh. I do wonder what will happen to him once he finds out that some of his theories are true."

"Hopefully, he'll stop."

They gazed at each other and chorused, "Nah!"

The wise curator placed the book on the nightstand. Then she noticed that Nyala had finally closed her eyes. She quietly stood, strode out of the room, and gently closed the door behind her. To her surprise, the group's caretaker sat outside, reading on a tablet.

"May, fancy seeing you here at this time. I was under the impression that you had gone for your afternoon walk. Nyala has fallen asleep if that is the reason for your visit."

"Hello, Mrs. Mozart. Actually, I came to speak to you." The caretaker stood. "I was wondering if you would accompany me on my walk. I'd like to discuss something with you."

"I would not mind a good walk, but who will watch over Miss Nyala?" She pointed at the room.

"I've taken care of that," May responded.

"Well, then, seeing as you have arranged it, give me a few minutes to change my footwear and apparel, dear."

The caretaker smiled. "Great. I'll meet you outside."

After a few minutes, Mrs. Mozart exited the Tektonites' compound. May was waiting next to a red metal door. The caretaker frowned inquisitively at the other woman's workout outfit.

"I came of my own volition if you need your conscience appeased," revealed Mrs. Mozart with a huge grin.

May chuckled. "Gypsy was right. She knew you would catch on."

"Of course, she was right. I would not have expected it otherwise, and yes, I concur. I need the walk."

"It's been several days, and you haven't left Nyala's bedside. We thought a change of pace might help a bit."

"Absolutely," said the woman. She zipped up her mustard jacket and started to take long strides. "Now, keep up."

The caretaker rushed to her side. "I wasn't totally being obscure. There's something I wish to discuss with you."

Taking deep breaths, Mrs. Mozart uttered, "By all means, but before you begin, I wanted to thank you for the treatment you have given Nyala. I have to say, in these last couple of days, I have seen vast cognitive and functional improvements."

"My pleasure," said May in a breathy way. "On that subject, she's the reason I want to talk to you."

"Go on."

"As you might know, part of my gift is not only to accelerate healing but also to discern if the illness is genetic or caused by some other factor."

"Correct, the pathogenesis of the disease." She took another deep breath and increased her pace.

May frowned because she knew the term until she realized who she was addressing. "That's right. Well, I find it interesting that upon examining Nyala's mental state, I sensed her psychosis wasn't developed by a genetic or external factor such as a force trauma to the head but something supernatural."

"Elaborate, please." Mrs. Mozart raised her hand in thanks to the car that stopped as she crossed the street into the park.

"I have a strong sense it was induced by a supernatural source like a Nephilim."

The wise woman remained quiet. May could tell she was thinking about the matter. The caretaker knew not to bother her when she was in this state. After several minutes of silence, May stopped.

"OK, Mrs. Mozart, I need to catch my breath." She exhaled loudly as she bent forward and clasped her knees.

The curator stopped and turned to May, not looking fatigued. "I had an inkling and appreciate your confirmation. However, I want to make it clear that I dismissed any notions that her words were bunkum or balderdash. Miss Nyala has a message and needs our assistance to articulate it."

"How are we to accomplish that?" Beats of sweat formed on May's forehead as she continued taking quick breaths in succession.

"You are the caretaker, dear. You tell me." The curator smiled.

"Deal, but you have to tell me why you are not fatigued."

Mrs. Mozart laughed. "I take an hour's walk with Miss

Gypsy at dawn pretty much every day." She winked. "Now, keep up. We have another forty-five minutes left."

"Why am I feeling hoodwinked?" asked May.

"That is because you were, dear. I missed this morning's walk, and now I'm having it with you," the wise woman disclosed as she took long strides.

13

AN UNLIKELY HOST

Dinner at the Tektonite compound was a busy affair. Each evening, people made their way to the dining hall to enjoy a hot meal and boisterous conversation and laughter. The doors were open to any needing food or companionship, but the mess hall was uncharacteristically full for a Wednesday evening. In the midst of the hustle and bustle, a trio of young women sat at a table with cards arranged in a grid.

"You've got this, Nyala," encouraged a curly-haired blonde with deep blue eyes. "Try to drown out the noise and focus on finding the matching cards."

Nyala drew a deep breath and attempted to ignore the commotion around her. Then, she stretched out her hand, flipped over one of the face-down cards on the board, and sighed in frustration. Finally, she scrunched her face and buried her face in her hands.

"I could recite entire works of history," Nyala lamented. "Now I can't even play a child's game."

"It's OK, Nyala." said the third, her narrow, deep-set

eyes fixed on her defeated companion. "Practice makes progress."

Nyala peeked out from under her hands. "Isn't it 'practice makes perfect,' Sparkles?"

"No, silly. You can't ever be perfect, but you can always improve, if just a little." Sparkles smiled, her round cheeks rosy. "Isn't that right, Olivia?"

Olivia nodded and placed her arm around Nyala. "You've been through something traumatic that your mind is still making sense of. Give yourself some grace."

Nyala breathed out and sat up straight. "Are you sure you're only fourteen? That's a lot of wisdom."

The blonde teen grinned. "I've seen more than most in my short life, and I've been surrounded by caring, wise women who've encouraged me every step of the way. By the way, May thought of the game. She hoped its simplicity would encourage you."

"And you have us encouraging you, Nyala!" cheered Sparkles.

Nyala chuckled. "Yes, I do, and I'm ever so grateful for it. All right, let's try this again." Nyala tapped her cheeks with both hands and concentrated on the cards in front of her. Then she flipped over a new card and beamed. Swiftly, she flipped over a second card, revealing the matching card.

"Yes!" cried Olivia and Sparkles in unison.

"I did it!"

"Yes, you did. I told you practice makes progress, silly," Sparkles teased.

The three women hugged. But, as they embraced, Olivia noticed a woman staring intently in their direction from across the dining hall. Olivia furrowed her brow, "Do either of you know that woman over there?"

Sparkles glanced over first and shook her head. Slowly, Nyala turned in the direction Olivia had pointed out. When she saw the blonde, middle-aged woman across the room, her eyes glazed over, and she started tapping her head with her palm. "No, no, not the voices again."

Chills went down Sparkles' and Olivia's spines as, for a second, they felt that they could hear whispers in the air, which quickly dissipated. Abruptly, Nyala stood and stomped toward the stranger. Olivia rushed after her.

"Why are the two of you here?" demanded Nyala as she glared at the woman and then glanced at the empty space beside her.

Olivia was right behind her. "I'm sorry. My friend's been having a tough time lately. She means you no harm."

"No harm done. I—" the woman started, but Nyala cut her off.

"Conduit of Haniel, Primal of Balance, what is your business here?" she yelled, causing the hall to become quiet. All eyes were now on them.

The new woman's face grew pale, but she composed herself.

At that moment, Joan, Gypsy, and Mrs. Mozart entered. Their attention was drawn to the scene playing out with Nyala.

Nyala grabbed her head. "Please, please be quiet," she pleaded. "She's whose mother?" the young woman asked no one in particular.

The stranger rose to her feet. "I see my presence is disturbing the young lady. I'll be on my way."

Nyala's eyes glowed with an unnatural green hue, though with her back turned to everyone else, only the stranger witnessed the transformation.

"Why are you here, Theresa, mother of Therion, the Son of Destruction?" Nyala asked emphatically, an unusual sternness in her voice.

Upon hearing the name Therion, Joan shot Gypsy a glance. The warrior was on her way toward the commotion.

"Ma'am, I think you should come with me."

Theresa glanced at the frightened faces around the room. "Very well. Lead the way."

Joan and Mrs. Mozart sat around the table in the multipurpose room. Theresa sat across from them. Behind them, Gypsy leaned against the wall, her eyes fixed on their enigmatic guest.

"I'll cut to the chase. Is it true? Are you Therion's mother?" Joan inquired.

"I am," Theresa answered, grimacing.

"Are you here for revenge?"

Gypsy tensed her muscles and placed her hand on the hilt of her blade as they waited for her answer.

"Revenge? Why would I…" Theresa started, then the realization dawned on her. "It was you people. You're the ones who killed him. You're the Daimon Killers' group." The blonde woman gripped the armrests of her chair as pain and rage swelled within her. The tension in the room was palpable. After a few seconds, Theresa regained her composure and released her hold. Finally, she took a deep breath. "I did not come here for revenge. I was sent here on a different mission."

Mrs. Mozart and Joan looked at each other. "Why did Diablos send you here?"

Theresa rolled her eyes. "I'm no longer affiliated with the Daimons and their cause."

"You gave birth to Diablos' son, their greatest champion. You expect us to believe you gave them a two-week notice and left?" Gypsy scoffed.

Theresa glanced at her, and her eyes lingered on the prosthetic.

"This was courtesy of your son."

The woman's face softened. "I'm sorry for your pain. Unfortunately, we were all deceived by Diablos. I've had a lot of time to reflect since then. I'm pretty sure even Therion's death was somehow orchestrated by Diablos."

The Daughters' brows furrowed.

"Why would Diablos kill his own son?" Joan questioned.

"I don't know the answer to that. I do know that Diablos secured an ally more powerful than you can imagine through Therion's death."

"Wait, what?" Gypsy blurted. "There's someone worse than Diablos?"

"There are beings beyond the Angels and Daimons."

"You mean Archangels," Mrs. Mozart interjected.

Theresa nodded. "My benefactor is one of them—Haniel, the Primal who represents Order and Balance. He fears Diablos has somehow enticed the oldest and most powerful of them to his side. She goes by Mara and styles herself the Primal of Death."

Joan looked at Mrs. Mozart. "What do you know about this, Mrs. Mozart?"

"Precious little, I'm afraid. There are only legends and conjectures regarding the higher-order beings. This is my first time hearing those names, although the term Primals rings a bell."

The women were silent for a moment, then Joan spoke again. "Even if what you're telling us is true, none of this answers why you are here."

"We were investigating Mara's activity when Haniel sensed the presence of the third of his kind here in this facility. It would seem the young lady who confronted me downstairs has been in contact with Apocalypse, the revelator. He hoped she was here for the same purpose: to free their sister."

"What kind of activity were you investigating?"

Theresa eyed the women. "Some violent attacks, but we haven't made much progress yet."

"Pray tell, what are your intentions toward Miss Nyala?" queried Mrs. Mozart.

"Is that the chubby girl's name? Apocalypse picked an unlikely host."

"Watch yourself!" Gypsy warned.

Theresa shrugged, "I mean no offense, but the girl seems a bit off, and she's not in the best fighting shape. I had to train for years to come to terms with my connection to a Primal. It seems like she's struggling with her grip on reality."

"Miss Nyala's struggles aside, you still have not

answered what you want with her."

"I don't personally want anything to do with any of you people." Theresa paused for a moment as if listening to someone. "And Haniel can't communicate with Apocalypse. It would seem coming here was a waste of time."

Theresa stood to leave, but Gypsy stepped into her way and stared her down.

"Let her go, Gypsy," commanded Joan.

The warrior stepped aside, and Theresa promptly left the room and exited the Tektonite compound.

Joan sighed and clasped her hands together. "What do you make of all this, Mrs. Mozart?"

The wise woman furrowed her brow. "There are forces in play beyond our understanding."

Olivia was sitting on the edge of Nyala's bed, softly stroking the woman's head. Nyala swayed her body as her leg shook rapidly.

"Why is she here? What does she want? He wants to kill her. Yes, kill her; that's his plan, but it won't work. Then he'll go after the seals. He'll do it again, try to trigger the Eschaton. No, no, no, no." Nyala muttered as tears streamed down her face.

Olivia looked at the young woman with compassion. "It's all right. Everything is going to be all right," she comforted. However, the teenager didn't feel things were going to be all right. Since Nyala's outburst downstairs, she'd sensed something foreign and strange from the ailing woman. If Olivia quieted her mind, she could hear a low rumble of whispers when she was next to Nyala.

"Will the mother kill the daughter? Will the son return?" Nyala continued, her breathing growing ragged.

May entered the room and sat on the bed beside Olivia. They lifted Nyala's head, gave her some pills, and remained in the room with her until she fell asleep.

"Poor Nyala. She was getting better, then she had this episode. I hope it's merely a relapse and not a sign of further deterioration," May whispered.

Olivia didn't respond, simply smiled courteously and continued watching over her friend.

14

NEW ORDERS

Libby pushed open the door to the conference room in the main residence building at All Agoria Academy. She wore a gray business suit, and her blue-black hair was up in a bun. The room's occupants turned in unison to face the newcomer. The newcomer scanned the room from left to right. Diablo's High Lords, Hades and Legion, were present, along with an assortment of high-ranking Nephilim, the Principalites. Libby walked past the men, placed her satchel on the table, and sat.

"Morning, and thank you for gathering on such short notice. As per Diablos' and Mistress Mara's plans, we have much work to do and not long to get it done," Libby started.

The men glanced at each other.

"Pardon our surprise, child, but we were under the impression that Lady Mara would be present," Legion stated.

"Mistress Mara has delegated all duties of coordinating

the acquisition of materials for Operation Lightbringer to me."

"I see," the Daimon responded. "Well, given your age and inexperience in these matters, you should leave those duties to us."

"I don't recall anyone questioning Therion's age or lack of experience." Libby shot back. "Your master ordered you to follow Mistress Mara's command. As her agent, I carry out her will and desires. If insubordination is the only thing you have to contribute to this endeavor, then your input is not required in these meetings."

Legion's eyes narrowed and he opened his mouth to speak, but Hades interjected.

"You petulant, foolish runt." The Daimon's eyes flared with rage. "You speak to beings who've been alive since the dawn of this world."

"Well, we're here to discuss the future, not rehash the tired mistakes of the past," retorted the young hybrid.

Hades ground his teeth and stomped toward Libby. He grabbed the table with one hand and flipped it, but Libby retrieved her satchel before it hit the floor. The woman smirked and stood to face the raging Daimon.

"Your temper tantrums have no effect on me, Daimon. If you lay a finger on me, you'll be sealed away by Sovereign Law. Even if you kill me, Death is my mistress's domain, so you'd accomplish nothing. All you can do is throw fits. We have work to do, and you're holding up my meeting."

"Katastrofi, I think this little girl needs to be taught a lesson." Hades smirked.

The Nephilim had been leaning against a wall through

this exchange. He was over eight feet tall and had a hulking physique. He stretched out his hands, and Libby rose several inches into the air.

"It's a pity force is the only thing you people seem to understand," the woman stated, unfazed.

She was surrounded by a purple aura. Her eyes glowed the same color, then her hair fell out of its bun, and it danced wildly in the air. Katastrofi's hold on her loosened, and she dropped to the floor. Then a thick fog covered the room, and she disappeared from their sight.

"I can sense that she's still here, but I can't see her," Katastrofi cried. "Where is she, Father?"

"I-I..." Hades stammered. "I don't know."

"Arggh!"

Hades turned to face his son. From within the smoke, a pair of arms had appeared. Katastrofi was kneeling on the floor, his head pulled back by his hair and a blade positioned at his neck. A thin line of blood had formed where the knife touched his skin.

"Aetos!" Katastrofi hollered.

A male hybrid in the room reacted. His body was covered in dark-brown feathers, and his hands bore large, sharp talons. The Nephilim stretched out his feather-covered arms and created a powerful gust of wind in the conference room. However, the smoke was undisturbed.

The female hybrid released her prey and sent him crashing to the floor with a mighty kick to the back. Then she disappeared into the smoke again. The men craned their necks, trying to discern her position to no avail. After a few moments, the remaining Nephilim yelped and grabbed their necks one by one. Each was each bleeding from a thin cut across their Adam's apple. Then, as mysteriously as it had appeared, the smoke dissipated, and Libby reappeared in the spot where she had been before the confrontation.

"I could have ended the life of every Nephilim in this room, and there was nothing any of you could have done to stop me," the woman announced. "I'm stronger than all of you. Stronger even than Therion was. However, I'm not him. I don't wish to command you with threats and terror. Clearness of purpose is a better motivator than fear."

Libby looked at the faces of each of the Nephilim in the room, then she faced the Daimons. "Now, High Lords, I don't want to waste any more of our time on petty squabbles. Please allow us to get on with our task."

Hades opened a portal and disappeared through it. Legion grinned wickedly, gave a small bob of his head, and exited the room via the door.

Libby glanced to her right, "Leon, Aner, would you please place the table upright so we can start our meeting?"

The two Nephilim did as they'd been asked, and they all sat.

"I have to say, Miss Libby. Diablos' plan is...well, it's not what I was expecting, given the events of the last few years," stated a Nephilim dressed in a white Italian suit with matching shoes.

"If there is anything I've come to expect from the King of Daimons, it's that he has plans within plans, Pytho," Libby responded. She glanced around the room and noticed a puzzled look on another of the Sons of the Lords. "You seem to have a question, Aner."

"Well, not so much a question as an observation."

"What is it?"

Aner sifted through several sheets of paper that Libby had handed out to them and arranged them in a small grid. "I've run the calculations in my head over and over. Unfortunately, what Lord Diablos wants to accomplish will require inordinate amounts of energy. More than humans can generate at the world's current level of technology."

Libby smirked. "I hoped your abilities would help you notice that." She pulled one more sheet of paper from her satchel and glided it to the Nephilim. "That's why you'll be in charge of procuring the materials and overseeing this construction."

The hybrid's eyes grew wide as he studied the diagrams on the page. "Will this... Can this..."

"It will, and it can."

Pytho spoke up. "Well, what is it? Don't keep us in suspense."

"Why don't you explain it to them, Aner?" Libby interjected.

Aner cleared his throat. "This is a design for a zero-point energy generator."

The other Nephilim in the room glanced at each other.

"Oh, is that all? Why didn't you say so sooner?" Pytho scoffed.

"Sorry. It's a device that can tap into the energy in the quantum vacuum. It's been theorized that this is the excess energy from Creation, the sheer power of the Sovereign One embedded in every single point in space. The amount of energy that can be harnessed from the volume of a cup would be enough to boil every ocean on the planet."

"That is correct," Libby added. "You and the lesser Nephilim under you are going to build it while the rest of the Sons of the Lords complete their tasks."

"But, my lady…" Pytho started.

The young woman held up her hand. "Libby will suffice."

"Yes, Libby. Countless Nephilim have abandoned our ranks. Not to speak ill of the dead, but…"

Libby sighed, "Yes, my idiot brother did an excellent job alienating his subordinates and inciting a mass exodus from our ranks. I've seen the reports. As many as sixty percent have fled."

"Before the band was brought back together, we were tasked with hunting down the traitors," Katastrofi added. "Are we supposed to just ignore their treachery?"

"Don't worry, my friend. Justice may sometimes seem slow in coming, but each of them will get what he deserves in time. For the time being, you have your new assignments."

"If I might be so bold, what will your task be, Libby?" inquired Pytho.

"Serving my mistress' Justice."

15

FINDING LAURIE

The illuminated ground sign said *UPSTATE NEW YORK PATH OF LIGHT.* It was mounted a few yards from the main entrance of the complex.

A woman wearing pitch-black apparel slowly passed a razor over her head. She was lurking within the darkness of the woods encompassing the campus. She carefully observed the latest truck that arrived at the security checkpoint. Though the freestanding sign in front of the guardhouse read *No Visitors After 8:00 PM*, a buzzer sounded, and shortly after that, the gates began to open.

Once the truck went through, she tossed the razor away, grabbed her backpack, and reached out with her bolt cutters, carefully avoiding the package labeled C-4. Both sides of her waist bore blades, one steel and the other quartz. The woman covered her bald head with the hood of the jacket and skulked her way toward the rear end of the main building. The intruder quietly cut a hole big enough to admit her through the chain link fence. After replacing the cutters in the backpack, she dashed toward the building and found a back door, stopping just in time to avoid the cameras.

She pulled out a small black box with a single red button out of her pocket. Aiming the box at the detectors, the woman pressed it, and the camera stopped moving. The intruder pressed a timer on her watch and raced to the back entrance, then popped the locks and opened the back door.

Her destination was the second floor, west wing, corner office. Scuttling to the nearest staircase, she bounded up and crept through the dimly lit corridor. There were no names on the doors, only numbers, exactly as she remembered them from the schematics she'd found on the internet.

Glancing at her watch, she quickened her pace. The phrase *Dr. Patrick Ostero must be killed. He must be stopped,* raced through the woman's mind as she sprinted to her destination. When she reached the door, she reached for her steel blade and walked through. She frowned that the room wasn't an office but a large open area from what she could see in the dark. The door behind her slammed shut and bright lights that blinded her came on.

"*FREEZE!*" came the command.

The intruder threw her blade without aiming while shielding her eyes from the lights pointing in her direction. The clatter when it landed echoed throughout the space.

"*I SAID, FREEZE!*" the voice repeated. "*ON YOUR KNEES, HANDS BEHIND YOUR HEAD!*"

Perplexed and outnumbered, she did as instructed.

Moments later, her hands were cuffed, and a tall shadow loomed over her.

"Ms. Davidson, or should I say Jewels, how great to make your acquaintance. We've been expecting you."

"Who the hell are you, and where is Dr. Ostero?"

"Oh, you mean Luminary Masmasu. Rather, the excommunicated Masmasu, in case you weren't aware."

The woman frowned but was silent.

"My name is Kenneth Owens, but you can call me Hormuzd." He strutted around her as he continued to speak. "You are a hard cookie to catch, but with your latest hack during which you retrieved those fake schematics, we were able to ascertain your next location."

"If he's excommunicated, give me the man, and I'll be out of your hair."

He stopped in front of her and squatted to meet her at eye level. "Oh, it's not that simple. You've cost us lots of money, and that's a big no-no." He slapped her across her face, knocking the hood off and revealing her bald head. "We suspected you were looking for that traitor Masmasu, but we are curious as to why."

She remained quiet, sucking her bleeding lips.

"I would kill you now, but my superior wishes to speak to you in person. He has other plans for you."

"If that's the case…" She spat blood into his face.

"Oh, Jewels, I'm going to have so much fun with you," the agent promised as he wiped his face.

"My name is Laurie," she corrected.

A dark smile appeared on his face. "No matter. By the time I'm finished with you, you will wish I had killed you." He straightened and glanced at the guards. "Take her away.

She'll be one of the first to take part in the Great Cleansing."

"If it isn't Rogue One," joked the female over the phone.

"Yeah, I hear that's what they are calling me now. How are you, Mist?"

"I'm doing fine. How are you holding up, Joan? I received a deceptive email from our *corporate office* that you are now in the kidnapping business," Mist replied sarcastically.

"We figured that would happen sooner or later, but it wasn't a kidnapping. It was more of a prison break, but I'll update you on those details at a later time. To be honest, that's not my biggest concern." She swiveled the chair and faced the office window. The New York leader fixed her gaze on the cloudy night sky.

"What's on your mind?" the Lancaster leader asked with concern.

"I meant with Erinys yesterday, and she handed me the *corporate office's* list of demands." Joan repeated the phrase in the same manner Mist had.

"That was their delegate." The Lancaster leader scoffed. "Those daughters of witches. According to their email, a delegate was dispatched to petition you to relinquish your authority and return to the proper order. Whatever that is."

"If that order means being under Erinys, they can forget about it. It seems she's now the new Tristate overseer." She watched the light drizzle bouncing off the glass. "The demands weren't the only thing Erinys mentioned. My friend, Horizon, Robin, Lucky, and Venus are dead."

"What?" came the shocked response. "How?"

"According to Erinys, they were killed."

"By Nephilim?"

"No." There was a moment of silence. "She alleges that it was Villainous, at my command." Joan heard a long sigh.

"I'm sorry to hear that, Joan. Any reason she suspects it was her?"

"I don't know. That's the main reason for my call. Do you know where she could be hiding, or have you heard anything from her?"

"No..." she replied, then, "Well, I did receive a postcard about a year and a half ago that read *Restitution,* signed with the name 'Laurie.' That's Jewels' real name. I didn't make anything of it, so I never mentioned it. It had no return address."

"Erinys also stated that she's been causing the Star of Nimrod trouble, and they are demanding that we turn her in. Any idea how we can get in touch with her?"

Mist exhaled. "I don't know. Maybe you could reach out to our friend Agent...I mean, PI Ortega. Maybe he could help."

"Hmm. I might just do that." Joan returned her gaze to the dark clouds at the sound of grumbles and growls. "I also wanted to inform you that Erinys learned about the special Kollourion concoction we created for the male hybrids."

"Oh, shoot! I'm sure she wasn't happy about that."

"As you can imagine. Be careful with the males you are

keeping in your compound. Sooner or later, they'll link you to me."

"We're prepared. What are you going to do about the demands?"

"I'm not sure. I'll have a talk with the women and let you know."

Joan ended the call with Mist and focused on the rising storm.

16

ALLERGIC REACTION

Before she could lick her bleeding lips, Jewels was struck again. The blow put her in a daze. She was in a dark and unventilated room, strapped to a wooden chair, with her hands bound behind her back. Her blackened left eye was swollen shut. She tilted her head to attempt to see the aggressor with the right and prepared herself for the next blow. She took a deep breath when she saw the arm rising again.

"Stop!" exclaimed the commander before she was struck. "That's enough."

The beaten woman spat blood on the floor. Her functioning eye was focused on the man sitting a few feet in front of her.

"Come on, Laurie. You can make this stop. I'm tired of sitting here, so I can only imagine how you're feeling. Tell us why you are looking for that traitor Masmasu."

Laurie gazed at him, head wobbling, and smiled with bloodstained teeth. "So ignorant and naïve. That man was part of your organization for years, and little did you know he worked for the enemy the entire time." She shook her head. "What's your name again? Hormuzd the freaking stupid." She laughed.

Agent Owen gestured with his head to the aggressor, who struck Laurie again. "This pain can go away if you tell me what I want."

"This is what you call pain." She chuckled. "This is a walk in the park in comparison to the pain I have experienced. If you don't let me go, you'll experience that same freaking pain." The woman tried to free herself. *"LET ME THE HELL OUT OF HERE!"* she yelled.

"Unfortunately, I can't do that. You see, the grand luminary has special plans for you. He requested to speak to you personally, and that's a great honor. He's searching for his missing daughter and believes that repulsive sister of hers might have maliciously influenced her."

"I have no idea who you are talking about," Laurie hissed at him.

"Even if you don't, we can always use you for sport." He leaned forward in his chair. "His Supremacy has great plans for your friends at the warehouse and that other group that moved out."

"You're wasting your time if you think I have friends."

He pursed his lips. "If you provide the intel on Masmasu, maybe, just maybe, we can become friends, and I'll put in a good word to keep you from the Great Cleansing."

She frowned. "The what?"

Owens stood up, then moved behind his chair, gripping the back. "It is a great celebration in which abominations like you..." he pointed at her, "will stand before the high council, face judgment for contaminating the Earth, and be executed through decapitation." He gave a shallow smile.

"OK …" She gulped, then sighed. "I'll talk, but just you. No one else can hear this."

He nodded to the guards to step outside. As soon as the door closed, he spoke. "All right. I'm listening."

"I don't trust these walls, and what I'm about to tell you is a secret. I have killed for this, so get closer."

He took a few steps forward.

"Closer, please!" she demanded.

He was a few inches from her.

The woman stared frantically around the room. "I need to whisper it to you. It's important that I tell only you," she pled.

Agent Owen bent forward, and when he did, Laurie smashed her head into his.

She laughed hysterically. "You are all ignorant fools. Your pursuit of greatness blinds you."

After rubbing the bump forming on his forehead, he smacked her across her face.

"Rest assured that you'll pay for that. You and your friends," the man promised. He grabbed his cell phone and walked out of the room.

"A postcard with no return address sent more than a year ago is little to go by, Amelia," said the man. His eyes were watering, and he had a rosy nose. He had a cup of hot tea with honey in his right hand and a tissue in his left.

"It was worth a shot," replied Joan, who was sitting

across from the man. "Ortega, do you still have any contacts within the bureau? Surely they'll have information on Laurie Marilyn Davidson?"

"Achoo!" He sneezed thunderously into the tissue. "I swear, pollen is hell dust. Every spring, it's these same damn allergies." After wiping his nose, he shook his head. "Unfortunately, I don't trust anyone in the agency when it comes to hybrids. It's one of the main reasons I retired."

Joan reached into her desk drawer, pulled out a box of tissues, and handed it to him. "I'm sorry to have bothered you when you are sick, but I'll be frank. We're up against a wall. Finding her could ease the tension."

He sniffled and put another tissue to his nose. "Awilda mentioned that it's been great having your help and that of the other women. I thought everything was going dandy."

"It was until two weeks ago, when we received an unsettling email from one of the women in London. Since then, things have been spiraling. The Global Daughterhood Committee is demanding that I and the other women in the council step down and submit to the leadership of Erinys."

He was about to take a sip of his tea but stopped. "You mean that crazy lady who wanted to kill children?"

She nodded. "In addition, Villainous appears to be back to her old games, causing trouble with the Star of Nimrod and killing some of the women who remained with the Furies. If we don't find her and hand her over to Erinys, not only will we have the Furies and other Daughters after us but the Star of Nimrod as well."

"And I thought I had it bad with the allergies." He put his cup on the leader's desk. "I'm sorry to hear that, Joan.

I'll do everything in my power to help you in any way possible."

"Thank you, Ortega."

"How's the kid holding up? She invited me to her graduation, but I was too sick to go." He picked up his tea again and took another sip.

"Unfortunately, she's avoiding us. I think she was shaken up by something that was said in a meeting. Maybe you could have a chat with her." Joan was interrupted by the ringing of her cell phone, and her eyes grew wide when she saw the caller ID. She lifted her index finger at Ortega and clicked the answer button.

"What the hell are you playing at?" asked a loud voice that Ortega could hear.

"I'm at a loss here, Erinys." Joan exhaled to keep calm.

"Instead of turning the woman in, you sent her to infiltrate another of those zealots' sites."

Joan raised her voice as she stood. "You are presuming that she's working for me in addition to knowing what in blue blazes you are talking about?"

"Don't act coy with me. That freaking zealot Kenneth Owens called, saying they've captured your witch and plan to execute her soon."

"The matter is settled. She's been captured, so what else do you want?"

"That wasn't the deal. Your job was to turn her in. She had a score to settle with us first."

The leader sighed resignedly. "Believe me about this. She is *not* working for me..." Before she could finish her sentence, the line went dead. She took a seat despondently.

Ortega cleared his throat. "Are you all right?"

She shook her head. "The Star of Nimrod captured Villainous."

"Yeah, I heard it over the screaming of the call, but did I hear her mention Kenneth Owens?"

Joan nodded with a frown. "That's right. Why?"

"That was my old boss, and he was one of the reasons I left the bureau. I figured he was working for the Star of Nimrod."

"Hmm. I'm curious why they haven't killed her already. It appears they are keeping her alive for a reason."

Ortega nodded as he thought. "It's a good question. Let me do some digging around. I might not have much on Villainous, but I have plenty on Owens. As they said, keep your friends close, but your enemies—"

"Closer," Joan finished. She glanced at her watch. "I have a meeting to attend, but let me know what you dig up."

"Will do, and regarding your earlier request, I'll have a chat with the kid."

The twelve members of the Daughters of the Watchers Tristate council were meeting with the Lancaster group via video conference. Joan had just finished updating everyone on Villainous' capture and the list of demands issued by the global committee. Every face in the conference was solemn.

The group leader removed her reading glasses and placed them on the rectangular conference table at which she sat. She then gave her attention to the women around her and to the screen a few feet from her.

"We stand on a precipice that will either end our affiliation with the Global Daughterhood or our commitment to a code of honor that, in our hearts, we know is true. This isn't an easy decision for one person to make." She looked around the room with a sincere and warm expression. "We have fought together, endured hardships together, cried together, and have seen things too wonderful to elaborate together. As we experienced these things together, this decision needs to be made together.

She stood and wiped a tear from her eye. "If I can be forthcoming, remaining with the Daughterhood is the easiest and safest thing to do. Otherwise, we'll be persecuted, chased, hunted, and even face death. Logically, it seems like the right thing to do, but I cannot, in good conscience, jeopardize matters of the heart.

"The changes and decisions we've made in the last few years were based on truth, and, in my book, truth is uncompromising. However, how we move forward from this day onward isn't up to me, and no one in this room should feel coerced or forced to decide whether through persuasive words or dire situations."

The leader gulped and lowered her head. "I cannot and will not accede to their demands." Joan gave the group a determined look. "I will immediately remove myself from leadership if you think I should."

"Ain't no education in the second kick of a mule," said a hefty silver-haired woman, glancing around the room. "If we stay, we haven't learned our lesson. Like my momma always says, 'Don't let the fox guard the henhouse.' I don't want to be part of a group that is bent on destruction. These demands they're making ain't pretty, y'all. This is only the beginning." The old woman gazed at Joan. "I'm with you, honey bun."

Joan smiled. "Thank you, Grace."

"I concur with my long-time companion," uttered a lanky, wise lady. "For years, we believed they were the persecuted ones, yet to my shock, I learned we were the instigators. These frivolous demands are only a ploy to keep the truth hidden." She turned to the leader. "Joan, I vote nay to their demands."

"Oorah! I'm with Mrs. Mozart and Grace," declared the ginger-haired, blue-eyed warrior.

"That's a nay for me as well, Gypsy," announced the caretaker. "Better to die in truth than to live a lie."

"Aye, May. I was pure scunnered by those demands." Mrs. Poppins turned to Joan. "Nay for me, lass."

"Nay." The woman sitting next to the children's caretaker quipped, "This is Crystal, and I approve this message."

One by one, the remaining members, along with the Lancaster group, agreed unanimously not to consent to the demands.

"Thank you, all," replied Joan. "This means we have to emplace contingencies and security measures…"

Before the leader of the group could finish, the conference room door was abruptly thrown open, and in bounded Nyala.

In a manner both pleading and commanding, she exclaimed, "She must be saved! She has a purpose. Please rescue her."

Joan glanced at May, who stood and walked toward the newcomer. She gave her attention to the Mozambican. "Nyala, we're having an important meeting. Can we discuss this later?"

Nyala shook her head. "The voice in my head told me she has to be rescued. It said to wait until you all decided first."

May was about to escort her outside when Mrs. Mozart stopped her. She had a very concerned expression. "Miss Nyala, can you elaborate further on this decision we needed to make?"

The girl nodded. "Yes, the decision to break away from the Daughterhood. The voice said this would be the turning point. Without it, all would be lost."

The leader turned to Mrs. Mozart and mouthed, "How did she know that?"

The wise woman looked from Joan to Nyala. "Who are we supposed to rescue?"

"The woman named Laurie."

17

THE CHOICE

The two-hundred-pound man with salt-and-pepper hair stopped before exiting the Tektonite compound when he heard someone yelling his name.

"Mr. Ortega! Mr. Ortega, hold up!" called a female.

He looked back with a frown. "Everything OK, Caroline?"

"We need your help," responded Gypsy. "Can you come to the southwest conference room?"

He coughed into a tissue and nodded. "Give me a minute. The look on your face tells me I need to fetch another tea."

"Make that two," requested the warrior.

After grabbing two cups of tea, Ortega walked up two flights of stairs and lumbered over to the southwest conference room. He glanced at the familiar faces and smiled at the women who were present: Joan, Gypsy, and Tassel. On the video call was Mist. The man strolled to the warrior and handed her tea.

"I was only kidding," stated Gypsy. "But I'm not going to refuse it." She grabbed it and took a sip.

"What's going on?" he asked curiously as he took a seat across from the women.

"Ortega, we had a situation come up, and we need your help," stated Joan. Concern marred her features.

"Anything, with the exception of running the New York City Marathon," he joked, though no one laughed.

"We need your help to rescue Villainous."

He chuckled out loud. "That's a good one, Joan." Seeing their sincere faces, he cleared his throat. "Wait, you are serious about this. Are we talking about the woman that orchestrated the attack on the group six years ago?"

"I wish I was joking," agreed Joan. "But Sovereignty has it that we are to rescue this woman."

"OK," he drawled. "I'm all ears when it comes to Sovereignty and my wife. How can I help?"

"We have no information about where to even look for Villainous. I was hoping you could provide us with any intel you have on Kenneth Owens. He could lead us to her."

"I can provide you with all the intel you need, but wouldn't it be quicker to hack the Star of Nimrod's system to find her whereabouts?" He gazed at Tassel.

"Negatory," responded the geeky young seer. Her laptop was open on the conference room table. "I have tried, but they've really enhanced their network security. It could be days before I made any progress."

He rubbed his chin and fixed his eyes on Gypsy. "What about your sister, Margaret? Wouldn't she know how to access their system?"

"Hmm, that's a good point." The warrior reached for her phone. "Let me give her a call."

After a moment, Gypsy got her twin on a video call. Seeing her sister's face always made her smile.

"Hey, sis. This is a lovely surprise." Margaret glanced at her watch. "I thought we were speaking later tonight."

"Hello, beautiful. Unfortunately, change of plans. We're in a pretty pickle and need your assistance." Gypsy moved her phone so Margaret could view those who were present. "As you can see, I'm not alone. I'll cut to the chase. By any chance, do you have credentials to access the Star of Nimrod's systems?"

"Unfortunately, my access was revoked after I left the organization."

"I suspected that was the case. Any way we can get into their system?"

She shook her head, then smiled. "Maybe there's a way, since you've piqued my curiosity."

The warrior scrunched her nose like a tiny accordion. "Does it make any sense that we're attempting to rescue an enemy from them?"

"No, but you are doing that thing with your nose, which means it's important. The old man is predictable. I saw that Tassel is present with her laptop. Can you hand me over to her?"

Gypsy handed her cell to the seer.

"Greetings, Margaret," Tassel said.

"Hello, Tassel. I'm texting you a link to a login portal, a username, and credentials. Can you attempt to log into the site I sent you?"

"Absolutely!" The seer viewed the text and frowned at

the username, *tammuz01*, and password, *5uperMacy!*. Tassel gazed at Gypsy's screen. "You don't think he changed his password? Isn't he the grand luminary now?"

"I changed his password once, and he screamed at me. Like I told Caroline, he's predictable."

"All right," the seer said cynically. After her fingers ran over the keyboard, she beamed with excitement. "Super! I'm in."

"As I said, predictable. I have given you the keys to the castle with those credentials, so have at it."

Tassel passed the cell back to Gypsy. "I owe you one, Margaret. If I don't get a chance to call you tonight, good work on closing down those three underground fighting rings."

"You got it, sis. If there's anything else I can do, let me know. Tell Reina I'll send her lover D'Angelo back to her soon. He's been a great help to us. Love you!"

"Love you, too! Bye." Gypsy ended the call. "Tassel, do you your thing."

"I'm already on it," responded the woman, who was already accessing the security intel they would need. She read the screen like greased lightning.

For several minutes that felt like an eternity, everyone nervously watched the techie. They were relieved when the seer hung a lopsided grin on her face.

Tassel waved the group over and pointed to the screen. "Security states that a female hybrid was captured yesterday evening in their upstate location. The hybrid was tagged 'Most Wanted' and marked for execution. She's being held at that location."

Gypsy turned to Joan. "That must be her."

"How fast can you get a tackle team to upstate New York and infiltrate?" Joan asked the warrior.

"It might take a day or so. I'll need to call in a few women, then study the building's plans while devising a—" The warrior was interrupted.

"Wait!" Tassel exclaimed as she continued reading. "I think there's a better way. It states here she's being relocated tomorrow night. I have the license number and make of the vehicle, the route, and the time of transport." The seer turned around to the group. "Wouldn't it be easier to rescue Villainous en route?"

Gypsy pursed her lips while nodding. "That's plausible." The warrior fixed her eyes on Joan. "What do you think?"

"Sounds reasonable," the leader agreed, placing her finger on her chin.

"Tassel, text me all the info and the number of guards," requested the warrior. "I'll start making phone calls."

"I'm sending that info posthaste," responded the seer.

As Gypsy was about to head out the door, Mist spoke. "Gypsy, the last time I confronted Villainous, she was under the control of an evil spirit. While I believe she was set free by Kitty, these latest developments might mean she has something worse controlling her. If that's the case, I advise taking Angel and Kitty along."

"Excellent point, Mist." The warrior eyed the seer. "Can you check on your girlfriends and see if you can get hold of Pretzel as well? I'm gonna need some good drivers."

"Immediately!" Tassel responded with a smile.

Tassel returned to the networking room she had made into her personal office. She missed her old lab with its vast racks of servers and computer equipment, yet she wasn't a complainer. She made the best of every situation, a good example being the massive improvement of the Tektonites' compound. Every room had Wi-Fi, and the meeting room areas had video conferencing. All the hardware and software had been upgraded to the latest and greatest, and she had managed to create many applications useful for various purposes.

By fourteen, she had learned every major programming language. This was her life, as well as serving the Daughters of the Watchers. The seer never knew her mother or heritage, and though she was a geek, Tassel was never able to find anything about her ancestry. All the seer knew was that she had been left on the doorstep of an orphanage and later adopted by the Daughters of the Watchers, who had become her home and family.

The seer placed her laptop on the makeshift desk and opened it. She opened her address book and scrolled to the section she had happily named *Best Friends*. Finding Angel's name, she clicked on the video call icon. After a few seconds, Angel's big grin was plastered on the screen.

"Hey, Tassel girl!" she greeted. She had a backdrop of mall stores.

"Angel! You are looking chipper! What are you up to?"

"I'm doing some shopping. What's going on with you? Wanna meet us? I'm with Pretzel." Angel turned the phone's camera in Pretzel's direction.

Pretzel waved. "Hiya, girlfriend. C'mon and meet us. I'll get you your favorite Jovian Bean matcha tea latte."

The seer sighed. "I would love to, but something has come up. Can you both find a private spot to speak?"

"Sure," Angel responded, and they found a secluded sitting area. Both friends sat and gave their attention to the seer. "What's up?"

"A very important mission has been sprung on us, one that needs the both of you."

Angel's expression became serious. She let out a long sigh. "What mission?" She sounded irritated.

Seeing the woman's agitated face, Tassel chose her words wisely. "Well, we have to rescue someone. Um, her name is Laurie."

"Who's Laurie?" asked Pretzel. "Do we know her?"

"Yeah," Tassel replied with hesitation as the side of her nose sprang up.

"Tassel, I know that look. Who is she?"

"OK, OK. It's Villainous."

"*VILLAINOUS?*" both women yelped.

"Are you crazy?" Angel asked, then lowered her voice. "Why in the world would we want to rescue that witch?"

"Let's just say Sovereignty is involved." The seer pursed her lips.

"Let me guess...Nyala. We've been using that word a lot since she arrived." The girl's jaw clenched, and her nostrils flared.

"I know it sounds crazy, but the council believes her, and I think we should too. I have a sense that she's on to something."

"I'm sorry, Tassel, but I'm out."

The seer took in a deep breath. "Oh, OK. What about you, Pretzel?"

Pretzel was quiet for a moment. "I'm with Angel on this one, Tassel. This doesn't sound logical to me. I'll have to pass."

"Tassel," Angel continued, "maybe you should think about this a bit more. It's time for us to move on."

The seer adopted a fake smile. "I'll speak to you guys later, then. I have to call Kitty."

"I'm very sorry, Tassel. I just hope you understand where we're coming from." Tassel nodded. "Reina returns from her Orlando business trip tomorrow. Why don't we schedule a girls' weekend trip?"

"Sounds good. Bye." She clicked the end button and gazed at her screen disappointedly.

The girl then clicked on Kitty's contact. After sharing pleasantries, the seer laid out the mission. The goth girl said nothing at first but then nodded in agreement.

"I understand if you don't want to," disclosed Tassel. "Angel and Pretzel both said no."

"Hmm. I must go," Kitty revealed.

"Really!" She seemed surprised.

"Yeah, really. I'll come over soon."

The warrior stood in the doorway as Tassel finished with Kitty.

"What's the deal with your girlfriends?"

"Kitty is in, but Pretzel and Angel are out."

"Oh, boy. This complicates things." Gypsy touched her temples in thought. "I know you don't do field work, but you *are* an excellent driver. Could you help?"

"Definitely!" The corners of her lips quirked into a smile. "I've always wanted to do some field work."

"Great. Once Kitty gets here, let's meet in the southwest

conference room to discuss the plan. Also, I'm using that new server to upload my security intel. Is that safe?"

The seer nodded. As soon as the warrior left, Tassel stood up and started doing karate chops. "All right! Field work," she said enthusiastically.

18

THE TASTE OF DEATH

"Nyala, I'm sorry, but I cannot take you," the woman stated. She leaned in and placed her prosthetic hand on the Mozambican's shoulder.

"Gypsy. I must go. I sense grave danger for this mission," she pleaded.

"More reasons you shouldn't be there." She grabbed a duffle bag off the floor and tossed it into the back of the black SUV. "I'm already taking risks by bringing along non-warrior members, and taking another could seriously jeopardize this mission and your safety." The warrior took a deep breath. "Unless you can tell me why you need to go."

Nyala grasped her head and paced in a circle, attempting to articulate her wandering thoughts. "I just don't know, but please! I beg you."

"Then it's a definite no. Also, I'm only taking two vehicles," the warrior pointed at the other SUV in the garage, "which can only take five passengers each. There are nine of us, and I need to leave room for Villainous. Now, excuse me. I need to fetch the shackles and duct tape. Villainous is still dangerous in my book." The warrior pushed the close hatch button and returned to the building.

The Mozambican remained in the garage, watching the women pack the other SUV.

"That's the last of it," she heard one say, and then she closed the back hatch.

"All right. Gypsy wants us to meet in the conference room to review the plan again before we leave," said the other.

Shortly after that, the two women entered the building. The Mozambican stood still, clasping her hands together as she wrestled internally. Beads of sweat formed on her brow. *They will all die if I don't go* was her primary thought.

No longer able to contain it, the woman then dashed toward the SUV and opened the back. She moved a few bags around and climbed on board. Lastly, Nyala pushed the close hatch door button and covered herself with the bags.

The Fury rushed out of the computer lab with a document in hand, bounded up to the second level, and ran to the leader's office. She didn't bother to knock but barged in, almost out of breath.

"Crimson, what the hell? I'm having a meeting." The leader's eyes darted toward the intruder.

Crimson ignored the other woman in the room and slammed the paper on the desk. "Erinys, they're planning on rescuing Villainous!"

"*What!*" the Furies' leader exclaimed with knitted

brows, then gazed at the details on the desk. "How did you get this?"

The girl placed her hand on her chest, struggling to catch her breath. "Well, it seems that geeky girl who worked in the lab here wasn't thorough."

Erinys continued reading, growing more upset. "This is something, all right."

"Although she erased the data from most systems, she missed one server. She did wipe the data but not the hard drive. Using recovery software, I was able to reconstruct what she found. At first, it was old data. Then earlier today, I reconnected to the network, and it synced automatically. When I looked, I found what you are reading now."

The Furies' leader slammed her fist on the desk. "Damn! I knew Joan was lying, and just to think I had given her the benefit of the doubt."

"What do you wanna do?" asked Crimson.

Erinys looked across her desk. "Glory, assemble the women and meet Crimson and me in the parking lot in a half-hour."

"You got it!" the other woman responded.

It was a lonely, narrow road in the middle of nowhere with no streetlights. The darkness of the night made it difficult to see the surrounding trees on both sides.

Two black SUVs blocked the road, and beside the vehicles were three women dressed in state police uniforms. Their holsters carried custom tranquilizer guns that could sedate their target in seconds.

"This spot is perfect for the roadblock. We're two miles from the interstate," informed the woman. "Tassel and Kitty, you'll remain hidden deep in the woods until you're called upon. Make sure to leave your comms active." She turned her attention to the women without uniforms. "Crystal, take Taffy with you. Arial, you are with me on the opposite side."

The warrior looked at her smartwatch, then gestured with her head at the uniformed women to turn on the vehicles' lights. The surrounding darkness was replaced by rotating flashing red and blue lights.

"All right, team, this is it. Remember, we're looking for a white van, and if the intel is correct, there will be four armed guards. That means everyone should have their tranquilizers locked and loaded. If they realize what's going on, they'll call for backup, but from this location, it'll take twenty minutes for anyone to arrive. By that juncture, we will be long gone."

Gypsy took a deep breath. "I'll handle Villainous." She lifted the shackles and tranquilizer, then turned to Kitty. "Once I apprehend her, I'll need you to be close by. Tassel, you are to get in Vehicle Two with our state patrol women and immediately head back to the compound. The rest will go back with me." The warrior glanced at the group. "If you have no questions, everyone to their spot."

The group darted into their designated positions, and for twenty minutes, it felt like the night before Christmas —all through the area, not a creature was stirring, not even a car.

Tassel and Kitty sat behind a tall Eastern Black Walnut tree. The goth girl fidgeted with her fingernails while the seer reviewed notes on the cell. Tassel's expression turned dark, and her eyes popped wide at what she saw on the screen. "*Oh, no, no!*" she blurted.

Kitty stopped her nail-biting and asked, "What's wrong?"

She ignored her friend's inquiry and spoke into her comm. "Gypsy, what server did you upload the mission file to?"

"I used the system named NY-DWTRI-01. Why?"

"That system was an old server I decommissioned when we left the warehouse. Someone brought that system back online, and it appears the file you uploaded was recently accessed."

"You mean to tell me that I handed our mission intel to the Furies?"

"I think so." Tassel gulped while the warrior cursed up a storm.

After a long sigh, the warrior advised, "We keep to the plan, but that means we need to keep our eyes peeled."

"No need for that," Kitty stated. A few yards away, she saw lights bouncing. She pointed. "Those look like flashlights, which means they are already here."

"Damn it!" exclaimed Gypsy. "Ladies, get your asses out of there. We need to abort the mission. I repeat, abort!" The warrior was distracted by the approaching headlights brightening the road.

The white van decelerated and then came to a stop at the roadblock.

"Gypsy, what do we do?" whispered one of the patrol women into her comm. She turned her head toward the vehicle. The lights of the van illuminated the open backs of the SUVs, and her eyes widened in disbelief. "We have another issue. There's someone in one of the vehicles. I believe it's that Nyala chick."

"What!" the warrior exclaimed. "Lily, let them through, but first approach the vehicle and advise that you are conducting a routine check. Take a quick glance, then let me through."

The woman in uniform proceeded as instructed and flashed her flashlight at the driver and passenger. "Hello, gentlemen. We're looking for DUI drivers, but you guys look fine. Give us a second to move the vehicles."

"Officer," replied the driver. "We know the local authorities in this area, and they made no mention of a routine check." He pulled out a Glock from his holster and shot her in the head.

He placed the van in gear and rammed into the SUVs as Gypsy screamed at the two uniformed women to move.

Smoke rose from the hood of the van. The driver shook off his daze and placed the vehicle in reverse. The van retreated, but before the driver could ram the SUVs again, two sharp darts flew in his direction and knocked him out. His foot hit the brake pedal.

Another guard banged on the back panel and yelled, "We're under attack!" He tried to remove his seatbelt but was met with an iron fist to the face, followed by several darts.

The van's back doors opened, and out came four men with semi-automatic rifles in head-to-toe tactical gear. They opened fire.

The warrior took cover in front of the van and yelled into her comm, "The intel did not include the drivers.

There are four guards with rifles. Take cover. Do not come for me. I repeat, *DO NOT COME FOR ME. RUN!*"

The guards stopped firing and gestured to one another to move to the front of the van, two on one side and two on the other. They paced forward, taking short and meticulous steps. When they saw each other through the side windows, one lifted his hand and began a five-second countdown with his fingers.

The warrior crouched, surrounded by oil and water on the ground. Her breathing was deep and steady. She knew her chance of survival was minimal, but she wasn't going down without a fight. She dropped the tranquilizer and extracted two blades, gripping them tightly.

Gypsy's eyes fixed on a panicked-looking Nyala. She banged on the SUV's window and mouthed the word, "*MOVE.*" The guards were too distracted with their countdown to notice the Mozambican. The warrior screamed, "Nyala, *NO.* RUN!"

3, 2, 1... The fingers went down, then the guards rushed forward. Then something unexpected happened—a strong gust of cold wind swirled around everyone. The water on the pavement turned into black ice, causing the armed guards to slip and fall.

Gypsy could see the vapor from her breath as her teeth chattered. Then purple smoke materialized before the warrior's eyes. Out of the blue, her mind rushed back to her fight with Therion and sensed an overwhelming fear. The more she thought, the denser the smoke became. Death was closing in; the warrior could taste it.

From the back window, Nyala saw Gypsy's impending demise. Unable to open the rear hatch, she struggled out of the back and into the seat. She quickly lowered the side window and yelled, "Gypsy, raise your arms. She's after you!"

Instinctively, the seasoned warrior followed orders. A sharp blade came out of the smoke and struck her prosthetic arm. It rebounded into her head and knocked her out.

A young woman appeared in the purple smoke, dressed in black apparel. Her flowing dark hair reached her lower back. She towered over Gypsy with a sharp silver blade in her left hand. The mysterious figure turned around and stared at Nyala with her stardust eyes, then vanished.

Nyala managed to open the locked doors and raced to Gypsy's aid. Unbeknownst to the Mozambican, the guards stood and shook their heads as they got up. They raised their rifles and aimed at the women in front of the van.

The Mozambican stretched her arms toward the two groups and stated, "Your quarrel is not with us. Go back to your masters, mortals bent on darkness, and address your evil intent with them."

Inexplicably, the men nodded, dropped their weapons, and bolted down the dark road.

"Are you OK?" asked Nyala as she assisted the warrior off the ground. She pressed down with her hand to stop the bleeding from a small laceration on Gypsy's head.

After rushing to the scene, Crystal stopped behind Nyala. "What the hell happened?" She bent to assist. "Is she still alive?"

"Yes, she is, but we must leave now. It will return," disclosed Nyala.

"How?" Crystal pointed at the smashed SUVs. "Both the cars are unusable."

"Please, we must get her up and get you all out of here. Your lives are in danger," the woman pleaded.

"We can try the van," said Crystal. She spoke into comm. "Ladies, rendezvous at the roadblock ASAP."

Within a minute, the group had gathered. Gypsy began to come out of it.

Crystal was the first to ask, "Gypsy, are you all right? What the hell was that?"

The warrior stood from the ground, holding onto Nyala, and shook her head. "I don't know. An apparition of some kind attacked me."

"An apparition like a ghost?" a spooked-looking Crystal inquired.

"I don't know, Crystal. It just came of nowhere." She turned to the Mozambican. "I should be upset with you, but you saved my life."

"Well, well, if it isn't Gypsy and the Holograms," announced a female from the woods.

"Erinys!" whispered the warrior.

Behind the leader stood a group of ten Furies. "You all make a lot of fuss about codes and honor and get into people's faces to hold to those standards, but you're a bunch of liars."

"This isn't what you think, and I swear to you that we would never hurt any of our women." Gypsy looked behind Erinys. "Glory, you know us. You were once one of us. Tell her that isn't the way we do things."

"I'm sorry, Gypsy, but I can't trust you anymore. Four of my long-time friends are dead, killed by the woman you are trying to rescue. She has killed our own before, and nothing was ever done. Now you are trying to save her. We can't let that happen."

Nyala raised her voice, "Please, ladies, we must leave this place. It's not safe for any of us."

Erinys addressed her. "You must be new, honey. If you are, let me be the one to say you are playing for the wrong team."

The Furies' leader had not finished when the cold wind picked up again. The trees rustled and unleashed a freezing mist that fogged the area. The asphalt iced over from the dropping temperature.

"This is that witch Villainous' doing," Erinys shared.

"Let me know how I'm doing it so I can stop it," called Laurie. She limped toward the group with her hands cuffed and her face bruised.

All eyes went to the notorious Villainous, but then the purple smoke reappeared.

"We must stick together, or some of you will die," Nyala told the two groups.

"What is that?" yelled the Furies' leader as the smoke increased in density.

Crimson chimed in, "That is that thing that killed Buitre."

Laurie laughed. "I felt this essence before when I almost died. This, my frenemies, is the taste of death."

The fog covered the entire area, and it was impossible to see beyond three feet. Many of the assembled women screamed or whimpered. Along with the fog, a tangible sense of fear encompassed them as horrors of their past crept into their consciousness like crawling spiders.

Silence took over the night.

There was a swoosh, then a thump. Then Erinys screamed, "Oh, my God! That's Glory's head." The women dashed in all directions.

Crystal told Gypsy, "We need to get the women out of here. I'll attempt to get the van started."

"You must not leave," advised Nyala.

"I'm afraid too, Nyala, but we have to escape this place now." Crystal sprinted toward the driver's side but was met by purple smoke and a blade to her neck. Her head separated from her body.

Kitty grabbed Tassel's hand. "We have to get out of here."

They ran toward the woods, and, jumping over tree limbs, faces slapped by branches, and dodging rocks, sprinted away, though visibility was minimal. They kept their eyes forward and didn't look back.

Gypsy remained with Nyala. She clasped the Mozambican's face with her right hand and asked, "I know your memories don't come easily to you anymore, but I need you to think about how we can stop this."

"I don't know, Gypsy!" She was shaking.

"Think, Nyala. I need you to think," the warrior commanded.

The woman nodded and closed her eyes, then took a deep breath.

Meanwhile, the two companions continued to run. Kitty lost Tassel's hand when the seer tripped on a tree limb. When the goth girl turned around, the purple smoke appeared behind her friend.

Tassel did not notice the aberration but stood up. The seer gazed inquisitively at her friend's bulging eyes.

"Tassel, get down!" Kitty yelled.

She reacted without thinking and turned to the smoke behind her and the blade moving toward her.

Nyala began writing on the ground with her finger. Gypsy sighed as she watched the Mozambican scribble on the forest floor. When she was done, the woman uttered authoritatively, "I, the Daughter of Apocalypse, mark this site." As she spoke those words, she put her hands down, and a bright light streamed out of her and marked the All-Seeing Eye. A *crack* resonated through the area, dispersing the fog and wintry temperatures.

She collapsed.

The purple smoke froze before Kitty. She could see stardust eyes glaring at her from the face of a young woman. The goth girl could sense the young woman's intent to harm her, but the assassin could not. With tears in her eyes and a quivering voice, Kitty asked, "Who are you?"

"I'm one who seeks justice," the assassin responded, then disappeared.

PART III

EQUILIBRIUM

19

IN THE BEGINNING

Countless Eons ago

Before there was anything, there was nothing. Empty space is not nothing; space is a thing. Nothing is not a thing. This state of nothingness endured, unchanging, then suddenly, something did change. Thus began a new temporal moment, the beginning of time.

The first place to appear was quite unlike the ones that came after. This space was not physical; it was a dimension of conscious energy. It was in this location that the first light emerged. Shortly after the appearance of the first, two more lights appeared one after the other, each equal in intensity to the first. The first light had a purple hue, the second was yellow-red, and the last glowed a bright green.

Then a voice spoke. Its speech was unlike a human's, projecting sound with their mouths that travels through the vibrations of air molecules. Instead, the communication reverberated through the dimension.

"Arise, Primals!"

The three lights pulsed with luminous energy and

started to take humanoid shapes. As this was occurring, three more lights appeared nearby. These were less intense than the original three, but each was majestic in its own right.

"Arise, Ancillas!"

The second set of lights started to throb and morph as well. Finally, a smaller, far dimmer orb appeared. This light was pale compared to others.

"Arise, Tritios!"

As this final light took shape, the energy of the dimension increased, and sounds and tiny lights began to dance everywhere. Then a swirl of life force emerged between the three sets of beings. This force shifted rapidly between them, leaving a bright red trail as it moved. Finally, the face of a young woman appeared amid the swirl as it stopped before the first of the Primals, a tall and elegant woman dressed in black.

"You are Dayyana, the first of the Primals, the aspect of the Sovereign One's Justice."

Next, the force moved to the Primal beside Dayyana. "You are Haniel, the second of the Primals, the aspect of the Sovereign One's Order." The face circled playfully around the last of the Primals. "And you are Apocalypse, the third of the Primals, the aspect of the Sovereign One's Understanding."

The three Primals bowed their heads in reverence. "What should we call you?" inquired Apocalypse.

"Hmm. I'm the Breath of the Sovereign One. You may call me Neshama."

Neshama turned, darted between the second set of lights, and stopped before them. "You, first of the Ancillas, the Warrior of the Sovereign One, will be called Michael. You, the second of the Ancillas, the Messenger of the Sovereign One, are Gabriel. And you, the Protector of the Sovereign One's works, are Sapha."

Last, Neshama went to the lesser light and circled it several times. "Last of the Great Lights, the Keeper of Annals of the Sovereign One, you are El-Samar Seper."

As Neshama finished naming the Great Lights, a mass of energy swelled behind them and took the form of a man. This individual's flesh glowed bronze, and his shoulder-length hair was white like wool. A white robe draped his body, and a gold sash adorned his chest. The Great Lights instinctively bowed their heads and paid their respects.

"My dear children," said the man in a soft, gentle voice. "Stretch out your hands."

The majestic beings did as they were told.

"Dayyana," he announced as a giant scythe materialized before her. "With this, you will ensure our Justice is always done."

A pair of scales appeared before the second Primal. "Haniel, may you always seek to maintain our Order and Balance."

"Apocalypse, you will bring Revelation of our ways and works." A quill pen and a long scroll appeared before her.

The man turned to the Ancillas. As he did, a flame exploded in front of them. The fire morphed into three balls that took new forms: for Michael, a radiant sword, for Gabriel, a trumpet, and for Sapha, a shield.

"Michael, you will bring retribution to any enemies who will surely arise. Gabriel, you will proclaim our message. Sapha, you will guard our works against harm."

Last, the man moved toward the dimmest of the Lights. He stretched out his hand, and a Codex appeared in it.

"El-Samar Seper, you will keep our knowledge and guide your co-laborers to complete the Works of Creation."

The seven lights accepted their gifts and again bowed their heads in reverence. The booming voice spoke again. "Let there be worlds."

A countless number of ornate doors appeared around the Great Lights. The doors varied in size and adornment but were all locked and colorless. Then, Neshama closed her eyes, and pulsing energy rays shot out of her and toward each door. When the energy reached each door, it took on color and swung open, revealing a portal to its corresponding world.

The man addressed the Seven again. "You are the first of our many servants. You are unique amongst those who will come after you, for you alone are Transworld beings, the Archangels of the Sovereign One. Six of you will lead from here, the High Heavens, intervening in the affairs of each world only when necessary."

He turned to Sapha and moved toward him. "You, Sapha, will be present in every world. Your essence will remain here, but you will have a counterpart on each world to protect it."

As he spoke this, Neshama dashed toward Sapha and circled him several times, then smiled and kissed him on the forehead. Sapha's light intensified and split into smaller orbs that shot toward the open doors and disappeared through the portals. Crowds of winged beings poured out of the doors, the Angels of each new world.

"El-Samar Seper," called Neshama, "There's much work to be done. Guide them."

The Great Light looked at the Codex in his hands for a moment, then opened it. Inside he found the designs, plans, and instructions for ordering each world. The crowds of Angels approached him with curiosity in their eyes, hungry to receive the Sovereign One's directions for Creation.

Innumerable Angels received instructions from El-Samar Seper and left for their respective worlds to carry out their directives. Michael and Dayyana approached the Keeper with their gifts in hand.

"El-Samar Seper, your assignment and gift are amazing," exclaimed Michael. "I have no idea what to do with mine." With a quizzical look, the mighty Archangel swung his fiery sword aimlessly several times.

"Tell us about the Annals," requested Dayyana.

"As far as I can tell, it's an infinite record containing the knowledge of the Sovereign One."

"A record of what?" Michael queried.

"Of everything," El-Samar Seper responded. "It contains the histories of every created world and every world that could have been created but wasn't. Also, within are the infinite paths the history of each world could take, the decisions each being in that world would make at each branching path, and the direction in which history will actually unfold."

"That sounds complicated. How does that small book hold all that?"

"The Codex doesn't show me everything at once. I have to think about a world, and when I open the book, it shows me the history of that place," explained El-Samar Seper. "When I come across a branching history, I have to think about the path I want to explore, and the next page will show it. Or, I can backtrack and think of a different path, and the following pages will reflect that choice."

Dayyana looked intently at the youngest Archangel. "Tell us about the worlds the Sovereign One has made."

El-Samar Seper's face lit up. "There are so many, and each is unique. The total duration of some worlds is measured in billions of temporal units. The entire account of others is a mere six or seven thousand. Further, some follow similar paths, and their temporal flow runs parallel."

The Keeper paused, then continued gleefully, "Some worlds have very little in them, while others will be teeming with life. There's even one with a talking lion!"

"What's a lion?" asked Dayyana.

El-Samar Seper locked eyes with the Primal. "I have no clue!"

All three looked at each other for several moments before bursting into laughter.

"The Sovereign One's works are majestic and mysterious," exclaimed Michael. "Is there anything in the book concerning what this sword is good for? Who am I supposed to be fighting?"

"I haven't looked very far ahead into the history of any world. Let me pick one and take a gander."

El-Samar Seper opened the book and flipped page after page, reading the history of one world.

"Hmmm, that's odd. This world ends abruptly. Let me check another."

The Archangel closed and opened the book and perused the pages. "This...this can't be right." He repeated the pattern of closing, opening, and scanning the book several more times. His face grew sadder each time.

"What's wrong, El-Samar Seper?" inquired Michael.

"I don't understand what I'm reading. The history of some of the worlds is not what it should be."

"What do you mean?"

"The Annals show me all branches of history. Every world has branches that lead to perfection. However, there are creatures in many worlds who shun the Sovereign One's plan and lead their world to ruin," explained the Keeper.

Dayyana gripped her scythe tightly, "What is the cause of this ruin?"

El-Samar Seper closed the book briefly and stared at the ornate cover before responding, "I'll have to look at many worlds before I can say for sure, but they all seem to have one thing in common."

"What is that?"

"They are worlds with creatures who can choose their own actions. They have free will."

20

DEATH BY A THOUSAND CUTS

The three young women scuffed through the familiar second-floor corridor. Its walls were now painted tan instead of pearl white. Each one held a cup of coffee to help strip away the early morning drowsiness, though their heartbeats infused them with an extra dose of adrenaline. The unexpected phone call had left them anxious and wondering. Finding themselves at the warehouse made the matter more confusing.

They gazed at Kitty as they approached her. She sat hunched with her hands covering her face as hot tears rushed through her fingers. She lifted her head at the sound of footsteps and stared at her friends with red eyes. That made the three young women hasten to her side and embrace her tenderly.

"Angel, Pretzel, Reina, she's..." Kitty started, shaking her head.

"Kitty, what's wrong?" Angel asked nervously, sensing her pain. "What happened?"

Her whimpers prohibited the young woman from

speaking, leaving all three to huddle around and embrace her even tighter.

Like lightning, a dreadful thought hit Reina. "Kitty, where's Tassel?" Her voice quivered.

The goth girl lifted her gaze to her friends with a loud gulp. "She's gone, guys. Tassel is gone."

"What do you mean she's gone?" Angel inquired desperately. Her eyes were welling with tears.

"Please don't tell me she's dead!" Reina exclaimed. Tears covered her face.

Pretzel steepled her fingers over her lips and shook her head in disbelief. "No, she can't be! She can't be!"

Kitty hesitantly nodded as the news struck her friends' souls, releasing a flood of pain.

They wept together.

The friends embraced in a huddle. No words of comfort were spoken, nor was anything said, but all sensed each other's overwhelming grief and loss.

After an hour, Kitty conveyed what had happened that evening. She bitterly related Tassel's and Crystal's deaths and her frightening encounter with the mysterious assassin. No matter how hard she tried, she couldn't put into words who or what she had seen. After a long pause, they turned to the door when a familiar face appeared.

"Joan!" exclaimed Pretzel.

"I, um, came to check up on Kitty." She began to cry.

Pretzel went to her leader's side.

Regaining her composure, Joan faced the group. "I'm so sorry this happened. She was like a daughter to me." She wiped her eyes, then continued. "Ladies, why don't you take Kitty back with you? I'll most likely be here for another hour or so, trying to make sense of what happened tonight."

"What did happen tonight?" inquired Kitty. "And I wanna know who killed Tassel."

"That is what we're trying to figure out in there." Joan pointed at the conference room.

"If you guys are discussing this, I want to be part of it." The girl stood and wiped her face. "I'm pretty sure we're up against something none of us have faced before."

"Kitty, go home and get some rest. We'll discuss this among the team and not with those Furies. They are not sympathetic. All they have done the entire time I've been there is bicker about why we were there."

Angel angrily asked, "Why *were* we there?"

Pretzel shook her head and placed her hand on Angel's shoulder. "This is not time."

"Joan, I'm not leaving." Kitty was adamant. "I can't let that thing attack again and take the rest of my friends. I wanna talk and share what I saw tonight."

The leader gave a reluctant nod. "Emotions are running high at the moment, so I ask that you follow my lead." She turned to the others. "Is there any chance I could convince you three to stay out here?"

In synchrony, they shook their heads.

"All right. Come on in and take a seat toward the back. Kitty, you sit next to me."

The women proceeded into a conference room filled with loud shouts. Around the table sat several Furies, along with a few of the Daughters who were bickering with one another. The tension in the room was thick enough to cut with a knife.

Gypsy sat quietly with an elbow on the table and her right hand on her forehead. Though she was a hardened warrior, her eyes were red. She had yet to remove the damaged prosthetic, nor had she said a word since she arrived.

After Kitty sat, Joan raised her hand to get the group's attention. When she was ignored, she exclaimed, "Ladies, *please!*"

As if the seventh seal had been opened, silence fell upon the room.

"There are plenty of questions and concerns to be discussed, but nothing will come about if we continue quarreling with one another. Six of our comrades, sisters, and friends have fallen tonight, so let's show them respect and try to understand what happened." She took a sharp breath. "Something out there is hunting us, and we need to know what it is to stop it."

"Most likely some powerful Nephilim," one of the Furies declared.

"It wasn't a man," Kitty said sternly. "A woman attacked us tonight."

"How do you know?" another Fury asked. "It was impossible to see anything in that thick fog."

Joan glanced at Kitty and whispered, "Follow my lead." She raised her hand again. "Why don't we begin by sharing what we saw, heard, experienced, or sensed tonight? It'll help us paint a clearer picture." The leader took a seat and turned to the young woman. "Kitty, why don't you begin?"

The goth girl cleared her throat. "Everything got convoluted when the temperature dropped to the point that Tassel…" she breathed shallowly to keep back her tears, "and I started to shiver. Fog covered the area, and out of nowhere, a mysterious purple smoke surrounded us. Though we couldn't see much, you could hear a blade coming out of a sheath. We started running, not knowing the killer was behind us. Tassel tripped, and when she tried to get up, she was killed. Through the fog, I could make out a blade coming toward me, but it stopped suddenly. In the smoke, I saw a young woman with piercing yellow eyes."

Pretzel's eyebrows shot up, vaguely remembering someone with those eyes.

"I asked who she was, but she only responded, 'One who seeks justice.' She then disappeared."

Crimson, who was sitting next to Erinys, spoke up. "The night Buitre died, I experienced something similar to tonight." The Fury gazed at Kitty. "I also saw a woman. She moves through a cloud of purple smoke at great speed, and I got the sense that she was feeding off my fear. Almost like the more frightened I became, the stronger she got."

A few of the women in the room nodded in agreement.

Erinys interjected, "If this thing can move so quickly, why not cause more harm?"

"I agree," added Joan. "Unless it was targeting certain individuals."

The Furies' leader gave Joan a disgusted look. "Her targets are all women who once belonged to or are part of your group."

One of the Daughters chimed in, "But why not Gypsy or Kitty?"

"Because I blocked her strike." Gypsy raised her damaged prosthetic. "It wasn't luck. I had help, and the person who saved my life also saved Kitty's in the nick of time."

"Nyala?" Joan inquired with a frown.

Gypsy nodded. "I misjudged her from the beginning. I think she might know who this mysterious killer is and how to stop her. Most importantly, she might be able to answer the question of who's plaguing us and why."

"Where is she, and why is she not in this meeting?" asked Erinys.

"She was unconscious for a while after stopping the assassin. Mrs. Mozart and May took her back to our compound about an hour ago to ensure she was OK."

"We need to talk to her at once."

Joan shook her head. "It's not that easy. She's the woman our London counterparts are alleging we kidnapped, but I suspect they did something that left her mind in shambles. Hence, the accusation of kidnapping."

Joan continued, "For those curious, Nyala was the reason we were there last night. As much as we hated to, we were there to liberate the one we call Villainous."

"Who got away again," Erinys interrupted.

Joan sighed. "Yes, but at least now you know she's not our assassin or executing my orders."

"She's still responsible for Dirae's death."

"She's responsible for the death of many." The leader took a breath to calm herself. "We did what we did because we believed it was the correct thing, though we didn't want to."

Those words resonated with Angel. For several days, she had struggled within herself to either live her own life or live like a Daughter. She greatly desired a regular life, yet she could not resist the urgency of her duty. The more she fought, the more the urgency consumed her heart like wildfire that burned deep into her bones. Although it wasn't what she wanted, she knew without a shadow of a doubt that this was her calling.

Pretzel noticed Angel's expression and asked, "Are you OK?"

"Ask me later."

"OK, Joan," interjected Erinys, rolling her eyes. "You have your ways, and we have ours. As of now, I have two murderers to contend with, Villainous and this thing that's hunting our women. You're concerned with the why, but I want to know how the hell the assassin knows when and where to attack?"

Joan nodded. "I agree, unless there's a spy among us. Something is drawing in this slayer, and we need to find out before she kills again. Until we stop her, can you keep the Global Daughters off our backs?"

The Furies' leader pursed her lips. "Under one condition. This assassin is killing our women, so I need real-time information. Therefore, I would like to assign Crimson as my personal liaison in your group. You've worked with her previously, so you should be comfortable with her. Any intel you obtain about these killings, please share it with her immediately, and she'll relay it to me."

Joan glanced at Crimson and nodded.

21

A MEMORIAL VISIT

Angel walked into Tassel's office and sat on the seer's chair. Her old laptop and multiple monitors were in sleep mode but were awakened when Angel brushed her hand against the mouse on the desk. A password prompt appeared, and behind it, a picture formed the background. She recognized it. The photo had been taken a year before on the women's trip to Niagara Falls to celebrate Tassel's birthday.

The young woman carefully examined the image, reliving the day. Then she reached out and touched the screen, smiling at the chaotic group photograph. It depicted a frowning Pretzel with a hotdog in hand, getting her blouse stained by Reina's clumsy handling of a mustard packet. While Kitty fidgeted with her nails, Cookie and Dough fought over a jar of cherries. Tassel was in the middle calling Angel over, who raced back from setting the camera's timer. The only thing that was remarkable about the photo was the backdrop of the Falls.

Angel wondered why, out of all of their photos, Tassel

had selected this one as her background. Why not the picture they had taken at the gala that evening or the one on the ferry as they toured the Falls? She smiled as a tear rolled down her cheek; she realized that was how Tassel remembered them. The image, in some way, illustrated their respective personalities.

"This was the perfect photo, Tassel," Angel wiped off the tear. She continued staring at the photo, specifically her late friend's face.

"That was a great weekend," said Pretzel from the doorway. She was wearing a black dress and heels. She was leaning her head on the doorframe, gazing at her friend.

"Yes, it was," responded Angel, who continued looking at the image. Then she swiveled around. "I miss her so much, Pretzel."

"Me, too." She walked into the room and sat by a nearby chair.

The room remained quiet until a perky blue-eyed woman entered. She also wore a dark dress. "Hey, guys, are you heading to the memorial service?"

"In a bit," answered Angel.

"Sit with us, Reina," requested Pretzel, making room for her on the chair she was sitting on.

The girl joined her and glanced at the room, remembering. "You know, Tassel called me that night. She was so happy. It was her first official field assignment." She swallowed while wiping away the waterworks. "Though I think she knew something was going to happen."

"How so?" inquired Pretzel.

"After we talked about our day, she sent me an email with an encrypted file containing passwords and other stuff. She mentioned how much she loved us and to remember that she could see things we couldn't." Reina sniffed, then wiped her nose. "When I asked her what that meant, she simply said, 'You'll see.'"

"Do you think she meant her death?" asked Angel.

Reina shrugged. "Maybe later, we can view that file. She might have left something there."

"That's a good idea, Reina," Pretzel stated.

Angel laid her head against the headrest and sighed. "*Dios mío*, I'm having that guilt feeling. I should have gone with her that night."

"Hmm. I've had those same feelings, especially after Gypsy informed me that I was supposed to be one of the drivers that night," shared Pretzel. "We can guilt-trip ourselves all night, but I think Tassel might have saved our lives."

"What do you mean?" Angel fixed her eyes on Pretzel. Her head was still on the headrest.

"If Tassel had not accepted the mission, Gypsy might have insisted and managed to convince us to join. Instead, she took our spot as if her death meant salvation for us."

"I know what you're saying, but to be honest, I now feel even more responsible. So, our refusal meant Tassel's death?"

"Then, we should honor her even more and remember her as a great friend who put her life on the line for us."

"I guess you're right." Angel smiled. "Then again, you're always right."

Pretzel winked at her. "Of course, girl."

"Hey, guys, what about this assassin?" Reina's eyes went

from Angel to Pretzel. "What are we going to do about her?"

"Whatever it takes," answered Angel.

"I've been speaking with Gypsy and Mrs. Mozart for the last three days, and I agree with something they shared. Nyala is the key to unraveling this mystery."

"Does that mean she's right about Therion's return?" Angel's eyes widened.

"If she is, she'll likely tell us how to stop him, but we have to help her. Tomorrow evening, there's an emergency meeting. I asked Gypsy if we could attend, and she consented. I think we should go. If we're going to stop whatever is hunting us, we need to do it together."

Angel took a long breath, then nodded.

"I'm in. For Tassel and Crystal," responded the blue-eyed girl.

Pretzel glanced at her watch. "It's that time. Let us remember and celebrate a great Daughter, seer, and friend."

It was late when the Daughters gathered in the southwest conference room of the Tektonite compound. Mist was in attendance, along with Cookie and Dough, who had arrived for Tassel's memorial service the previous day. The council members occupied most of the conference table, and the rest sat against the walls.

Everyone present waited and watched as a young girl struggled to project Joan's laptop. It was a grief-stricken moment as everyone recalled how effortlessly Tassel would execute the task. The flushed girl apologized a few times and finally displayed the image on the large screen.

"Thank you, Hadassah," remarked Joan and gave the girl a polite smile. The leader glanced around the room, taking note of those in attendance, then took a seat. She put on her glasses and opened a folder before her.

"I appreciate everyone making it on such short notice. Also to Awilda, the Tektonite overseer, for being with us, and Crimson, who will be our liaison with the Furies. Under the circumstances, I would've held this meeting some other time, but urgency called for it to discuss a new threat. An enemy we've never faced before, much faster, more powerful, and not detectable by our Spiritual Psychological Awareness. What makes this new enemy more menacing and mysterious is that it's not a Nephilim but a woman who has targeted our group specifically."

The leader cleared her throat as she reviewed the notes. "In the last three weeks, she has killed twelve women, all of whom belonged to the Daughters of the Watchers Tristate group at one point or another. Each one was killed in a similar fashion, beginning with Horizon and Robin, or Buitre as she was known among the Furies. The last two were our beloved Crystal and Tassel. At this stage, we don't have a concrete motive. Suffice it to say we're being hunted. Fortunately, by Sovereign will, two of our Daughters survived the attack of this assassin, and we believe they survived because they were protected by the same woman—Nyala."

Joan removed her glasses and glanced at the group. "If we're to survive, our defenses and battle tactics need to change. It will take more than might or power; it will take a transcendental strength that Gypsy saw the night she was attacked, one we believe Nyala possesses."

"Lass, how are we to accomplish this?" asked Mrs. Poppins. "The poor girl has a difficult time remembering even simple things."

"With our help," responded the leader. "She has improved since she arrived, and I think we can collectively help her get better."

"Well put, Joan," articulated Mrs. Mozart. "In addition, let us be observant and prudent about how we support Miss Nyala. Regrettably, I employed unfruitful strategies to reach her when she first arrived. However, I soon noticed something rather remarkable. Thanks to May's keen observation, Miss Nyala has really taken to young Miss Olivia and Miss Sparkles. I believe this connection has empowered her to make great strides on her path to recovery. I made the audacious mistake of preferring sophistication over simplicity. Let us be observant in such matters."

"Mrs. Mozart," started Gypsy, "on that fatal night, Nyala called herself the Daughter of Apocalypse and created an All-Seeing Eye around her. Even that old hag who visited us the other day claimed Nyala had some connection to that being. Do you know who Apocalypse is and what the symbol means?"

The wise woman placed a finger over her lips. "There are ancient writings that speak of the Seven Great Creatures, beings created before our world's space, matter, and time were in existence. These seven beings are also known as the Archangels, and among them is one named Apocalypse. Some suggest this Archangel is a revelator, though I'm not sure. Regarding the symbol, it is the sign of the Eye of Providence, meant to symbolize that the Sovereign One watches over mankind. Unfortunately, I'm not acquainted with how it relates to this Archangel."

"Could Nyala be the daughter of an Archangel?"

"There are no written documents of these Archangels interacting with mankind except for Gabriel and Michael, much less having offspring. My only knowledge is of early accounts involving seers coming in contact with a great revelator. I suppose that could be this Apocalypse."

"Mrs. Mozart?" It was May's turn to ask. "All of the victims were decapitated. Could that shed any light on these mysterious assassinations?"

"Intriguing question, May, and one I have been pondering much of late. Historically, the practice of decapitation or beheading was a form of capital punishment. In fact, the term 'capital offense' is derived from the Latin word caput, which means head." The wise woman turned to the goth girl. "In Miss Kitty's brief encounter, the assassin articulated that she seeks justice."

A slight commotion stirred in the room, and someone voiced a question without identifying themselves. *"Justice for what?"*

The wise woman raised her hand for silence. "I deduce that this assassin's execution style is deliberate and penal, though the reason is a mystery."

Awilda, the Tektonite leader, waved her hand and, in her Spanish accent, conveyed, "If you'll just give me a chance to share. Many Tektonites were persecuted and beheaded by many religious groups and the empire's officials during the ancient Roman Empire. These martyrs hailed from different nationalities, languages, and traditions. Still, they were all persecuted for the same reason; they followed the way of the Tekton.

"The question you need to ask yourself is, what do all the victims have in common? Or what experience do you share with the women who remained in your old warehouse? If you could answer that question, you could probably figure out the reason for the persecution."

Like synchronized clocks, every Daughter's eye gravitated toward the Daimon Slayer.

"*¿Quién, yo?*" questioned Angel, shocked.

Joan did not speak the language, but she understood what the woman was asking. "Well, not exactly you, Angel, but the visit of the Carpenter's Son. The event changed not only the course of your life but ours as well. It created a ripple effect that has led us to this path. It's the only commonality we share."

"What of it?" asked Angel, overwhelmed by everyone staring at her. "Why would this thing be after us because of that visit?"

The leader shook her head. "A good question and one we can't answer at the moment." Joan turned to Crimson. "Please inform Erinys to note all the women who were with us the night the Carpenter's Son appeared to us."

Crimson wrinkled her nose. "Wait, you really believe that he appeared to you guys?"

"Yes, he did." The leader turned to Awilda. "Thank you for your insight. It's the best lead we've had so far." She glanced at the group. "Group, one more thing. Until we know when and how this assassin attacks, we're suspending all future missions. We cannot take additional risks. Crimson, I'd pass that message on to Erinys."

22

A PRIMAL DISTURBANCE

Four Days Ago
Libitinia stood motionless in the dark corridor, struggling with a sense of failure. It was the first time she had ever experienced that emotion. She was hesitant at first, but eventually, she let out a sharp breath, wiped the bloodstained blade on her black pants, and proceeded down the dark corridor. The ornate torches on the walls revealed her downcast and puzzled appearance.

Before she exited the corridor, she put the blade back in its sheath, and as soon she entered the great hall, the young woman took a knee and bowed her head. Libitinia paid homage to the majestic woman on the bone throne. Her rich wine-colored hair wrapped around her body as she sat. The woman appeared distracted as she rested her pale left hand on one of the skull armrests and elevated the other to eye level.

The lady was gazing at a transparent image levitating above her palm, an hourglass dispensing its last droplets of sand. When the top bulb released the last grain, it became ash gray. The bottom bulb cracked, dispersing the sand. A moment later, it was repaired and grew bright.

As usual, it made the Primal clench her teeth. A flickering light appeared and drifted into Mara's being. Taking a deep breath, she waved her hand, and the image disappeared. The woman shifted her sight to the kneeling girl.

Mara knitted her eyebrows. "I sense you are distraught, my daughter."

"My lady, I've failed you." Libby's gaze remained on the floor.

"Explain yourself, child."

"I did not fully execute the assignment. Two of the eight remain alive."

Mara graciously waved her hand, and above her palm appeared an image that was different from the first. A group of bright and colorful hourglasses, the top bulbs leaking sand into cracked bulbs, though the white substance did not spill. One was different from the rest; though it was brilliant and vivid, the bottom bulb had a gaping hole, yet the grainy material remained within. The lady glared at the image, then flipped her hand, vanquishing the hourglasses.

"Was the assignment too much for you to handle?" Mara had a perturbed expression.

"Not at all, my lady. One deflected my strike, and the other prevented me from striking." Libby lifted her head and frowned. "It was as if they could sense me."

"Impossible!" Mara raised her voice more than usual. "Their transcendental senses are ineffectual, nor are they capable of restraining you."

The girl gave a heavy, thoughtful sigh. "There was

another woman, my lady, one whose aura was different from the rest. I think she had something to do with it."

"A different aura?" The lady leaned forward, staring at the young woman. "Describe this aura to me, Libitinia."

"It was a brilliant and vivid green. I've never seen anything like it."

Mara froze, eyes wide, as a strange, cold wind circulated through the hall. All the torches mystically extinguished, and the floor crystallized. Abruptly, the lady stood from the throne and marched toward Libby.

"On your feet," she ordered, then grabbed Libby's hand and disappeared.

In the twinkling of an eye, they emerged on a dark and narrow road. They proceeded toward the hooting of owls and the rustling of trees gently swaying in the breezes of the early morning hours. They stopped when they saw three stalled vehicles.

The white van's hood and grill were smashed, and its headlights flickered. A few feet from the van stood two black SUVs with deflated front tires and smashed fenders. Most horrific were the bloodstains that coated the asphalt, though there were no corpses present to show for it.

The most dreadful spectacle for the lady was the insignia of the All-Seeing Eye on the ground. Taking a few steps forward, Mara crouched over it. She stretched out her hand, and with her finger, carefully followed its patterns.

"Is something the matter, Mistress?" Libby stared inquisitively at the Primal. She had never seen her mother look so disconcerted.

The lady wiped her hands and stood upright. "You were

not stopped. You were interfered with," she revealed. Arms up, Mara slowly turned in a full circle while inhaling. "I can still smell her scent."

"Who interfered, and whose scent are you referring to?"

The Primal turned to her daughter. "One of my siblings. My youngest sister, to be exact."

"Your sister, my lady?" the girl questioned, brow furrowed.

"There were three of us, powerful and luminous Primals brought forth at the beginning of time. I was the eldest of the three. Then came my brother Haniel, and last was Apocalypse, the youngest." Her eyes momentarily became glassy. "Though bestowed with different essences, we were in unity, and for eons, we endured in a bond of love and ecstasy, even after El-Samar Seper abandoned his abode."

"May I be bold and ask what transpired?"

"Injustice, my child. Injustice."

The Primal walked to the edge of the road and gazed at a tree with no sign of life. The dead branches gave the tree the look of a cross.

She returned her gaze to her daughter. "You have asked why I'm downcast after my visits to the Chronal Halls?"

The girl nodded. "That's correct, Mistress."

Mara lifted a hand, and above her palm appeared an image of an hourglass capped with wood and adorned with gold leaf. Its light dispersed the darkness around them and shone brightly on the Primal's choleric features. She stared at it with both attraction and resentment.

With the image still over her hand, the lady looked up. "You see, He once made me an oath that wicked mankind was destined to die, and I was to execute judgment. For thousands of years and without flaws, I accomplished my responsibilities. From kings to peasants, young or old, the pious and irreverent alike came under my dominion."

The Primal turned to Libby. "But one day, He changed the rules on me. When it came to His own destiny, He reversed it. He broke his oath, His unshakeable word, as He likes to call it, and forced me to enact an unrighteous judgment."

Her eyes returned to the white sand from both ends of the bulbs flowing into the middle. "This hourglass belongs to Him. Its physics are unfathomable, and its light stretches out and touches unworthy vessels. This, my daughter, is the thorn in my side. The cause of my discontentment." With a flick of her wrist, she waved away the image. "El-Samar Seper and I are on different paths, but we both agree that certain injustices need to be rectified."

Mara strolled toward Libby and placed her hands on her shoulders. "You did not fail tonight, but similar to me, you were cheated." The Primal pointed at the marks on the ground. "I'm confounded by my sister's presence here and her meddling in matters she does not understand. Primals oversee from above, not from a world."

Libby looked quizzical.

The Primal began to pace in a thoughtful way. "Since she's here, I suspect she'll be an obstacle going forward."

"What do we do, my lady?"

The lady knitted her fingers below her chin. "We have to change our plan of execution. Up to this point, you have engaged them on their turf. To succeed now, we need to draw them to us."

23

VOICE OF REASON

Present Time

The cafeteria was filled with hybrids of all ages as the Tektonites hosted their annual celebration for that year's graduates. The group encompassed elementary kids and college alumni, all coming together for this afternoon's lunch. Among them was Angel, who had graduated two weeks prior, accompanied by the usual suspects. At her table sat Olivia, a petite, golden-haired girl, who had recently graduated from eighth grade, and Sparkles, Reina's business associate. Though none were in a celebratory mood, they had promised Awilda they would attend.

Unbeknownst to Olivia and Sparkles, a few feet away was Nyala, and while her table was full, she kept to herself. She sat quietly, occasionally smiling politely at those passing by. Nonetheless, she seemed displaced.

Nyala, it's me, she heard in her head. Closing her eyes, she shook her head. *Don't be afraid. I'm with you. Call my name*, continued the gentle whisper in her mind.

"Please, not now," the young woman mumbled and placed her hands over her ears. The others at the table stared while the Mozambican shook her head in despair.

Nyala, arise. Now is the time. The enemy approaches, and you must protect them. The inner voice had risen in pitch.

The Mozambican paled, and she cringed with her elbows on the table. She moved her trembling hands to her shaking head. "Please leave me alone!" she exclaimed, which got the attention of those around her. "You are not real. Get away from me!"

"Hey, are you OK?" asked one of the women at the table.

The girl did not respond but continued to speak to herself in a paranoid manner. Nyala brusquely stood and rushed out of the cafeteria.

"Hey, guys, what's going with Nyala?" asked Reina as she watched the Mozambican dash out of the room.

"I'm not sure. Something must've upset her," remarked Pretzel.

"*¡Ay bendito!*" Angel expressed in concern. "I feel for her."

Olivia and Sparkles remained quiet, gazing at each other in bewilderment.

Pretzel returned her attention to the table. "What's with the long faces, ladies?"

The girls ignored Pretzel's question and chorused, "Did you hear the voice too?" At the same time, each nodded.

"What voice?" inquired Kitty.

"You didn't hear it?" Olivia responded.

"Olivia, Sparkles, what's going on?" Angel was visibly upset.

"It was a kind woman's voice speaking Nyala's name," revealed Sparkles.

"That's right," confirmed the curly-haired girl. "It said 'Arise, Nyala,' and something about 'protecting them.'"

"'Now is the time,'" added Sparkles.

In haste, Pretzel stood. "Come on, let's go! All of us." She glanced at everyone at the table.

"Where are we going?" asked Reina, who was about to chow down on her burger.

"Nyala needs our help. You heard what she said about not being real. She thinks those voices are only in her head. That could explain why she was upset." The girl gazed at Olivia and Sparkles. "If you two heard the voice, it might mean something, or maybe someone is trying to reach her."

"Can I finish my burger first?" Reina inquired with a pout.

"Reina!" Pretzel raised an eyebrow.

"All right, all right!" She slammed the burger down and headed out with her group.

The Mozambican sat alone on her bed, sobbing. She had not stopped since she'd arrived.

Pretzel was the first to enter the room, and the group joined her, surrounding the disheartened girl.

"Hello, Nyala."

The Mozambican raised her head and stared at Pretzel with blotched red eyes. "What's wrong with me?"

The girl walked over and sat on the edge of the bed. She caressed the Mozambican's face. "What if I told you nothing?"

She sniffled. "I was an Oxford graduate at the age of eighteen, and now I struggle with writing my own name.

I'm broken, and, worst of all is this voice in my head that doesn't go away." Nyala slapped the side of her head with her palm.

"Hey, don't hit yourself." Pretzel gently grabbed the young woman's hand. "Nyala, you are not broken, and I believe you only need a bit of guidance." She gestured Olivia and Sparkles over. "The voice in your head is real. These ladies heard it too."

"What?" Her eyes popped wide.

"That's true, Nyala," started Sparkles. "It's a soft, gentle woman's voice, right?"

The Mozambican nodded in astonishment.

Olivia added, "It mentioned something about 'Don't be afraid, I'm with you,' and 'The enemy approaches, you must protect them.'"

"That's right, but how can you hear it?"

Both girls shrugged.

"I don't think we fully understand what's happening here, but someone is trying to reach you," chimed in Pretzel.

"Pretzel, look at me. Even if the voice is real, how am *I* supposed to protect anyone?" The Mozambican lowered her head, dejected.

"You protected Gypsy and me," stated Kitty. "So, I know you have a special ability."

Nyala pinched the bridge of her nose. "But my thoughts are all over. Nothing seems to make sense. How can I help anyone when I can't even help myself?"

Sparkles approached her and grabbed her hand. "Growing up with my mental disability was never easy for me. I never did well in school and have problems staying focused. Though it took longer to accomplish a regular task, I kept moving forward." She gave the perky blue-eyed girl a quick glance. "With the help of Reina, I have my company now, and I help people. People like me. I suggest you focus on that one thing that makes sense and don't worry about the things you don't understand."

"I'm having trouble focusing on the smallest thing."

"Hmm..." Angel interjected. "As a schoolteacher, one of the methods I've learned to use for kids who have problems focusing is to place them in comforting settings. It could be as simple as having them stand or sending them to the spot in which they feel most comfortable to do their assignment."

"For me, it's eating chocolate and playing video games," stated Reina.

"Long walks do it for me," added Angel.

"Sitting at Battery Park with my friends," disclosed Pretzel.

"Gardens," muttered Nyala in deep thought. "I enjoy gardens."

"There's a beautiful garden in the middle of this compound. Would you like to go?" asked the curly-haired girl.

"Yes, I *would* like that."

The garden was situated in the center of the Tektonite compound. Enclosed within the four walls of the building, it received plenty of sunlight. Spring flowers were in full bloom, scenting the area with a pageant of smells and illuminating it with an exuberant display of colors. Along with the gentle sunlight and warm breeze, the location was welcoming.

The women sat at a round table in the middle of the garden, large enough to fit all seven of them. The Mozambican's complexion took a turn for the better in the atmosphere and setting. She closed her eyes and enjoyed the bird chirps that filled the air.

"This reminds me of someplace," she stated.

"Back home?" asked Pretzel.

"No." She continued with her eyes closed, "It is far away. It is rich in colors and rosy smells, and the air is full of music. A place where birds not only chirp but sing. You would touch the followers, and they would caress you. And the peace! Yes, that beautiful peace." Nyala opened her eyes and glanced at the group. "He was there."

"Who was there?"

The girl shook her head nervously, not wishing to say.

"It's OK. We're not going to judge you."

"It was the Sovereign One."

Their eyes bulged.

"Do you remember anything else?" Pretzel asked.

"We were together for a long time. We spoke, we laughed, we cried, and we even joked." She smiled at the last part. "His words were always comforting. Also, there was a woman, elegant and beautiful. She showed me around and told me of things past, things present, and things to come." Nyala paused in thought. "Wait, the sound of her voice..."

"What about her voice?"

"It's the one I hear in my head."

"Do you remember her name or anything else about her?"

The Mozambican said nothing, though the group could see she was thinking. "She's a Primal, one of the great seven lights. She was the one who took me to see Him." Nyala glanced at the group. "Her name is Apocalypse."

"Mrs. Mozart mentioned that Apocalypse is known as a revelator who has, at times, visited Daughters who are seers. Could that be the same one?" asked Angel.

"I think so," answered Pretzel. "I believe Apocalypse is trying to reach Nyala."

"But I'm not a seer," Nyala disclosed.

Olivia walked to the Mozambican, knelt beside her, and clasped her hands. "Since I was a kid, I've heard voices in my head and have the strangest dreams. At first, it was very scary. I used to hate it and wanted it to go away until I learned that I didn't have a curse but a gift. A gift to help others. When I accepted that, the voices in my head made sense. Even the dreams I used to call nightmares took on a different light."

"I understand what Olivia is saying," added Angel. "When I learned that I was the Daimon Killer, it freaked me out. Then I began to worry about how I was supposed to become this mysterious thing. The words of Grace gave me great comfort. *'If this mystery is your lot, it'll be revealed to you in due time what needs to be done.'* I know it's frightening, but don't let fear keep you from what you need to do."

The Mozambican nodded and took a deep breath. She then closed her eyes and whispered gently, "Apocalypse, I'm here."

A bright green light appeared before Nyala, and from

within the light emerged a very tall female dressed in a fawn-hued robe. She was of dark complexion, and her black hair was bound up in a crown. The Primal turned her sparkling serene eyes to the young woman and smiled. "Hello, Nyala. Nice to see you again."

24

A CARPENTER'S HELP

"Good to have you back, D'Angelo," said the woman in a Spanish accent as she was engulfed in the embrace of the extremely tall man.

"Great to be back, Awilda." He smiled at the Tektonite leader, then sat in front of her desk. He turned his head to the man on his right. "Thank you again, Mr. Ortega. It was one of those red-eye flights, so I appreciate the early pick-up at the airport."

"Sure thing." He tapped the hybrid's belly. "I see the Mid-West has been feeding you well. You seem to have gained some weight there."

D'Angelo chuckled. "Yes, it did. Good food, I have to say."

"You're one to talk, *mi amor*," stated Awilda. "Since retirement, you've gained twenty pounds. I'm considering making you this year's Santa Claus."

"What?" Ortega placed his hands over his stomach. "This thing is a shield to protect my inner six-pack."

Everyone in the room laughed.

"I'm hearing great news about the closures of those underground fighting rings," remarked the woman. "I hope there will be none left soon. Any news on Sefani's siblings?"

"Nothing yet, but she's as tough as nails. Very persistent and still motivated. Margaret, Leo, Sefani, and a group of hybrids they've recruited headed to LA to follow up on some leads. I hope they pan out."

"Same here." She cleared her throat while drumming on the desk. "I know you just got back and would like to spend time with your fiancée." He smiled at the comment. "But I need your help."

He snickered. "She video-calls me every day. We've made plans for tomorrow, so I'm free today. What's going on?"

"Well, I received this letter about a week ago." The Tektonite leader picked up the correspondence off the desk. "It was sent by a man named John, who claims to be sheltering male hybrids. He's requesting medical and food supplies and urgently asking for our help. Typically, we depend on our forth-tellers to locate hybrids in need, but none have mentioned anything about this site."

"Do you think it's a trap?" D'Angelo asked with a frown.

She sighed. "I have thought and prayed about this and I sense the urgency, but to be safe, I was hoping you could scout the area." She turned her attention to her husband and winked at him. "You can take this big log of mine and put his hidden six-pack to good use."

D'Angelo laughed. "It will be my pleasure." He turned to Ortega. "How soon can we leave?"

"We can leave right now. My six-pack just got offended." He winked back at his wife.

"Here." She handed D'Angelo the correspondence. "Take this letter with you just in case. The address of the location is there. As you'll see, it's located in western New Jersey, borderline Pennsylvania. I've taken a look at the map and noted a lot of farmland in the area. So, if there's any truth to these claims, I suspect it's a good remote location to be hiding hybrids."

"Do you think it's worth bringing any of the female hybrids along?" asked D'Angelo, taking hold of the correspondence.

"The women have been much preoccupied as of late, and I don't wish to disturb them with this. I only want you to scout the area and determine the location before we send any supplies."

"Sounds like a plan," he answered and stood, along with Ortega.

After driving on the main interstate for two and half hours, they exited on a long, winding road landscaped with the warm greens and wild colors of spring. Though they questioned the accuracy of their navigation system several times, the men continued driving even when the roads they turned onto were gravel or dirt. After cruising for ten minutes, Ortega stopped his black SUV when several large tree limbs blocked the path. Both sides of the road were lined with trees, making it impossible to navigate around them.

"Either the GPS guided us wrong, or we've been duped," stated Ortega as he gazed at the blockage.

"Ya, mon. Three hours on the road for this." D'Angelo shook his head in disappointment. "You mind if I stretch my legs for a minute before we head back?"

"I'll join you," responded Ortega.

Both stepped out of the car and took in the fresh air of the late afternoon. The aroma from the woods was splendid, along with the pleasant sound of a distant river. As Ortega admired the scenery, he noticed tire tracks through the blockage. He took a closer look and called his partner over.

"These tracks look fresh," he said, crouching with his finger on the ground. The man looked at the tree limbs. "Do you think you can move those?"

D'Angelo examined the blockage. "I think I could."

"I would help, but I have to protect the six-pack," Ortega joked.

His partner laughed and grabbed the first tree limb. He sniffed but was too late to sense the assault rifle pointing in their direction.

"Drop the limb or get shot, dreadlocks!" said a man from among the trees.

"And don't go for the gun, fat boy!" said another male. "I have a clear shot at your gut from this location!"

Ortega gently removed his hand from his back holster.

"Just to let you know, it'll take more than bullets to stop me," disclosed D'Angelo.

"Not if they are laced with quartz, dreadlocks!" The man sounded closer this time. "I can smell what you are, buddy." The gunmen reached D'Angelo. "State your business or get blown away."

"We're looking for John," responded the Jamaican.

"John? How do you know that name?" the gunman asked.

"He sent us a letter." D'Angelo went to reach for it in his back pocket but was stopped by the rattling of the gun.

"Easy there, pretty boy! Hands up where we can see them."

"I'm just reaching for the letter. I'm with the Tektonites, and so is that guy's wife. We're here to help." The Jamaican kept his hands up, and out of his right eye, he saw that the masked man was wearing military fatigues.

"I thought Tektonites were regular folks, not Nephilim."

"I'm a hybrid, not a Nephilim. I was never sealed."

"Levi, check his back pocket and see if he has a letter," ordered the gunman.

D'Angelo frowned when a young man half his size searched his back pocket. He noted that he was only a boy.

"I got something," said the kid and raced to the nearby gunman.

When he read the correspondence, the man lowered his weapon and removed his ski mask. The man's face was covered with blisters and sores, as if he had bad allergies. "All right, boys, you can come out now," commanded the man.

Six teenagers wearing camo emerged from the woods, all with rifles in their hands and faces in the same condition as the man.

"Sorry for the fright, gentlemen. We don't ever get any visitors," said the gunman, who was the only adult in the group. "My name is Tommy, head of security." He handed the correspondence back to the Jamaican. "We weren't aware the Tektonites had hybrids with them. We were expecting supplies, not people."

"My name is D'Angelo Brown, and this is Daniel Ortega." He pointed to his left. "It's very unusual for us to get letters from unknown sources requesting supplies. We needed to make sure you were real."

"Oh, I get it. Wanna make sure we aren't spies or something like that," Tommy replied with a smile. "No worries. Let me show you who we are." He turned his attention to the teenagers. "OK, boys, let's move these logs outta the way."

The teenagers lifted the heavy limbs effortlessly and tossed them aside like twigs. In a matter of minutes, the road was clear.

"You gentlemen mind if I hitch a ride with you? The campsite is about a mile down the road. I can take you right to it." Ortega nodded. "Boys, make sure to cover the road again. Devon, you're in charge." He gazed at a kid of about sixteen.

Soon all three were cruising a long, narrow, and bumpy path with no indication of ending. Trees, bushes, and shrubs covered both sides of the grassy road. As they drove, Ortega carefully studied the man in the rearview mirror and saw that he was fairly young.

"Hey, Tommy, how old are you?" inquired Ortega.

"I just turned twenty, sir. Celebrated my birthday a few weeks ago."

"Well, happy belated birthday."

"Thank you, sir."

"Aren't you a bit young to be head of security?" The ex-agent asked with a deep frown.

"Unfortunately, it wasn't by choice but from capability."

With a scrunched nose, D'Angelo turned to face the young man. "What do you mean, capability?"

"The older ones either have missing limbs or aren't able to lift their arms, much less handle a rifle."

"But aren't the rifles the cause of those blisters on your face?"

"Well, sir, it's the price we're paying to keep our own safe." He pointed forward. "Right through there."

As the vehicle curved along the road, it opened to a large valley with mountains and peaks as the backdrop. In the center was a rustic farmhouse encircled by a picket fence, and a few yards away, a large red barn with sliding, white-striped doors. Several other buildings occupied the area, and there were acres of farmland. Livestock freely roamed through the grounds, including cattle and horses, a few drinking from a lake glistening in the afternoon sun.

"Beautiful, ain't it?" said the young man, feeling at home. "You can pull up to the house." As soon as the SUV came to a full stop, Tommy stepped out. "I'll get John for you. Just give me a minute." He raced up the ramp that covered the front steps and through the open door.

A few minutes later, Tommy came out pushing a lanky light-skinned man in a wheelchair he barely fit in. Standing, he would be at least seven and a half feet tall. He had a rugged unkempt beard, and his brown hair reached his shoulders. The man's beady eyes looked dark and menacing, but his voice was welcoming and gentle. "Welcome, gentleman, to Ebenezer Camp." Tommy stopped him a few feet from the vehicle. "My name is John."

Both men came out of the vehicle and shook John's bony hand.

"Hello, John. My name is Daniel Ortega, and this young man here is D'Angelo Brown. We represent the Tektonites. Was it you who sent us a letter?"

The man nodded. "Yes, I did. I was informed your group helps our kind."

"We help all in need," clarified Ortega. "Though, I'm curious how you learned about us."

"A stranger came through these parts. He saw our needs and mentioned that the Tektonites could help." He tapped Tommy's hand. "Take us to the barn."

"Who was he?" asked D'Angelo as they followed the man in the wheelchair.

"He didn't give us a name but simply stated He was a friend. He was a simple man, hair color and length the same as mine, and a short beard. A great woodworker. He fixed a few things around here, but above all, he was a kind person you could speak to for hours." He looked at Ortega. "Anyone you know?"

With a smirk, Ortega nodded. "Yeah."

"Anyhow, He gave us your address, and, well, the rest is history." Tommy stopped the wheelchair in front of the barn doors. "I was very vague in the letter, Mr. Ortega. We don't just shelter male hybrids in this camp." He rolled his left sleeve back and revealed a smudged, distorted mark on his left hand. "But also marked Nephilim. I was once a sealed one."

They gazed at the mark.

"Dealing with hybrids is one thing but dealing with a Nephilim is another." John gulped as he uttered that last phrase. "I wasn't sure if we would get the help if I stated that in the letter."

"As I mentioned, we're here to help those who request it," stated Ortega.

John motioned with his head to have Tommy open the barn doors. "What you are about to see may be disturbing, but I hope you can understand our need."

The doors opened to the scent of oak and pine mixed with antiseptic and rubbing alcohol. The barn had two floors with windows all around, and both were covered with the same thing: wounded men, either on stretchers or lying on mats. A few had missing limbs, mainly the left arm. Others had contorted faces that resembled those of animals more than men. The rest were paralyzed.

"Take us in, Tommy." As John moved forward, he elaborated, "Most of those you are seeing were sealed Nephilim. Mighty men so strong they could singlehandedly lift cars. Three years ago, our fathers disappeared, and so did our powers. That was half of it. When we were sealed, we gained superhuman anatomy to sustain our enhanced abilities. Those with animal-based abilities gained the matching composition, but when the powers were taken away, it left many with progressive muscle weaknesses and loss of bone density." He pointed to a few men on his left.

"Others like me lost the ability to walk due to our weight and height, getting acute arthritis or severe spinal injuries." He pointed at others. "Those with missing limbs are mostly deserters. Once the *Huios ton Olethron* revealed the deceptions and was killed, many of them left the faction and removed their seal by cutting off their arms. They no longer wished to be identified as Nephilim. Most importantly, they didn't want to be tracked by their masters."

The injured Nephilim silently and pitifully stared at them. "A few whose fathers vanished returned to the academy seeking to be resealed, but word has it they were killed." He looked soberly around the room. "Heroes of old who have become the scum of the earth." John tapped the young's man hand again. "Take us out, Tommy."

Once they were outside, John continued, "Many of us have no birth certificates, social security numbers, or public records, so technically, we don't exist. As you can imagine, some with nothing to live for have taken their lives. The helpful carpenter was kind enough to remind us that our lives still have a purpose after I told him what an evil person I once was." He smiled as if he were recollecting the exchange while Tommy closed the barn's doors.

"Mr. Ortega, the Tektonites are our last resort. We're short on medical supplies, food, and other essentials. Thank the heavens that these young men were not sealed, or they would've been in the same condition as we are. They've been a source of great help." He pointed at Tommy. "With the right medical assistance, we're hoping others could help us carry the load. Without what we requested, we don't know how long we can survive out here."

Ortega crouched before the wheelchair and grasped the man's hand tenderly. "John, I promise we'll get you the help you need, and if a good carpenter took His time to help you, so can we."

25

LUMINOUS PRINCIPUM

Tammuz walked ostentatiously into the council conference room wearing deep purple vestments adorned with precious stones and metals. Around his neck was a necklace with a pendant shaped like a blazing sun with a large ruby at the center. The thirteen men in the room stood in his presence. Toward the corner was a young man with coffee-colored hair, thick glasses, and a name tag that read *Senior Network Technician*. Along with the others, he saluted the grand luminary.

"We salute you, Grand Luminary, keeper of truth, warrior of purity, and holder of the Great Light."

The grand luminary took a seat on an ornate leather chair at the center of the large oval conference table. "Thank you, gentlemen." He gestured, and everyone except the technician took a seat.

"I'm pleased to have this first high council meeting with my top advisors and confidants." He placed his hand over the pendant. "With the help of the light, I was inspired to deem you my Luminous Principum, 'Chief Lights,' gifted with the virtues of understanding and knowledge. Your loyalty and dedication to the Great Light have guided you to become part of this council. You should be honored."

The men in the room clapped.

"I have called you together to discuss recent events, mainly the escape of Laurie Marilyn Davidson. The woman has cost us thousands in property damage, and after Agent Owens' brilliant capture," he gestured at the man on his right, "she managed to escape our grasp. As per my email, can someone please tell me how this happened?"

Agent Owens spoke up. "Grand Luminary, first and foremost, thank you for the honor of having me on this council. Like you, I was appalled to have heard of Ms. Davidson's escape. Therefore, I instigated a thorough investigation into the matter, and it seems we had another network security breach."

Tammuz pinched the bridge of his nose. "Three years ago, I ordered our network security-enhanced obligatory initiate password updated every three months and instituted multi-factor authentication. How could this happen after we invested in those security protocols? "

"Hello, Grand Luminary. Eddie Lopez here, and I wanted to first thank you for the honor of being part of this council." He pointed at the corner. "After you consented, I asked David Wilkerson, a senior network technician, to be present and elaborate on this latest breach."

"Speak freely, son," requested the grand luminary.

"Thank you, sir," said the technician nervously. He fixed his glasses, though they did not need adjusting. "Well, sir, everyone in the organization abides by the security protocols you've mentioned. All network accounts have a password rotation every three months and are configured to utilize MFA, that is, multi-factor authentication, with the exception of one."

"Whose account?" Tammuz had a deep frown on his face.

"Well, sir, *yours*. If you recall, we attempted several times to have you comply with these security measures. You refused due to the complexity of the MFA and password changes. As you enlighteningly put it, it interfered with your ability to communicate promptly with the Luminosity family. Unfortunately, your account was used to access data concerning the detainee."

"I was informed that my account had special security, so it could be exempted." His face reddened with embarrassment.

The technician gave a nervous smile. "Well, sir, whoever told you that might have just wanted to appease you. Unfortunately, no such security exists."

The grand luminary's expression grew turbulent. He took a deep breath and gave the technician a polite smile. "Thank you for the information. I'll make sure to address these security concerns. You may leave."

"Thank you, sir."

Once the young man left, the grand luminary glanced at the group. "Our holy writ states that we should not bring harm or make false accusations against the great anointed light. I was lied to, my friends, and I will not tolerate such insubordination. Thus, darkness has crept in." He glared at the man across from him. "Mr. Lopez, I want you to fire that kid immediately after this meeting. Loyalty, honesty, and speaking truth to the grand luminary are essential aspects of the growth and sustainability of the organization."

"Yes, Grand Luminary," responded Eddie Lopez.

"Agent Owens, regarding our escapee, do you have any information about her whereabouts? It's imperative that we find the woman."

"Not exactly, sir, but grant me a few days. I might know the people hiding her. First, however, there's something I would like you to see."

Tammuz frowned. "OK. Go on."

Agent Owens stood and grabbed a remote control off the table. He pressed a button, and a screen lowered at the front of the room. "We managed to pull the surveillance video from the vehicle the prisoner was being transported in. The footage you're about to see is from the night of the escape." He pressed a button that dimmed the lights and played the image.

The video displayed a woman in front of the van, raising both arms, though one was silver. Purple smoke appeared, and a blade emerged and damaged the arm. The image fast-forwarded to a thick fog covering the area, followed by the purple smoke, which was moving at an alarming speed. Though there was no sound, the group gasped when blood spattered wherever the purple smoke stopped. The clip fast-forwarded again. This time, they saw two women, one with light skin and the other dark. When the woman with the dark complexion knelt, a substantial surge of energy formed in front of the van. After that, the clip was blank.

The agent pressed several buttons on the remote

control, which stopped the video and turned on the lights. "Grand Luminary, I condensed this video to the important footage. What you saw in this video clip is a new class of hybrids we have never seen before. I managed to enhance the quality of the image, specifically the purple smoke, and there's something peculiar to note." He clicked the remote and changed the image on the screen. "If you take a closer look, there's a woman within that cloud." He pressed another button, which displayed a new scene, the dark-skinned woman kneeling and emitting energy.

"Sir, for the longest time, we understood that only male hybrids had heightened abilities, but as you can see, female hybrids have developed enhanced and superior abilities to their counterparts. We knew about the Utukku Slayer, but our intel suggests her abilities only affected male hybrids. When she destroyed Utukkus, it would strip the progeny of their enhanced abilities."

He glanced at the group, then gave his attention to the screen. "As you can see, these enhanced female hybrids are much faster, stronger, and more powerful. If my intel is correct, they are more formidable than the offspring of Azag."

The grand luminary pressed his index finger to his temple. "Agent Owens, can our weapons stop these enhanced female hybrids?"

"It's too early to say. Other than this encounter, our field agents have yet to meet this type of enemy, but I do propose that we reinitiate Project Nimrod."

"I thought that project was scrapped when the traitor Masmasu took the plans."

The agent gave a small chuckle. "We thought so too, sir.

Thank the light, during the renovation of the headquarters building, we discovered a vault containing thousands of records with detailed information on this project. Our scientists believe we can resume this project as soon as tomorrow."

"Grand Luminary, I'm James Edwards," said the man four seats from Tammuz. "I thought that project was scrapped because it was an abomination to our bylaws. It required partaking of hybrid blood, which our writ forbids."

Tammuz's eyes turned to the screen, and he watched the woman kneel and create that burst of light. "While our holy writ forbids partaking of hybrid blood, this was a warning to the rest of the world and not to us, the Children of the Light. Our blood is pure, and we must remember that our purity will one day cleanse the Earth of its impurity. Our purity cannot be contaminated. On the contrary, it purifies."

"I couldn't agree more, Your Excellency," stated Agent Owens.

"I deem it prudent to reinstate Project Nimrod as soon as possible. As trials begin, look for those loyalists within our ranks whose purity is above reproach to test the serum."

"We will do as you say, sir."

26

A TRAP IS SPRUNG

Rays of moonlight broke through the windows in the women's dormitories at the Tektonite compound. A digital clock on a bedside table read 3:32, and the floor was quiet save for the occasional snore. However, this serene scene was shattered when the clock advanced to the next minute.

Nyala jolted out of her sleep, gasping for air. She scrambled to her feet and rushed toward the door, but not before knocking into the table next to her. This sent a clock, a phone, and a watch crashing to the floor and stirred her roommates from their slumber.

"Nyala, is everything OK?" asked a curly-haired girl as she rubbed the sleep from her eyes.

"I'm being summoned. I have to go, Olivia," Nyala responded as she exited the room.

"Whoa, whoa. Wait up." The young lady came wide awake and jumped out of bed to catch up with Nyala. Olivia dashed out of the room, but the woman was nowhere in sight. *How'd she move so fast?* she thought to herself. The girl rushed through the hall and bounded down the stairs, desperately scanning for her friend. Panic rose inside her heart, but then she heard Nyala's voice in the garden. Olivia darted in the direction of the sound. She found the Mozambican woman kneeling amid the flowers.

"Yes, Apocalypse. I understand the risks. I'm willing."

Olivia slowed and approached Nyala from behind. "Is everything all right?"

The dark-skinned beauty stood and turned to face her young friend, her deep, dark eyes meeting the curly-haired girl's bright blue ones. "Apocalypse had to speak to me. I can hear her more clearly here in the garden. Mara is releasing her energy in a way that only another Primal could detect. She's been cautious not to reveal her location all this time."

"She's signaling?"

"Yes, Apocalypse thinks so. I need to go and meet her."

"Wait, let's tell Joan and everyone else. They can come up with a plan and get you where you need to go."

Nyala shook her head. "There's no time. Besides, those bonded to a Primal don't need transportation or portals to travel within the same reality."

With that, she disappeared from Olivia's sight. The teenager gasped, her eyes wide with fright. She froze, struggling to comprehend the ramifications of Nyala heading off on her own. Her brow furrowed, and she started to turn to get help when a bright green portal appeared beside her. Olivia stared at the swirling vortex. Seconds later, Gypsy stepped out, wearing skin-tight leggings and a crop top. She was holding several blades. The portal abruptly closed behind her.

"Gypsy, how?" queried Olivia.

"Nyala showed up in my apartment and told me she needed me. I barely had time to throw on clothes and attach my prosthetic. Then that portal appeared, and here I am."

As Gypsy finished her sentence, another vortex opened. Angel, Kitty, and Pretzel stepped through. They were casually dressed in jeans and shirts.

"You, too?" Olivia cried.

"None of us could sleep, so we went out for drinks and then took a long walk in Central Park. Then Nyala appeared in front of us and said she needed us, and a portal opened," explained Pretzel.

Materializing out of thin air, Nyala appeared between the five women, her eyes glowing green.

Gypsy asked, "Nyala, what's going on?"

"Mara has summoned Apocalypse to meet with her. However, it's probably a trap to kill me and stop Apocalypse's interference in Mara's plans. This will probably be very dangerous, but I can't do it alone. Will you please help me?"

The four females nodded. "Of course, Nyala. We're with you."

The dark-skinned woman's eyes glowed more intensely, and a green swirl opened behind them. "The portal is for your benefit. I'll see you there." She disappeared again.

Gypsy handed blades to the other adults, and all four turned to face the portal. The last time they'd stepped into a strange vortex was when Therion was sealed. They steeled their resolve and started toward the light, then Olivia rushed past them and ran into the portal.

"No! ¿*Esta loca?*" yelled Angel.

"No time to worry about her state of mind. Come on!" exclaimed Gypsy.

Theresa awoke to a rushing wind and the bedcovers blowing off her bed, leaving her cold and confused. She glanced around her hotel room and saw the Archangel Haniel standing resolutely several feet from her bed.

"Geez, that's one helluva wake-up call."

"Dress yourself. Mara has made her move."

"What do you mean?" the blonde woman said as she jumped out of bed and reached for her clothes, which rested on a chair nearby.

"My elder sister is making her location known, likely in an attempt to lure in the younger one and her avatar."

"So, it's a trap. Do you think Mara's attempting to lure us in as well?"

"Improbable. I've masked my presence in this world. The element of surprise is our greatest advantage."

Theresa bent down to tie her shoelaces. "You make it sound like we'll be launching a sneak attack. Aren't you Primals effectively indestructible?"

The Archangel frowned. "You leave Mara to me. Your target is another. The mortal agent imbued with her power must die so Mara can be free."

Theresa stopped tying her laces and glanced up at Haniel. "So, that's what this has all been about. This was why you needed me. You can't harm a human, so you needed one to do the killing for you."

"Trust me; this is the only way. Mara's agent is an abomination, a blot on the balance of the world. If they are allowed to live, they'll bring ruin to this world...and others."

Theresa's eyebrows shot up, and her heartbeat accelerated. "The place where you left me to train...was that on a different planet?"

"Yes and no. By world, I don't mean another floating rock in this space-time reality. The place where you trained is part of a different space-time—a different dimension, if you will. My role is to maintain the balance of the created order across all worlds. Mara's influence in this world threatens the entirety of Creation. I believe this agent binds her to this world. Thus, they must be destroyed."

Theresa wrinkled her brow; she felt nostalgia, as if a thought deep in her mind wanted to claw its way out but was blocked from doing so.

"Think on these matters no further. We have a job to do. One that will determine the fate of this realm."

It took several seconds for Angel's eyes to adjust to her new surroundings as she exited the portal. They were standing in what appeared to be a large training room. Angel and the other women were in the middle of the chamber. Nyala and Olivia were standing several feet from them. To their chagrin, the room's perimeter was littered with Nephilim and a Daimon in human form. Directly in front of the group stood a tall, pale woman dressed in black and a young woman with stardust eyes and purple hair.

"Sons of the Lords, attack!" commanded the young woman.

The Nephilim lunged toward the women, bloodlust in their eyes. One approached from the air, swooping down like a bird of prey. Katastrofi, the son of Hades, leaped into the air and made a fist, intending to slam it into the floor and knock the women off balance. Leon rushed at them on all fours and pounced at Nyala and Olivia, claws-first. However, before the assailants reached their targets, green vortices appeared before each of them, and they fell through. The portals swiftly closed behind them.

The Daimon's skin melted and he ripped his humanoid form off, revealing a large set of batlike wings, deep-set red eyes, and a mouth filled with rows of sharp, jagged teeth. He gained several feet in height and increased his musculature significantly. "Where did you send my son, you witch?" The monstrous beast darted toward the pair. "Sovereign law be damned; I'll beat you until you return Katastrofi."

His hulking hands were mere inches from Nyala's face when two more portals appeared in the room, one in front of Hades and another parallel to the floor in front of Angel and the other women. The Daimon slipped through the first portal and stepped through the other one, then crashed to the floor. His momentum caused his outstretched hands to break through the floor, leaving him kneeling in front of the women with his hands stuck. Hades lifted his eyes, and terror filled them as he recognized Angel.

"Daimon Killer!" he yelped.

Kitty touched Angel's shoulder.

"Hades, lord of Europe and Asia, High Lord of Diablos' council, your deeds have been weighed, and you have been found wanting."

"No!" screamed the Daimon as he tried to free his hands to no avail. An invisible force held him in place. "You can't do this to me."

"Not only did you abandon your abode and follow your master in his folly, but you instigated countless genocides and atrocities among the peoples in the territories you controlled. For this, the Sovereign judges you today and sentences you to confinement in Tartarus until the day of judgment."

As Angel finished her pronouncement, Hades' body contorted in unnatural ways, producing a sickening crunching as his bones collapsed on themselves. The Daimon's wings shriveled and retreated into his body, and the musculature he'd amassed during his transformation atrophied. All that was left of him was a withered, vaguely humanoid shell. A putrid smell filled the room as the fallen Angel's skin rotted off his body, revealing a shadowy mass of energy. No longer stuck to the ground, the shade attempted to lunge at Angel in a final act of defiance. Before the dark mass could reach her, it compressed into an orb that pulsed several times before imploding and disappearing.

"I like these odds a lot better," Gypsy quipped.

Mara glared at the Mozambican woman, fury in her eyes. "Your powers of foresight are truly a wonder to behold, sister." Sarcasm oozed from her words.

"You can take over now," Nyala muttered.

The woman's eyes glowed green. Light shot out of her mouth and her braids unraveled, leaving her hair streaming against the pull of gravity. She opened her mouth, but it was no longer Nyala's voice. "Your folly has not escaped the notice of the High Heavens, Dayyana."

Mara sucked her teeth. "I set aside that name until Justice is returned to Creation."

"You have been blinded by your focus and El-Samar Seper's deceptions. You are not acting as a harbinger of Justice but one of destruction. Depart from this path, or you will bring ruin to this world."

"My path is just. I was given a purpose when I was created, which is now in jeopardy. You'd expect me to sit idly by?"

"I expect you to trust the wisdom of the Sovereign One, even if His plan seems inscrutable to you."

"This can't be His plan. There must be some interference, some nefarious scheme. I will root it out and return things as they should be."

Nyala shook her head. "Even if that means working with a traitor who seeks to exalt himself?"

"Diablos is a means to an end, nothing more."

Olivia had stood next to Nyala throughout this exchange. As amazed as she was by the dialogue between the Primals, the teenager was more concerned with what she saw in her friend. Nyala's body was trembling and sweat accumulated on her forehead. The stress of allowing the Primal to use her as a conduit was proving too much for her mortal frame. The supernatural glow in Nyala's eyes flickered and she teetered, but Olivia stepped closer and propped her up.

Mara smirked. "Your vessel is far inferior to mine, dear sister." The Archangel waved her hand at the young woman standing next to her. "Libitinia is the height of perfection. This human you inhabit is weak and frail."

Libby stared at Mara as she spoke. A frown adorned her face.

"I've had enough of this. Daughter, bring them swift Justice."

"As you command, my lady."

Fog filled the training room, and Libby disappeared.

"Here she comes," warned Gypsy. "Our SPA won't work against her, and she can attack from within that smoke at any time, so get into a defensive huddle and protect each other's backs."

Gypsy, Pretzel, and Kitty huddled, but Angel stayed by herself.

"Angel, get into formation," Gypsy ordered.

Angel's eyebrows shot up, and she moved her head back and forth as if she were tracking something.

"What are you doing, girl? Get in here," Pretzel yelped.

Without looking at her friends, Angel asked, "You guys really can't see her?"

"Wait, what?" Gypsy inquired, her mouth agape. "Are you able to sense her?"

"No, not sense. I can see a silhouette in the smoke. It's moving incredibly fast, but I can track it with my eyes. Pretzel, duck!"

The mocha woman obeyed Angel's command and

narrowly avoided a blade that seemed to materialize out of thin air and just as quickly disappeared.

"Oh, crap, she's coming after me now," Angel exclaimed.

The Daughter raised her knife and parried a blow, but the strike staggered her. The first blow was followed by a second and a third, each subsequent strike forcing Angel into awkward angles due to the force. The next hit caught the woman flat-footed, sending her careening toward the floor. The unrelenting attacker followed up immediately, aiming at Angel's neck. However, the blade was stopped short by a hand.

"Awfully violent, aren't we?" quipped a strange woman with blonde hair and piercing blue eyes. Angel thought she recognized her. This had to be Therion's mother.

"It's easy to beat up on women you outclass. How about you try your hand at facing another Primal's conduit?" Theresa challenged. Then, the woman performed a circular motion with her arms and clapped her hands forcefully. The smoke dissipated, revealing an astonished Libby.

At that instant, Haniel appeared across from Mara and Apocalypse.

"You finally show yourself, brother," Apocalypse began.

Mara's countenance grew paler. "Haniel, what are you doing here?"

The Primal of Balance spoke sternly. "I should be asking you that question, sister. Your purpose often had you leave the High Heavens, but after enough time, it was simple to surmise that something had happened to you."

"How did you find me?"

"The creation of that abomination signaled to the rest of the Archangels where you were." Haniel pointed at

Libby, who was engaged in a furious battle with Theresa. "And with her death, you'll be free of this place and can return to your rightful abode."

The Primal's eyes grew wide as she glanced over and saw Libby being pushed back. Haniel's agent was countering all her abilities and attacks and had her on the defensive.

"My daughter!" Mara exclaimed, but before she could rush to Libby's side, Haniel raised his hand, and scales appeared before them.

"This is a matter between mortals now. You will not interfere." As he spoke, a beam of yellow-red energy shot toward Mara. Before the ray could reach her, she produced her scythe, and her purple energy countered Haniel's.

"You dare pit yourself against me, the eldest of the Primals?"

"I'm not against you. On the contrary, I'm trying to free you from this infernal cage." Haniel glanced at Nyala. "Apocalypse, help me contain her until my conduit finishes the deed."

Nyala's breathing was labored, her body taxed to its limit by the incursion of the Primal. Still leaning on Olivia, she turned away from the two elder Primals and glanced at the struggle between Theresa and Libby. The blonde woman had overpowered the hybrid and taken hold of her blade.

"Theresa, has Haniel told you who you are fighting?" asked Apocalypse.

The woman stopped and yelled, "I'm a little busy, and Haniel's not the most forthcoming of individuals."

"When you were brought here, you were impregnated

with three embryos manufactured by human ingenuity and Mara's intervention. When your son Therion was born, you were told the other two fetuses were stillborn, the price you had to pay to produce the offspring of Diablos."

Theresa narrowed her eyes at Nyala, then looked at the injured young woman on the floor in front of her.

"That was a lie. Only one of the fetuses died; the second stands before you. She is the sister of Therion and your daughter."

The blonde woman's mouth dropped open, and tears welled in her eyes.

Across the room, Haniel continued his struggle to contain Mara. "Theresa, her parentage is irrelevant. She is a danger to the cosmos and must be destroyed to realign the scales and bring order."

Theresa glared at the Primal. "So, you knew? You knew, and still, you trained me. You knew, and still, you commissioned me to kill a child I carried in my womb."

Haniel looked on in horror as Theresa tossed the blade in her hand aside. "Pick up the weapon and strike her down now! I can't hold Mara much longer. Theresa, Apocalypse, this must be done."

Mara's eyes burned with fury. She gritted her teeth, then screamed, "Stay away from my daughter!" As she bellowed, her energy beam became more intense, which caused an explosion of the combined energies of the two Primals. The blast quickly spread outwardly from the point of impact.

Apocalypse shielded the women behind her. However, Olivia threw herself in front of Nyala and shielded her from the energy with her own body. The blowback pushed the teenager forcefully against Nyala, and they both crashed to the floor. Angel and the other Daughters braced themselves and were protected by Apocalypse's energy. The building shook from the resultant shockwave, knocking the Daughters off their feet, but after several seconds everything settled.

Theresa was still standing, mostly unfazed by the blast, but she'd shielded her eyes with her forearm. She lowered her arm and looked for Libby, but she wasn't there. Then, the woman glanced at the dueling Primals, but only Haniel remained. Finally, the Archangel turned toward her.

"You've failed me!" bellowed Haniel at Theresa. "More importantly, you've failed this world. I have only one path now. I will seek the seven seals." With that, he disappeared from their sight.

Angel was the first of the women to recover. Her eyes tracked around the room until they finally settled on Nyala and Olivia on the floor. The Mozambican was stirring and rising to her feet, but Olivia lay deathly still.

"Olivia!" Angel exclaimed.

The other Daughters rose and dashed toward the fallen teen. Gypsy reached her first and checked her pulse and respiration. "She's not breathing."

Angel reached her next and put her hand behind Olivia's neck. "Help me turn her over." The four women flipped her body quickly but carefully. Angel tilted the curly-haired girl's head back and started administering CPR.

She alternated between breaths and chest compressions, as she'd learned in her training. After half a minute, which felt like an eternity, Olivia gasped for air several times before starting to breathe on her own; her respiration was ragged and labored. However, the teen did not regain consciousness.

Pretzel stood, rushed toward Nyala, and clasped her shoulders with both hands. "Please, Apocalypse, if you are still there, you have to send us home."

Nyala staggered and slumped headfirst into Pretzel's chest, but not before a green vortex appeared behind her.

"Kitty, help me with Olivia," ordered Gypsy before turning her head toward Theresa. "It seems your ride left without you. Help Pretzel carry Nyala and come with us. Maybe you can explain to us what the hell just happened."

Theresa's face was pale. "He's gone. He'll start the Eschaton."

Gypsy wrinkled her brow. "The what?"

Pretzel's voice cracked as she translated, "The end of the world."

PART IV

WAR

27

THE BIRTH OF DEATH

Countless Eons Ago

The usual stillness of the High Heavens was abruptly disrupted. The serene state of its energy was gone, and an agitated vibe filled the dimension. Dayyana, the aspect of Justice, sensed the disturbance and tried to commune with the other Archangels. However, they were all off on errands among the world ensemble, save for El-Samar Seper. The elder Great Light approached the youngest of the Archangels but immediately perceived something was wrong.

"El-Samar Seper, can you feel that?" she inquired. He did not respond since he was distracted by furiously scanning through the pages of his Codex.

Dayyana drew closer to him. El-Samar Seper slammed the book shut and rushed toward her. His behavior and demeanor startled her, which was a new sensation. When he reached Dayyana, El-Samar Seper grabbed her hand, deposited a small token, and closed it into a fist.

"The time has come," he stated ominously.

"What do you mean? Do you know what's happening?"

"Yes, soon your purpose will be revealed, and you will put your gift to use. However, it will all be stripped from you one day by a Great Injustice. We will speak again when that day comes."

Haniel, Michael, and Gabriel appeared from the portals to different worlds.

"I felt a great disturbance," exclaimed the Primal of Balance. "What's happened, and where is El-Samar Seper?"

Dayyana turned back to where the Keeper of the Annals had been but saw only the Codex.

Two Millennia Ago

The moon was nearly full. Its cycle would be completed the following day. However, the night was dark since the sky was covered in clouds. Two shadowy humanoid figures stood on the tallest tower in the middle of Jerusalem, looking out at the city.

"Lord Diablos, it's begun. He's finally been arrested, and soon he'll be killed. We've done it," uttered one of the shades.

"Yes, Apollyon, the day is finally here," Diablos confirmed. "You have always been my most loyal servant, ever ready to leave your duties of oversight of the western lands to attend to my plans."

Apollyon glanced at his master, "Of course, my lord." If the Daimon didn't know better, he'd have sworn that he detected melancholy in his master's tone.

"Do you remember what I taught you about the High Heavens?" Diablos inquired.

The Daimon nodded.

"I'm going to summon one of the Primals now. No matter how I'm addressed, you will keep your mouth shut. This is not a being to be trifled with."

Diablos extended his hands and channeled all the Daimonic power he could muster. A vortex of energy formed at his fingertips, abruptly shot into the sky and tore a hole through the cloud canopy. Moments later, the space next to the two Daimons started to bend and crackle with energy. A portal formed, and out stepped a black-clad woman holding a scythe. She glanced around before fixing her eyes on Diablos.

"El-Samar Seper, or part of you. It's been an age."

Diablos reverted to his human form and bowed his head. "It's been far too long, my lady."

Apollyon was as terrified by the majestic being before him as he was surprised by his master's deference toward her.

"Why have you contacted me after all this time, Great Betrayer? Why should I not enact Justice upon you right now?"

"We both know that's not how the Sovereign One works," retorted the Daimon. "And I have contacted you because the time of the Great Injustice is upon us."

Dayyana's eyes narrowed.

"I'm sure that by now, you've enacted Justice in countless worlds and have become accustomed to your purpose and role in Creation. But in a few of this world's days, the Sovereign One will ask more of you than has been asked of any Archangel before or will be again. After it happens, use the pendant I gave you to access the Chronal Halls, and you will see the end of your purpose."

The Primal stared intently at her former friend. "You would have me betray my master and abandon my abode, as you have. You think much too highly of yourself."

"No, my lady. Quite the opposite. I would have you hold firm to your role, even if the Sovereign One disregards you. My plan has never been to act against Creation but to save it from the madness that plagues it."

Dayyana doubled over in laughter, composing herself after several seconds. "Oh, you poor, misguided thing. Do you really think you can change the Sovereign One's design and will? Why would he listen to you?"

"You are right. He did not heed me before, much less now. If I was his equal, he would have no choice but to listen." An evil smirk marred Diablos' face.

"You truly have lost all sense. Goodbye, El-Samar Seper."

"Goodbye, Lady Dayyana."

A Transworld portal appeared behind the Primal, and she stepped through without looking back.

Apollyon breathed a sigh of relief as she disappeared.

"Come, Apollyon. I'll teach you how to summon her in the future. The next time you see her, she'll be going by a different name."

Several Days Later

A parade of disembodied specters queued silently down a long dark hallway. The walls on either side of the corridor were adorned with stone depictions of arms stretching out as if to grab the waiting souls. At the front of the line was an arch with a scroll parchment on the floor directly beneath it.

One by one, the shades took turns standing beneath the arch. When they did, the scroll on the floor would measure the weight of their soul. Those found to have heavy souls were pulled through a shimmering portal that led them to eternal rest. However, those of insubstantial spirit were whisked away by an ominous dark portal to eternal torment.

This procession had continued unmanned and unabated since time immemorial until one soul, unlike the others, reached the arch. This spirit shone bright like the sun, or it would have, but its splendor was muted by the ethereal grime that covered it thoroughly.

When this specter stepped on the scroll, the arch shook, and cracks appeared on its cornerstone. The mechanism could not determine the weight of the soul, as it seemed to be of both incalculable worth and immeasurable wickedness. Seconds later, an Archangel's portal appeared next to the arch and Dayyana stepped out, scythe in hand. Her frustration bubbled on her face. She'd not needed to attend to these matters personally before.

"What is this?" the Primal asked as she glanced at the spirit under the arch. "How are you here?"

The specter turned to face the Archangel. "This was planned from before the foundation of this world, Dayyana."

"But why?"

"It's the only way to fulfill the righteous requirements," the ghost responded.

"I don't understand. I-I'm the aspect of Justice. How can this be just?" Dayyana stated as she pointed at the filth covering the specter. "You are the epitome of perfection, yet you've taken on the injustice of the whole world."

"It's so those who are unjust may become worthy. Those who've lost their way can return home one day."

Dissatisfaction plowed Dayyana's brow.

"The procession of judgment must continue, Dayyana. You must judge me now. Strike me with your scythe."

The Primal peered at the implement in her hand, then glanced at the soul. "How can I judge you with the very gift you gave me?"

"Because this is your role. You are the only one who can do it."

Tears welled in the Archangel's eyes, a phenomenon she was not aware she was capable of. Dayyana turned her face and swung the mighty reaping instrument, which struck its intended target. The dark, ominous portal opened and pulled the specter through.

As the apparition vanished, it said, "Always remember, even when you've lost your way, you can always return home." Then it was gone, leaving behind a sobbing Dayyana. The Primal calmed after several minutes and peered into the distance. Then she opened her hand, and the token El-Samar Seper had given her before disappearing from the High Heavens appeared in it.

She stared intently at it for a few moments, studying its design. The token depicted an hourglass framed by two snakes devouring each other's tails, positioned in the shape of an infinity symbol. Finally, she closed her fist and disappeared from the corridor of the dead.

"What is this place?" Dayyana thought aloud as she teleported to an unfamiliar place.

The Archangel was in a colossal chamber connected to numerous hallways around its perimeter. In the center of the room stood a massive hourglass that was colorless and broken. The woman examined several corridors and saw the same thing in each one, a collection of hourglasses in various states of use and disrepair. Many were broken, some were pristine but empty, and others had sand trickling from the top bulb to the bottom.

"These must be the Chronal Halls, the record of everyone who has ever been judged or will be judged."

Dayyana navigated various corridors and discovered that no matter which one she entered, they all looped back to the central chamber. She also realized she could witness the lives of individuals whose hourglasses had expired.

The Primal lost track of time as she navigated the halls, but she was interrupted when a sudden flash of light illuminated the space. She returned to the main room, and her jaw dropped. The large glass was mended and full of sand. Rays of light emanated from the timepiece, flooding the room and the attached corridors.

"He's alive!" Dayyana exclaimed, eyebrows raised. She was preparing to depart when out of the corner of her eye, she noticed energy discharges from the hourglass making their way toward the corridors. When the tendrils touched previously broken sandglasses, they were repaired and infused with the light from the central timepiece.

"Wait, this isn't right," the Primal uttered. She approached one of the newly restored pieces and peered into its history. "This person deserves judgment. Why is the light of life touching them?" Panic crossed Dayyana's face as she analyzed the restored hourglasses one after another and deemed them all unworthy.

"This is wrong! This is Injustice."

The Archangel watched in despair as the light encroached on the corridors of the judged. Even some hourglasses that still had sand were affected by the intrusive energy. As some of them emptied, they remained incorruptible and whole.

"This has to stop," Dayyana muttered. Then she remembered El-Samar Seper's warning of the Great Injustice. "Something is tampering with Justice. I have to rectify this until I can find a solution."

The Primal agonized, her face twisting. She paced, head down, watching her feet move one after the other. Suddenly, she stopped.

"I can't leave things as they are," Dayyana started. "Justice must be done, but death is being denied its proper place in judgment." Her eyes narrowed, and her brow furrowed. "I will find a way to fix this, even if I must become Death."

Unconsciously rubbing her fingers against the infinity snake charm, the Archangel announced, "I need a name that reflects my resolve. Dayyana is too soft. From now on, I will be known as Mara."

28

TOO MUCH INFORMATION

The morning scene at the Tektonite compound could only be described as organized chaos. As Joan and the other council members gathered and awaited a report on the events that had transpired before daybreak, May and several Tektonites hustled to care for Nyala and Olivia.

"*Dios mio, ayudenla por favor,*" cried a distraught Angel, her cheeks red and her eyes puffy. She hovered over May as the doctor checked Olivia's vitals.

"Angel, we have to debrief the council," admonished Gypsy from behind the distraught woman.

"I'm not leaving Olivia's side," Angel responded without turning around. She remembered when she had first encountered the teen as a frightened little girl all those years ago. She felt guilty that she hadn't spent much time with her in recent times. "I haven't told her how proud I am of the woman she's becoming, and that's the first thing I'm going to do when she wakes up."

Gypsy sighed. The warrior left the bedside and started

toward the door. Kitty was leaning against the wall next to it.

"I'll go with you," the goth girl declared.

"Thanks. Pretzel is seeing to Nyala, so I think it will just be the two of us. Let's go."

The pair headed down the stairs toward the conference room, where the leadership was waiting anxiously. They entered the room, closed the double doors behind them, then proceeded to sit in front of the council.

"How are Olivia and Nyala?" Joan inquired.

"May says Nyala is just exhausted and should be all right after some rest. She doesn't know what's wrong with Olivia. Her vitals are all over the place, but she has no external wounds. She thinks we might have to take her to a hospital so they can check for internal damage."

The leader drew a deep breath.

"My dear, help us understand what happened," Mrs. Mozart interjected.

"I was sleeping in my apartment, and Nyala appeared in my room, just like she appeared in front of us when we were in Europe. She woke me and said she'd be going to confront Mara and wanted my help."

"Did you try to talk some sense into her?" Grace inquired.

"I didn't get the impression she'd have listened to me. Besides, given what I saw after, I could have done nothing to stop her."

Joan chimed in, "No offense to Nyala, but she's not a warrior."

Gypsy shook her head. "Well, somehow, Nyala opened a portal and then disappeared."

The room broke out in a low rumble of murmurs.

"What do you mean she opened a portal? And she disappeared how? Did she walk into the portal?"

"I can't explain it, but I think the entity she's been communing with was working through her. The portal was for me. She could vanish and appear elsewhere instantly without it."

Joan covered her mouth with her hand and stared incredulously at Gypsy.

"Did you see this entity, this Apocalypse?" Mrs. Mozart queried.

"Not exactly. The Archangel talked and acted through Nyala. At one point, a divine light poured out of her eyes and mouth, and she stopped feeling like a Daughter to my senses. At that moment, she was something else."

Joan sighed. "Let's continue with the report. What happened after you stepped through the portal?"

"I appeared here in the compound, in the garden. Olivia was already there. Moments later, Angel, Kitty, and Pretzel appeared through another portal. Then Nyala joined us and opened a portal for us four, but Olivia rushed past us and dove into the vortex."

"Where did the portal lead?"

"I'm not sure, but it was a training room of some sort. Mara, Hades, the Sons of the Lords, and a woman were there. The woman was the attacker who's been killing Daughters."

Gypsy told the council about the confrontation, the banishment of Hades, and the revelations of Theresa, Libby, and Haniel. "Further, I think now how this assassin was able to determine our precise location and hunt us.

"Can you elaborate?" questioned Mrs. Mozart.

"Just as Apocalypse has Nyala as her conduit, Mara, the Primal of Justice and Death, has her own. In Crimson's debrief, each assassination occurred right after there was a death. On the night Crystal and Tassel were killed, Lily was shot by the men of the Star of Nimrod. Her death lured Mara's conduit."

The room was silent for several uncomfortable minutes. No council members knew what to make of the night's events.

Finally, Mrs. Mozart broke the silence. "The blonde woman we met before. Is she still here?"

"She's in the dining room," Kitty answered, "I'll go fetch her."

The young woman exited. Silence filled the room again.

"Gypsy, I don't know what to make of this. After that fiasco years ago with Therion, I would have thought you would know better than to rush into an unknown situation through a strange portal," Joan chided.

"Nyala would have gone with or without me. I have a feeling the events that transpired have more significance than we can fathom. I made a judgment call in the moment, and honestly, given a chance to do it again, I'd make the same choice."

At that instant, the doors to the conference room opened, and Kitty sauntered in, followed by Theresa. The elegant woman looked pale and despondent. The air of confidence she had worn the last time she had been in this room was nowhere to be found.

"Thank you for joining us. Please take a seat." Joan motioned at an empty chair next to Gypsy.

Theresa ambled over and slumped down on the seat.

"Could you help us understand what happened?"

As Theresa opened her mouth, the doors opened again. All present stared wide-eyed as Nyala hobbled in, aided by Pretzel.

"Nyala!" Gypsy cried as she bounded out of her seat and rushed to help her friend. They made their way to the empty chair, and Nyala sat next to Theresa.

The Mozambican smiled at Theresa. "Apocalypse wants to return what was taken from you." Without warning, she grabbed the blonde woman's hand. Theresa's eyes nearly popped out of her head, and she fell off her chair and to her knees.

"*Ikasha murbtre hshan,*" the woman bellowed as she clutched her head.

The council members glanced at Pretzel.

"I...I have no idea what she said. That's not a language I can interpret with my gifts."

Theresa drew a deep breath. She steadied herself against the chair and got back onto the seat. The woman stared at the floor for a few more moments, then raised her head and addressed the council.

"I remember everything. I'm not from this world. I was brought here by Mara because I served someone very much like Diablos where I'm from. My memories were erased soon after I arrived. I was implanted with knowledge of this world and the English language. The shock forced me to cry out in my native tongue."

Joan and the other council members glanced at each other and then at the woman. "I'm sorry, we don't understand. Another world?"

Nyala chimed in, "This world, this dimension, is not the only one that exists. The Archangels come from a place called the High Heavens. At the beginning of time, the Sovereign One created it and them. Then, he created the world ensemble, a countless number of planes of reality, each with their own timeline, history, and Sovereign plans."

"So, the multiverse theory is correct?" Pretzel interjected.

"Not exactly. It's not like what you see in popular fiction or even science books. Each world is different and unique. Time runs differently on many of them. Some have civilizations like ours, and others are different in ways our minds can't comprehend."

"So are there, like, other versions of me out there?" Kitty interrupted.

Nyala shook her head, "Each person is unique. There is no one else like any of us in any other world. The Sovereign One loves variety."

"How do you know all this, Miss Nyala? Also, you sound much more like your old self," Mrs. Mozart questioned.

"The Sovereign One showed me. When I went to return the spear, I met Apocalypse, and she brought me to him. After the revelation, a Nephilim used his abilities on me. He was working with Cherry."

"I don't know what to make of this," Joan exclaimed as she put her hands over her head. "I think I finally understand how hybrid women feel when they first learn about their parentage. This is too much."

Mrs. Mozart clasped her hands together and leaned

forward, "Ms. Theresa, we interrupted your account. Could you please continue?"

"No problem. I was brought here to bear the Son of Destruction. Apparently, the seed of Diablos destroyed any human cells it came in contact with, and only someone from another world could bear his child. However, I was lied to about the procedure. I was implanted with three embryos; one was Therion, and the other two reportedly died. I just learned that one of them survived and was raised by Mara as her own."

"You don't mean..." Joan started.

Gypsy interjected, "The killer who's been targeting us."

"This lady better not have any more kids," Kitty quipped under her breath.

"I'm not sure what her deal is, but I met her once before. Years ago, when Therion kidnapped me, she fed me and let me use the bathroom." Pretzel added.

"Yes, well, that's all fine and dandy, but she's gone from that to hunting us like criminals," Gypsy exclaimed. "She would have killed Angel if Theresa hadn't stepped in."

Joan motioned for everyone to settle down. "Theresa, why did Haniel leave you behind?"

"Haniel picked me as his conduit but never told me what he wanted me to do. He only mentioned that he wanted to free his sister from whatever was binding her to this world. It turns out he thought that meant killing her...*my* daughter."

"Wait, I don't understand something. Don't hybrids always take after their mother physically? Why does she look nothing like you?" Gypsy asked.

"The doctor who performed the procedure said something about replacing the insides of some of my eggs with those from another priestess. Also, Mara did something to them. I don't know all the details, but the scientist boasted he'd made the first embryo with three mothers—Mara, the other priestess, and me."

"What will Haniel do now that you've refused to kill her?" Joan inquired.

Theresa sighed and steepled her fingers. "He's going to destroy this world by unlocking the seven seals."

"Can we stop him?"

"I don't know if it's possible. He was given the authority to usher in the Eschaton in worlds that have fallen irreparably out of balance. It's the failsafe when a world is in utter disarray."

A dreadful quiet flooded the room as despair and awe gripped the hearts of the council.

Nyala motioned at Gypsy and used her help to get out of her chair. "The world hasn't ended yet. I have to see about Olivia. Only Apocalypse can save her now."

Joan glanced at Gypsy and nodded. The warrior helped the woman out of the room and up the stairs to where May was tending Olivia. The duo entered the room, and Angel sobbed quietly as May frantically searched for her phone.

"Her vitals just disappeared," Angel blurted as Gypsy and Nyala entered the room.

"Don't bother calling Emergency Services. There's nothing human medicine can do for her. Her ailment isn't physical," Nyala pronounced.

The Mozambican approached the bed.

"What is wrong with her?" May inquired, phone still in hand.

"The energies of two Primals are raging within her, disrupting her body's connection to her soul."

Olivia's lips had turned blue, and her face was deathly pale. Nyala closed her eyes and laid her hands on the teen's forehead and belly. A green glow enveloped Nyala's hands, and a flash of energy entered her body. She drew a deep breath, and the color returned to her face. Nyala glanced at May.

"Apocalypse infused some of her energy to balance the other two. Now the strength of her spirit will determine if and when she regains consciousness."

Earlier that morning

Mara and Libby appeared in her throne room after the confusion caused by the explosion during the confrontation with Haniel. Libby spat out some blood and wiped her mouth as she sank to the cold floor and rested her head on the skull throne.

"*How dare he?*" hollered Mara as she thrashed about the room. Unbridled rage danced in her eyes. "He thinks he can just show up with his little pet and harm my daughter!" The Archangel let out a primal roar that shook the space and caused the bones in the walls and the throne to rattle.

Libby was holding her side, nursing bruised ribs. She had never been hurt this badly. However, her physical wounds were not causing her the most discomfort. The young woman stared as her mother, the eldest of the Primals, paced about with a deep frown on her face. Mara settled down after several minutes, then faced her daughter.

"Do not fret, Libitinia. We will have our revenge against this insult, which is of the highest order. Haniel missed his one chance at success with his foolhardy scheme. He will not get another."

Libby propped herself up, wincing in pain, and looked at Mara. "Mistress, tell me about the High Heavens."

Mara glanced at the young woman curiously. "Certainly, my daughter." The Primal approached the throne and sat. "It's a dimension of conscious energy. We did not have physical bodies there. Instead, our spiritual essence was manifested in its purest form, though we perceived each other as having roughly humanoid shapes.

"Seven of us were the first created, though one was divided among the countless created worlds and became the leader of the Angels in each one. We existed in perfect harmony with each other and with the Sovereign One. That is until El-Samar Seper abandoned his purpose and form."

Libby lifted her gaze to meet Mara's eyes, "Why did the other Primal call you Dayyana?"

"It was the name given to me by Neshama, the Sovereign One's breath. But that was before…" Mara's voice trailed off, and she stared into the distance.

"Mistress, why does the other Primals' presence here distress you so much?"

"They are interfering in this world's affairs. Archangels are called to serve all the worlds. They should return to their place."

"Couldn't they say the same of you?"

Mara's eye twitched, displeasure marring her face for a

moment. Then a token appeared in her hand. "I'll return shortly."

Libby's eyes narrowed. She'd never stopped to analyze the symbol Mara used every time she visited the Chronal Halls, but this time she took note. She'd seen the symbol many times before as she worked with Diablos. Mara disappeared, leaving the young woman alone with her thoughts in the cold, dark room.

29

HOW A WORLD ENDS

In another time, in another world

Tall crystalline structures graced the horizon as far as the eye could see. The buildings varied in size and color and were arranged in discrete geometric shapes. The grouped edifices combined to create a three-dimensional megastructure that was only fully perceptible from a low orbit.

Ten circles were arranged in three columns, three on either side and four in the middle. Connecting the circles were rectangular arrangements of the same crystalline buildings. Under the entire development lay a complex network of caves dug into the bedrock that supported the megastructure. A humanoid figure stood atop the tallest spire. It had fiery red eyes, wild jet-black hair, and facial features similar to a lizard's.

"We were so close," the lizard person hissed as it stared into the night sky. It was a clear evening, and the planet's two moons, Telperion and Laurelin, were full. A massive earthquake hit, causing the structure to shake violently for several seconds. Some of the glassy buildings creaked ominously, and in the distance, the top of a tall spire broke off and crashed to the ground.

Behind the figure, a door opened, revealing a pair of individuals and a winding staircase. The two figures who stepped through the door resembled the first, with their lizard-like appearance. However, they were much smaller, and their eyes were deep-set and of a yellow hue.

"Lord Mephisto! The power turbines are starting to fail, and there are reports of structural damage throughout the Tree. What should we do?" one of the newcomers desperately inquired.

"We do nothing, for there is nothing we can do," admitted Mephisto.

The pair glanced at each other, their forked tongues flicking in and out of their mouths.

"But, sir! If this continues, the structure could suffer irreparable damage."

Mephisto sighed. "There was an old legend, a cautionary tale, really, of a saurian who attempted to fly in between the goddesses of the night." The lizard pointed at the two satellites shining brightly in the sky. "The elders of the village warned her that such an endeavor was folly and would only invoke the wrath of the goddesses.

"However, the saurian was stubborn and persisted in her undertaking. She constructed a winged chariot to carry her through the air, but as fate would have it, a meteorite fell from the sky when she attempted her first flight. It killed her and destroyed the vehicle."

"It was a righteous punishment for her hubris," interjected one of the smaller saurians.

"That is the moral of the story. Of course, the whole concept is nonsense. Those two luminous orbs are no more goddesses than you are. I've allowed the superstitions of your people to persist because it helped me manipulate you to attain my goals. Ironically enough, the kernel of truth in the legend has become true. I reached too high, and now the destruction has come."

"We don't understand, my lord. Are the goddesses punishing us? You taught us that building this complex and sacrificing our children and homes was what the divines wanted from us."

"The divines want nothing. They are nothing more than dead rocks floating in space. I, on the other hand, wanted to attain the highest state, and I nearly achieved it. The Tree would have allowed me to pierce the veil into the High Heavens and make my claim."

Mephisto turned to face the duo. His bright red eyes burned more intensely. His saurian appearance melted, and his height doubled. Batlike leathery wings emerged from his back, and he opened his mouth, revealing rows of sharp, menacing teeth. The two saurians stood wide-eyed and trembled in fear at the monster in front of them.

"What are you?" one of the quivering creatures managed to sputter.

"I am..." the monstrous being began before another earthquake rocked the planet, an order of magnitude more potent than the previous one. First, the foundations of the megastructure began to buckle, and then entire sections toppled over and crashed into the lower parts. That set off a chain reaction that reached the spire the trio was standing on. The building shook violently and crumpled, sending the pair of saurians plummeting to their doom. Mephisto was held aloft by his mighty wings.

As the creature beheld the destruction, he noticed an odd shift in the shadows below. He looked up, mouth agape, as Telperion crashed violently into Laurelin, destroying them both and sending pieces of the satellites hurtling toward the planet. The winged beast hovered between the destruction and the onslaught from above for several minutes, then a tall humanoid appeared before him.

"Haniel..." hissed Mephisto, his eyes scorching with fury.

"It is done. The seventh seal has been unleashed, and this world will soon come to an end. I will not allow you and your ilk to affect the Balance."

Mephisto growled and contorted his face into a wicked grin, "You think yourself so lofty and self-righteous, but tell me...how many worlds have you destroyed? You've extinguished more lives than I could even imagine."

"I've only done what was required of me to maintain order. You and your kind are the final cause of such destruction. Witness the end of your schemes, you wicked traitor." And with that, the Archangel disappeared.

Now alone, Mephisto let out a mighty wail that shook the rubble below him. Anguish filled his gaze, and despair marred his face. He looked at the night sky again and saw the distant twinkling lights disappear.

"So, this is how it ends." Mephisto closed his eyes as a wave of invisible energy crashed into the planet from all sides, disintegrating all matter down to the smallest particles. The being's physical body was obliterated, and the destruction was followed by a gravitational collapse, condensing the planet into a speck smaller than a quark. All matter, fundamental forces, and fields ceased to exist. The only thing that existed was a dark orb of energy, casually effete and unable to interact or affect anything around it because nothing was left. Mephisto, ruler of the Molochs and enslaver of the saurian race, was left a whimpering mass for the rest of time.

Present time, Present world

Haniel stood resolutely on the moon's surface, overlooking the Earth and its inhabitants.

How many worlds has it been? he thought. *How many more will it be?*

The Archangel stretched out his hands, spreading his fingers and curving them inward. Then he closed his eyes and concentrated his energy on the space between his hands until a ball of yellow-red energy formed. The mass separated, and seven balls took shape. The seven spheres spun rapidly, then abruptly shot into the cosmos. One of the spheres made its way back to Earth and stopped somewhere in the middle of the Indian Ocean. However, the others traveled out into the reaches of the universe.

Haniel vanished from his location on the moon and appeared over the turbulent waters. Another majestic figure appeared next to him.

"Prince Gabriel. To what do I owe the pleasure?"

"You know why I'm here, Haniel," responded the chief messenger of the Sovereign One. "I warned you not to involve yourself in the matters of this world."

Haniel's eyes narrowed. "Am I acting outside the purview of my purpose?"

"No, not exactly."

"Have I not been given the authority to deem when a world has become a danger to the balance?"

"Well, yes."

"Then, what is your quarrel with me, Great Prince?"

"I fear you will precipitously condemn this world to destruction."

Haniel glared at Gabriel. "Has the Sovereign One sent you with a message for me? Does He forbid my actions here? If that is the case, I will desist."

"No, the Sovereign One has not spoken to me about your activities."

"Then help me understand why you are interfering in my affairs. I have never sought to receive the Sovereign One's messages, nor have I attempted to impede their distribution. Why do you hinder me?"

"We Archangels have each operated as we deemed fit, according to our purpose and design. However, we have never acknowledged how the loss of El-Samar Seper's instruction in the High Heavens has left us without specific guidance in certain matters. Nevertheless, I sense there is still a Sovereign plan for his world."

Haniel's gaze softened, and he placed his hand on Gabriel's shoulder. "Gabriel, I recognize that you might be correct. However, I cannot risk the order and balance of the world ensemble to your sense. Therefore, I will trigger the Eschaton in this world. Yet, if it is the Sovereign One's will that it remain, He will intervene in the way He deems correct."

Gabriel gazed intently into the Primal's eyes, then nodded. "Very well, Haniel. His will be done."

"His will be done."

The Ancilla bid Haniel farewell and disappeared. The Archangel descended through the raging waters until he reached the deepest point of the Java Trench. There, he found the sphere of energy that had made its way to this location. The Primal closed his eyes, placed one hand perpendicular to his chest, and rested the other on the orb. Then he began the ritual to open the seal that would usher in the end of this reality.

30

TERRA FIRMA

"Puttus, come over here," called Reina, gazing at the sunset dropping between the mountains encompassing the valley. The vivid rays bathed the lake in a golden hue. "This is the type of spot I would like to get married in." She gestured at him from the front of the vehicle.

D'Angelo stepped out of the driver's side of the truck, strode to his girlfriend's location, and wrapped his arm around her waist. "It *is* amazing, Rei. I thought you'd want the church and large hall."

"Nope." She leaned her head against his chest. "You should know me by now. I'm a simple girl. An outdoor wedding surrounded by my loved ones, that's me." She gazed at his dark and chiseled features. "Are you OK with that?"

He stared into her blue eyes and smiled. "Yeah, I'm OK with that." He leaned down and kissed her.

"Hey, hey!" Ortega quipped as he pushed John out of the picket fence house. "You two are supposed to be working. Those supplies won't move on their own."

"Leave them alone, *mi amor*," Awilda said, striking him lightly on his side with her elbow. "You and I were the worst when we were dating." She winked at the young people. "Mia and Timothy, you didn't hear that."

The siblings laughed.

"Hon, you're damaging my reputation."

His wife rubbed his stomach. "Love, you damaged your reputation long ago." She kissed him on the cheek.

"There we go with more overweight jokes."

John looked at the young couple. "My apologies if I'm prying, but I heard you from inside the house. If you like, you are more than welcome to hold your wedding here."

D'Angelo and Reina glanced at each other gleefully, then gazed at the man in the wheelchair.

"We'll consider that, John," responded D'Angelo.

As they exited through the gate, Awilda asked, "John, this is a large and beautiful piece of land. How did you get it?"

The group stopped behind the white truck full of supplies. "Regrettably, it all belongs to me."

"Regrettably?" inquired Ortega with a raised eyebrow.

"My family was once part of the *Mystikés Oikogéneies*. That is Greek for Secret Families who served the cause of the Underworld. As a contribution, my grandfather offered his only daughter to one of the Lords. She was my biological mother. As a reward, my family was given money, fame, and great status in this nation." He glanced around the valley. "This was one of the pieces of property my grandfather acquired."

"May I ask what happened to your family?"

"My loyalty tribute in becoming a Nephilim, to my

shame, was to eradicate them all. I was young and naïve, a pawn in the hands of manipulative overlords." He lowered his head. "I unquestioningly followed their orders." He gave his attention to Ortega. "Regrettably, I inherited all the land, as well as my family's wealth and possessions."

"How do you feel about it all?" Awilda asked further.

"The guilt and the shame are unbearable. Two years ago, I considered burning this place down." He again surveyed the property. "A home built on blood money. I just hope the good deeds of my latter years compensate for the evil deeds of my younger ones."

The Tektonite leader gazed at him. "From what I can see, you've done a great job of using your resources to help others." The woman looked around. "What was intended for evil is now being used for good. Good always overcomes evil, but I do think your incentive is misplaced."

"How so?" asked the man curiously.

"No one on this Earth is free of evil. Whether our infractions were great or small, evil is evil. For example, take a great Tektonite named William Wilberforce, a British politician known for his efforts to abolish the slave trade in Britain. In his youth, he spent much of his time in self-indulgence, gambling, and drinking after inheriting his grandfather's wealth. At the age of twenty-one, he was elected to Parliament, and four years later, William had an encounter with the Tekton. His commitment and convictions to the Tekton way were pivotal in abolishing the slave trade."

The woman placed her hand on John's shoulder. "Wilberforce once said, 'True Tektonites consider themselves, not as satisfying some rigorous creditor, but as discharging a debt of gratitude.' You see, John, no number of good deeds can ever remove the guilt from your heart. Only the Sovereign One is able to do so, but live the rest of your days free of the debt of gratitude for the second chance at life you've been given."

The man smiled and nodded his head. "Thank you for those words and the supplies you brought us. I'm forever grateful."

"Speaking of supplies, where should we store them?" asked Ortega.

John pointed his frail finger at a structure a few yards from the main house, a wooden building with a large opening like a garage door at its center. "You can pull the truck over there. That's where we store all the supplies. If you don't mind, I would like you all to accompany me. There's something I would like you to see."

D'Angelo drove the truck while the rest of the group strode to the shelter. With shaky hands, John managed to pull a small black knob from his pocket and handed it to Timothy. "If you don't mind, my boy, press the button."

Timothy pressed it and was surprised. "I didn't see any wiring running to the building, so I didn't expect it to have electricity."

"This whole campsite runs on solar power. All of the buildings, including the barn, have solar panels," informed John. "We also have power generators with enough juice to produce energy for days."

When the garage door opened, the group gaped. Inside was lumber, steel, window frames and glass, a vast number of bricks, bags of concrete, and other building materials.

"Are you building a city?" asked Ortega in awe.

John laughed. "About two years ago, when I was still capable of moving on my own, I had a dream so surreal and realistic that it gripped me to my bones." He swallowed hard as the thoughts trickled in.

"I saw the end of the world. Chaos and despair gripped the major cities. Nations and countries fell to war and violence. The whole world plunged into anarchy." He pointed a shaking finger at the sky. "I heard a voice from the heavens that said, 'Good terra firma you have. Build upon it, and plant vegetation so it can become a haven to many.'

"The dream terrified me, but nothing happened at first. Groups of Nephilim appeared and needed my help. I took it as a sign that the dream was real, so I started accumulating material. Unfortunately, I ran out of money, and at the same time, I started losing my ability to walk. Eventually, I had to stop." He gestured at Ortega. "If you don't mind, can you move me to the back of the building?"

Ortega did so, and the others followed. Shortly after, they all gazed at acres of arable land. Some parts had dried plants, while others appeared to have recently been cultivated.

John chuckled. "I will confess, I'm not a farmer. Last year's crops were a total waste. That's why we're in need of food supplies. I'm hoping to have better success this year."

The man stopped talking and gave his attention to a tall and brawny figure walking out of the distant woods. He squinted at it.

"One of yours?" inquired Ortega.

The man shook his head. "No. Most of the older

Nephilim are unable to walk or have a missing limb. He might be lost."

D'Angelo took stood a step, and his eyes widened. Reina gazed at his perturbed face. "Puttus, What's wrong?"

"Rei, that's one of the Sons of the Lords. That's Katastrofi."

Reina extracted two quartz blades from the sheaths on her back.

"Don't hurt him!" John cried as he stared intently at the expression of the distant Nephilim.

"What?" Reina asked. "That buffoon is one of the most dangerous."

John shook his head compassionately. "Not anymore. I have seen that expression many times. That, my friends, is the face of someone who's lost everything."

After a few more steps, the mighty and great Katastrofi dropped to the ground.

John called, "D'Angelo, please help him."

D'Angelo dashed over to the fallen and stared in shock at the severely mangled appearance of the fallen Son. His body convulsed, and he groaned in intense pain. The hybrid picked him up and ran back to John.

"My boy, take him to the barn. He's in terrible pain. We must sedate him, or he'll die in anguish."

31

THE LIGHT OF MAN

A crowd of nearly five hundred sat in an auditorium on folding chairs, pointing at a makeshift platform. The stage was adorned with potted plants and wood pallet decor. A handful of individuals graced it and animated the crowd with easy-listening tunes, pop songs, and inspirational quotes from well-known historical figures.

After several minutes, one of the animators invited Lash up to the stage. The grand luminary of the Star of Nimrod eschewed his flamboyant accouterments and instead wore a pair of ripped jeans, sneakers, and a fitted t-shirt that read, *Be the light you want to see.*

"Welcome, friends! We're so glad you could all join us today for the inaugural gathering of Luminosity. My name is Lash, and it is an honor to address you today. All of us here stand at the precipice of something much larger than ourselves." Lash glanced around the room, making eye contact with as many people as possible.

"We live in a world that tries to convince us that darkness is winning and the light is gone. I say, enough of this lie! There is light in this world. That light is in you and me. We only need to recognize it in ourselves and others. Turn to the person next to you and tell them, 'I see your light.'"

A low rumble reverberated through the space as the gathered people shook hands and repeated the platitude to one another. Lash maintained a look of humility, though inside, he reveled in how easily the crowd was eating up his every word.

"My beloved friends, we here at Luminosity are no different from anyone else. We've simply recognized the light, and now we invite you to shine like the stars in the night sky and radiate like the noon sun. We will teach you how to discover the glow within yourself.

"Soon, everyone around you will be amazed as they enjoy your life's luminescence. You might be asking yourself, is this possible for me? We say it is! The crime is that society has attempted to dim your light to keep you a slave to consumerism and fake light sources. You don't need an outside lamp. You are the light of this world!"

Lash paused as many people in the crowd stood and applauded. They were existing members placed as plants to invigorate the group.

"Dear friends, would you do something with me? Let's be silent for a moment and close our eyes."

The majority of the crowd did as they were asked.

"Normally, we only see darkness when our eyes are shut. I want you to focus on your breathing, your heartbeat, and the subtle movements of your muscles. Now let's go deeper. Feel the flow of energy as your brain transmits thousands of electrical signals up and down your body. That is the source of your light. I want you to visualize and manifest it in the darkness of your mind's eye. Take your time."

Several seconds later, on cue, one of the plants shouted, "I-I can see it. *I see the light.*"

Moments later, another plant told the crowd, "Oh, my goodness! I see it too."

Then, as the consultant predicted, others in the crowd joined in. Their heightened emotional state made them susceptible to suggestion and manipulation. Before long, nearly half of the group had claimed to have seen the light.

"Open your eyes. You are no longer my friends. You are my siblings! You have begun your journey to be a lamp in this world, which is in desperate need of darkness-dispelling light bearers."

The group hooted and hollered. Some embraced, and others high-fived. Then the animators came up on stage again, led the group in a repetition of positive words of affirmation, and dismissed the meeting.

The plants in the crowd made small talk and boasted about their supposed experience. They suggested that they'd be returning to future meetings and encouraged others to do so. Lash mingled with the people, shook some hands, and offered clichés and banalities. After a small group of sycophants departed, a tall, well-dressed man approached the leader.

"Lash, I was very impressed with your speech. You have the charisma and likeability to go far. My name is Mateo." He offered his hand and gave Lash's a firm shake. "My friends and I have been looking for an institution with the potential for explosive growth for quite some time. I think we might just have found it."

Lash smiled. "Thank you, my brother. I see the light in you. I have a feeling we have much to offer one another."

"Here is my business card, Lash. Have your people make an appointment with my executive assistant. We can discuss Luminosity's bright future—pun intended, of course." The men gave each other knowing glances and laughed.

As Mateo walked away, a petite woman walked up behind Lash.

"Well done, Mr. Boswell. You've just landed your first whale."

Lash turned around. "Rani, your prepared remarks were exquisite."

The Indian woman shook her head, "It's an easy formula. The power is not in the words but in the speaker. You mesmerized the crowd."

Lash smiled, pleased with himself. However, his face dimmed, and he stepped closer to the young woman. "Listen, we need to meet soon to discuss some potential image issues with…unsavory characters who were once part of the organization. They've all been excised, but I'm afraid their wicked deeds could come back to tarnish our reputation."

"Don't you worry, Mr. Boswell. We specialize in decreasing your liability to skeletons from the past. Our organization knows how to deal with scandals, discredit wannabe whistleblowers and disgruntled employees, and suppress past, present, and…" Rani smiled and pointed at a pair of pretty young women who were waiting patiently to talk to Lash, "future accusations. We'll be in touch, Mr. Boswell."

Lash left the auditorium and walked toward the headquarters building. The moment he entered, Lash, the humble leader of Luminosity, disappeared, and Tammuz, the grand luminary of the Star of Nimrod, manifested. His assistant placed a purple robe around his shoulders and handed him a tablet. Tammuz swiped the screen several times, stopping to read certain essential pieces of information. Finally, the luminary handed the tablet back to his assistant and headed for the elevator.

Once inside, Tammuz pulled a key out of his pocket and inserted it in the panel, which revealed an iris scanner. The man raised his eyes to the device, and the elevator doors closed. A minute later, the doors opened again in a subterranean complex beneath the main headquarters.

"Grand Luminary, you grace us with your presence."

"Thank you for your kind welcome, Eddie. I received your message. Is it true that the first round of testing is ready to begin?"

"Yes, Your Radiance. Masmasu's notes were impeccable. We were able to replicate his work quickly. In fact, our researchers have even made adjustments that we hope will improve the odds of success. Project Nimrod is a go."

"Wonderful. Who are the test subjects?"

"They are survivors of the attack in upstate New York."

Tammuz nodded, "The light of man is with them."

Eddie motioned toward a nearby room. "Please come this way, Your Radiance. We're ready to begin."

The pair entered a dark room with several padded chairs and seventy-inch LED screens. Each screen showed an all-white room with a man strapped to a metal chair by his hands and feet. Five intravenous lines protruded from each subject's arms, legs, and lower back. Next to the men, machines tracked their vitals.

"On your command, Grand Luminary."

Tammuz nodded and motioned with his hand. Eddie flipped open a clear lid near the wall, revealing a green button, and pushed it. The contraptions in each test chamber activated, and a dark-red liquid flowed into the test subjects' bodies. Several of the men screamed in agony, and one passed out. Halfway through the procedure, the vital signs of one of the men spiked and bottomed out. Medical personnel rushed into the room to assess his situation. One of the doctors turned toward the camera and shook his head.

"Should we stop, Your Radiance?"

"No, see it through. These people volunteered for the glory of man."

Three other men exhibited a rapid heart rate and a blood pressure spike, followed by a flatline. Only one of the subjects survived the procedure. Tammuz stared intently at the screen as the man contorted his face and screamed. Suddenly, the subject broke out of his restraints, picked up the metal chair, and crumpled it in his hands like a piece of paper.

He threw the balled-up chair against one of the concrete walls, leaving a sizable indentation. Then he rushed toward the wall and punched it with his bare fists. Each strike cracked the concrete, and the indentation became a hole. Before the test subject could exit the room, he fell to his knees and gripped his head. He let out a blood-curdling scream before blood started gushing out of his mouth, nose, ears, and eyes. Then, he slumped to the floor and lay motionless.

Eddy glanced nervously at the grand luminary.

"Your Radiance, this was just the first test. I'm sure with time, we can…"

Tammuz interrupted him. "That was majestic."

"Pardon?"

"Did you see the strength he displayed for that brief moment? That's the strength those abominations have lorded over us since the days of Nimrod, but no more! Redouble your efforts, tweak the formula, and find more test subjects. The time of man has come."

As Tammuz replayed the display he'd just witnessed in his mind, his smartphone chimed. He glanced at the screen; it was a message from Agent Owens.

> **Grand Luminary, our agents have discovered Ms. Davidson's location. Should we send a team to apprehend her?**

Tammuz tapped furiously on his device.

> **No. Instruct your team to follow and keep tabs on her. Her time will come when the new breed of man is ready to cleanse this world of the abominations for good.**

32

DIGGING UP DIRT

Mist drove a half-hour south from the Lancaster compound and finally pulled into a long, dusty driveway that led to a one-bedroom cottage. The woman didn't bother to check the mailbox tagged with the name Davidson but continued toward the old wooden structure in her blue Jeep.

Stopping in front of the house surrounded by wild grass and crops, she removed her shades, shut off the ignition, and sat for a moment with the windows open to take in the fresh air of the country. Her tranquility was disturbed by seeing the windows of the cottage open. She remembered shutting the windows on her last visit. She grabbed her quartz blade from the glove compartment, got out of the vehicle, and stealthily paced toward the house.

She gazed intently through the small glass opening on the faded brown door for any sight of movement. Seeing no one, she opened the door slowly to avoid creaking, to no avail. The wood floors were no different, though she tiptoed in. Her eyes gravitated to a half-full iced lemonade jar on the kitchen counter with water droplets forming on the outer surface of the container.

She gripped the blade tighter. Curiosity etched her features when she saw a stranger in the grassy yard through the kitchen window. She let out a long sigh when she recognized who it was, but she continued to grip the blade firmly. She opened the kitchen door that led to the backyard.

The stranger held a shovel and was working diligently on making a hole. She stopped when she heard the screeching door. She did not turn but simply asked, "You come to finish the job, Charlotte?"

"That's up to you, Laurie. If I must defend myself, I will," answered Mist standing a few feet from her old partner and ex-friend.

Laurie grunted as she stabbed the shovel deeper into the hole she was working on. "It seems you and your friends are adamant about capturing me. They missed their chance in upstate New York."

The Lancaster leader placed her blade on a scruffy wooden table next to a glass of lemonade and took a seat on a shabby old chair. "They weren't there to capture you but to rescue you."

The woman chuckled. "Aren't you just a mushy greeting card? Can't you see I'm beyond rescuing?"

Mist glanced over the trees at the blue afternoon sky. "Someone up there doesn't seem to think so."

The woman stopped digging and moved to the next spot. "I guess you are the one I should thank for keeping up my grandmother's place," she continued, almost out of breath. She shoved the digging tool into a fresh patch.

"Yeah, I came here after I moved back to Lancaster, and I try to visit at least once a week. It's one of the few places that produce fond memories." The Lancaster leader took note of the many holes in the yard. "If you are hoping to make a garden, you are going about it the wrong way."

"A garden is not what I'm digging for." Laurie wiped the sweat from her brow and continued digging. "I didn't expect to find the place still standing, much less in livable condition."

"Then why are you here?" She had yet to see the woman's face but noticed a limp in her step as she moved to a different spot.

"Believe it or not, searching for a treasure." Laurie turned her head, revealing her damaged left eye and bruised face. She quipped, "I just need a black patch and the hat to finish the pirate outfit."

Mist's eyes became glassy when she saw how disfigured Laurie was. She didn't bother to offer medical assistance, knowing she'd get a condescending response. "Why were you captured by those zealots?"

The woman grunted as she started the new hole. "I'm searching for a man named Dr. Patrick Ostero, also known, or he was known, as Luminary Masmasu."

"What about him?"

Thrusting the shovel into the dirt, she limped over to the table and took a sip of the lemonade. "You are looking well. The long hair suits you," she uttered and strode back to the shovel.

"I can't return the compliment. The bald look is not you."

"Don't have time for the salon." She smiled and

answered her earlier question. "Dr. Ostero was responsible for making the twins."

"What twins?" Mist frowned.

Laurie snickered. "You guys are really behind." She continued digging. "Dr. Ostero is a deplorable scientist who worked for the Daimons for years. He helped Apollyon bring forth the Son of Destruction and his twin sister. I suspect she was that thing who killed your friends a few nights ago."

"How do you know about that?"

"The man likes to talk when he tinkers, and I, being one of his subjects, had to endure his incessant ramblings." Again, she grunted, but this time, it was because of the pain in her leg. She continued working.

Seeing her struggle, Mist stood and snatched the shovel out of her hands. "Let me do this." Laurie glared at her. "If I had asked, you would've given me a snooty response. Take a seat and let me find whatever you are looking for. I'd hoped to put a vegetable garden back here, but since this is your house, I guess making holes it is."

Laurie sighed and sat on the chair Mist had vacated.

The Lancaster leader deepened the hole Laurie had been working on. "Why was he experimenting on you?"

The woman remained quiet for a while but eventually responded, "He hoped to replicate what I had for others."

Mist stopped digging and gave the other woman a hard stare. "You mean to tell me he wanted to find a way of imbuing others with evil spirits?"

"It didn't work. That's why you could not find those missing European girls."

Mist gripped the shovel. "Damn, Laurie! You have a fine

way of saying things."

"Look, I'm not happy about my actions if that's what you want from me!" She took a long breath. "Why am I even sharing this with you? Just get the hell out of here and let me live out my remaining days in misery."

The Lancaster leader pinched the bridge of her nose and sighed. "I'm sorry. I didn't mean to work you up, but if you meant what you wrote about restitution, help me understand what this doctor was up to and why you are looking for him."

"You can stop there. The old lady couldn't walk that far." The woman pointed at a new area. "Try that spot over there."

Mist followed orders. "What are you looking for?"

"Some stuff my grandmother buried to hide it from my junkie mother. I was the only one she told."

"Right," responded Mist and continued digging.

"After his failed attempts, Dr. Ostero was ordered to stop when a new and more promising means was discovered," she disclosed and took another sip of the lemonade.

"What was it?"

Laurie shrugged. "I've no freaking clue, but whatever it is, he must be stopped. I lived with that disgusting thing for years, and the anguish I experienced was incredible. I tried killing myself a few times but was further tortured instead since I no longer had a will of my own." She gazed blankly at the weeds in the yard. "It was as if I was under the control of someone else."

Mist was about to offer her sympathy, but Laurie raised her hand and stopped her. "Call it the price for my sins. I deserve death, and it will come once I've killed Dr. Ostero."

The Lancaster leader stopped digging when she heard a thud and the shovel stopped moving. "I think I found what you are looking for." Mist excavated around the object and discovered a small metal chest. With the shovel, she unearthed it and handed the box to Laurie.

Laurie slowly and meticulously opened it, revealing a slew of precious stones— glistening sardius, sapphires, diamonds, rubies, and emeralds. Mist gaped at the gleaming stones.

"The last of grandmother's jewels," Laurie told her as a tear raced down her face. "How I hated my mother for selling most of my grandmother's collection, and here I am, about to do the same thing."

"Why? Didn't you tell me once that your grandmother's jewels were a family heirloom?"

"I have no family left." She abruptly closed the container. "And I need the money to find Dr. Ostero."

"I'll give you the money. Don't sell the stones."

Laurie stood. "Keep the place. I'm pretty sure it means more to you than it does to me. I have no further use for it."

As the woman walked away, Mist called after her, "Hey, wait." Her ex-partner turned. She grabbed a pen from one pocket and a receipt from the other. The Lancaster leader wrote down a phone number on the back of the paper and handed it to the woman. "If you ever need anything, call me."

Laurie's lips quirked as she grabbed it. "Bye, Mist."

As she strode to the cottage, Mist whispered, "Bye, Jewels."

33

JUSTICE SERVED

The last several days had been a whirlwind for Joan and the other council members. The losses, revelations, and remaining mysteries weighed heavily on their minds. Joan had always prided herself in being a woman of action and decisiveness, but for the first time in her life, she was at a loss as to how to continue. The Daughters gathered in the conference room and addressed minor housekeeping issues before coming to the items on everyone's mind.

"Honestly, I got to tell y'all that I feel like a cockroach in a hen's pen," Grace began, breaking the uneasy silence. "I've seen and heard more than my fair share in my century on this planet, but this feels overwhelming."

Joan's eyes were drooping, the physical and emotional exhaustion of recent events taking their toll. "I think we all feel that way, Grace. May, what can you tell us about Olivia's condition?"

The doctor sighed and glanced at her colleagues. She had hoped to be able to deliver good news. "There's been no change. So far, she's stable, but I'm afraid…" May's voice cracked. "This is beyond me. All that's going on? It's beyond any of us." Her voice trailed off as she choked back a sob.

"Mrs. Mozart, please give us some good news. Have you discovered anything that might help us?"

"I scoured the records at my disposal and found nothing. Then I remembered something. When Miss Nyala and I were looking into the Spear of Destiny in the London archives, we came across a book titled *Records of the Primals*. As serendipity would have it, it is not a forbidden text, and there was a copy in the Lancaster Daughters branch."

"Thank the Sovereign One! What did you find?"

"Not much, I'm afraid, and what I did find does not bode well. The text says that there are three beings known collectively as the Primals: Dayyana, Haniel, and Apocalypse."

"Who's this Dayyana? I thought it was Mara," Gypsy interrupted.

"I asked Miss Nyala about that, my dear. Apparently, some event caused Dayyana to change her name to Mara. The rest of the book mostly deals with speculation and conjecture. However, one part caught my eye. Legends mention that Haniel is also known as Ανοιχτήρι των σφραγίδων, the Opener of the Seals."

"Well, that's it then," Mrs. Poppins chimed in. "We're truly living the end of days."

The silence was heavy in the room until Awilda, who'd been observing the conversation, spoke up.

"Joan, may I?"

"Yes, please, Awilda. I'm afraid we're all at a loss."

Awilda drew a deep breath and gazed into the eyes of every woman in the room. "From the very beginning, Tektonites have lived with the ever-present expectation of the Tekton's return. We've embraced the concept of living our lives as if today were the last but planning for our future work as if the world would last another million years.

"In the past and even today in many parts of the world, Tektonites lived with the constant awareness that evil forces were actively trying to destroy them. Empires rose and fell, kings lived and died, yet we've remained.

"Maybe the end of the world *is* finally at hand. The question becomes, what kind of end do you want to have?" The leader paused and let her words sink in. "As long as it lasts, we'll continue to do good and help. Evil wins when good people do nothing. If this is our end, let it be one that is full of joy, gratitude, and hope for the life to come."

The women in the room felt a sudden cool breeze sweep over them, although the doors were shut. However, the lethargy and self-pity melted from their souls, and the light of life shone in their eyes again. Joan let out a sharp breath, shook herself, and stood.

"Awilda, thank you! That was exactly what we needed to hear. It is true that there are adversaries we cannot hope to defeat. However, that only means it's not our battle. We will continue doing what we can and leave the rest in Sovereignty's hands."

The other women in the room nodded, and some dried their tears. Then the door of the conference room burst open.

Kitty popped into the room unannounced, "Um, sorry

for interrupting, but I thought you'd like to know that Olivia's awake."

"OK, let the girl breathe, Angel," instructed Pretzel.

The Latina was alternating between hugging and kissing the recently awakened Olivia.

"*No te metas*. Let me have this. I've been so worried." Angel cried without releasing the teen.

Olivia's voice was muffled. "I guess I was out for a while."

"Girl, you've been unconscious for days. You gave us all a fright. How do you feel?"

"I'm starving."

The women chuckled.

Angel grabbed Olivia's shoulders and looked into her bright blue eyes. "Don't you ever scare me like that again! What were you even thinking, rushing into that portal?"

The curly-haired teen looked at the two adult women. "I felt I needed to be there for Nyala. I knew I couldn't help fight whatever was on the other side, but I could support Nyala and protect her."

"Ugh, you stubborn, headstrong, wonderful, brave child. No, *young woman*," exclaimed Angel.

May rushed into the room, and her eyes glistened as she glimpsed the teen. The doctor sniffed and composed herself.

"All right, everyone out."

"*¿Que?* Oh, come on!"

"I need to check my patient, and you are crowding her.

Besides, she needs liquids and food. You can go to the kitchen and fetch some for her."

The pair obeyed reluctantly, but not before Angel squeezed Olivia one last time.

"I know you are probably sick of being in bed, but I need to examine you. Let me fetch some things, and don't move," May instructed as she left the room.

Olivia nodded, then threw herself back onto the bed. She rolled over on her side while she waited for May to return. She played with her curls, which were matted and tangled from lying down for so long. Unnoticed, arcs of electricity bounced between the strands of her hair; purple, yellow-red, and green streams collided and clashed, leaving behind nearly imperceptible sparks.

Theresa leaned against the outside wall of the Tektonite building with her head arched up, her eyes not focused on anything in particular. She was deeply lost in thought and did not notice when Nyala strolled up beside her.

"Can you sense it too?" asked the dark-skinned woman.

"I've been feeling a strange unease. Do you know what it is?" answered the blonde without glancing over.

Nyala nodded. "Yes, it's similar to the signal Mara sent to lure in Apocalypse but much weaker."

"So, it's her."

Nyala joined her on the wall. "Yes, it's your daughter."

"I can't kill her."

"I know."

"You can't fight her on your own."

"I know."

Theresa lightly banged her head against the wall. "Damn it. Is killing her really the only way?"

The Mozambican looked at the ground. "I'm not sure it was ever the way. I don't know what I'm walking into this time, but I know I need to go. Even Apocalypse can't tell what's going to happen after this point."

Theresa pushed off the wall, sighed, and turned to Nyala. "If you're talking to me, I assume you don't intend to bring your friends."

"Libitinia has caused them too much pain for them to be objective. Besides, this is a struggle between Primals, and it seems fitting that the daughters of the Primals see it through to the end."

"Well, what are we doing wasting time here? Let's go."

Nyala's eyes glowed green, and a portal appeared. She went to take a step but lost her footing. Luckily for her, Theresa caught her before she fell.

"Thanks. I don't think we can expect a repeat of last time. Unfortunately, I can't channel Apocalypse's power efficiently. This portal might be all I muster."

"We'll make do."

The pair stepped through the portal, and a deep chill penetrated to their bones. They were in a large, mostly empty chamber with a gloomy-looking throne. Libby stood in front of it. The portal closed behind them, stranding them with their formidable adversary.

"You came. I wasn't certain you could sense my call. And you came without backup. Feeling confident?"

Theresa scanned the room warily, but there appeared to be no immediate threat. Nyala took several steps toward

Libby and stopped a few feet shy of her. "You didn't summon us here to fight. I could tell that much. So, why did you?"

Libby squinted at Nyala. "You're not glowing, so it's just you. I wanted to speak to the Primal."

"I'm not channeling her power, but she can hear you."

"I-I have to know," Libby started. "Is my mistress...is Mara in the wrong?"

"She's sincerely mistaken," Nyala responded.

"Explain."

"Mara...no, *Dayyana* has fundamentally misunderstood something of grave importance. However, it's likely all been instigated by Diablos or El-Samar Seper, as he was formerly known."

"So, you're saying my mistress is being controlled." Libby's gaze fell to the floor. Her eyes glazed. "Is it because of me?"

Theresa's eyes went wide, "You called us here, prepared to die. Didn't you?"

"I-I've served Mara faithfully since I was a child. Everything I've done has been because I believed my mistress' cause to be pure and just. She's the embodiment of righteous judgment. But now, others of her kind are opposing her, calling into question her actions. Did I corrupt her? Am I the reason she lingers in this world and commits injustice?" Libby's eyes moistened, and she clenched her teeth. Her heart raced as she braced herself for the answer.

Nyala was moved to compassion by the sincerity in the young woman's words. "Haniel certainly thinks so. However, Apocalypse disagrees. She sensed a corrupting influence on Mara, but it's been there since long before you were born. Something anchors her not just to this world but to an obsession that consumes her."

Libby breathed a sigh of relief. Her heart slowed from a gallop to a trot.

"Why have you been killing female hybrids?"

"Mara believes their lives should have ended years ago during an incursion by the Daimons. However, someone interfered. Even with all her power and understanding, she didn't know what had happened. It eats at her."

"Those women were saved by the Carpenter's Son."

Libby's eyes grew wide, and her jaw dropped. "It can't be. He's... Why would she oppose him?"

Mara appeared in the throne room, fresh from a visit to the Chronal Halls. The infinity snake token was still visible in her hand. Her eyebrows pulled down, and her nose wrinkled at the sight of Nyala and Theresa. Then, she shifted her eyes to her daughter.

"Libby, the enemy is here. Strike at our adversary."

"At once, my lady."

Immediately, smoke covered the space, and Libby disappeared. Theresa rushed toward Nyala to shield her. However, they did not anticipate where Libby would appear. The young woman materialized above Mara, blade in hand, and thrust the weapon at the Primal's hand, striking the token. The pendant shattered.

Dark energy gushed out of the broken pieces. Libby took the brunt of the blowback and flew backward, crashing headfirst into the bone throne and demolishing it. The energy raged out of control for several seconds, enveloping the chamber's four inhabitants. The next thing they knew, they had been transported to a hall with a massive glowing hourglass.

"No!" bellowed Mara, staring in horror at the shattered symbol in her hand.

Libby lay on the floor, unconscious. Nyala and Theresa stood a few feet from the furious Primal. Mara initially ignored them to focus on the broken pendant. Then her black eyes moved slowly from her hand to the two women, fury plastered on her face.

"What did you do? My daughter is incorruptible. How did you deceive her?"

Nyala stood tall though fear gripped her heart. "We told her the truth."

Mara sucked in a breath. "You speak to me of truth when even now, you are unjustly covered by His light." The Archangel reached out, and a timepiece hurtled toward her from one of the room's many corridors. The hourglass released sand from the top bulb to the bottom. A sliver of light connected it to the giant hourglass in the central chamber.

"This hourglass is you," Mara explained. "The sands hold the record of your life. Every injustice you've committed, all of your misdeeds etched indelibly. And yet, you are connected to His life. It's not just you. You human parasites are legion. Can you explain this injustice to me? Can you explain this *truth*?"

Nyala glanced at the enormous glowing hourglass, the sands eternally flowing in both directions. The ornate design of the frame filled her with an inexplicable sense of peace. "This is the Carpenter's Son's," she muttered and turned toward the Primal.

"You've no doubt looked at the injustices and transgressions of countless humans in the sands. Have you ever looked at the story His sand tells?"

Mara huffed. "There is no Injustice there. He's utter perfection."

"Yet, there is an incalculable amount of sand. Surely it tells some story."

"I-I can only see the evil perpetrated. I see nothing else. It's all I need to see."

Nyala glanced at the broken pieces in Mara's hand. "Maybe that's because that's all someone wanted you to see."

Mara's brow scrunched. The Archangel looked at the item she'd carried since time immemorial. Then, she tilted her hand and allowed the broken pieces to fall to the floor. Finally, with trepidation, the Primal touched the shining timepiece, then gasped. Tears flowed down her pale face.

"It's beautiful." Mara withdrew her hand and composed herself. "But this changes nothing. Your kind isn't worthy of His light. It's not just that you participate in His life."

"Because of our injustices and evil?"

"Precisely."

"What is the worth of His life?" Nyala inquired.

"Infinite."

"What is the value of His Justice?"

"Incalculable."

Nyala pointed down several corridors. "If you added the injustices of every hourglass, would they overshadow His Justice?"

Mara answered without hesitation, "Never."

"So, if a being of infinite Justice pays the price of finite

Injustice with his own life, isn't it unfair to think the unjust world has to pay?"

Mara opened her mouth to speak but stopped.

"Since he overpaid the penalty, shouldn't Justice be considered done when He gives His life for it?"

"I-I..." Mara glanced at the central hourglass again. "What have I done?"

The Primal slumped and covered her face with her hands.

Theresa approached Nyala and put a hand on her shoulder. "You did it."

"It was already done. She just needed to see it."

Mara straightened and peeked at her daughter, who was still unconscious on the floor, and then at the pair of women. "My folly has caused much harm. I was blinded, and now we're doomed to haunt these halls for all time. That trinket was my only way in or out of this place."

Three rays of light shot from the radiant timepiece, and golden portals opened. One portal opened next to Libby's still body, one behind Nyala, and another behind Mara. Theresa marched over and lifted the young woman off the floor. The blonde woman turned to face the dark-skinned Daughter.

"Nyala..." Theresa started

"Take her. She's caused much hurt. Maybe someday you can both join us," Nyala said with a sad smile.

Theresa locked eyes with the Primal across the room next.

"Take care of our daughter," the Archangel requested as she took one last gander at the woman she'd cared for since birth.

"I will, Mara."

The Primal shook her head. "It's Dayyana."

Theresa and Libby disappeared into the golden vortex.

"Goodbye, Dayyana." Nyala turned around and walked into the portal behind her.

"Goodbye, child. And thank you."

The Archangel turned to face her portal, then steeled herself and walked through. She found herself back in the High Heavens. In front of her stood a man in a white robe with a gold sash. She looked at him sheepishly, but the man opened his arms, ran to her, and embraced her.

"Welcome home."

34

A MESSAGE OF LOVE

Crimson ran her hands through her dark hair and gazed at the media player on her laptop. She had listened to the recording several times and still couldn't believe what she was hearing. The Fury took a deep breath, inserted a USB drive into her system, and saved the media file on it. Upon hearing approaching footsteps, she turned to the door of the makeshift office.

"Crimson, do you have that file ready for me?" asked Joan, entering the room and glancing at her watch. "By the way, thanks for helping Nyala get this file from her cloud drive. She had no idea about the recording, much less that it had uploaded automatically."

"Joan, I know you are in a hurry, but is this all true?" She extracted the USB from the laptop and gestured at it. "This whole conflict between the species of the hybrids was all a ploy?" The Fury shook her head in disbelief.

"I'm afraid so. We learned about it some time ago, which explains why the committee is so adamant about getting us out. They wanted to keep our mouths shut." She took the USB drive from Crimson's hand. "However, I wasn't aware how thorough and deliberate the London group was in their deception."

"All these years, and now I come to find out it was a lie." Her expression turned from confusion to anger.

"We were all deceived and moved as pawns." The leader shook the drive. "But that's going to change." Joan placed the USB in her pocket. "When are you heading back to the warehouse?"

The Fury was silent for a moment, staring at her clasped hands. "I'm not sure if I want to go back," she finally responded. "To be frank, I don't know where I belong now. This is all too confusing."

The leader nodded in understanding. "I know many don't believe the story, but when the Carpenter's Son visited us at the warehouse, He warned me about a deep deception and how much it was going to shake me.

"Since then, I have discovered deceptions upon deceptions, each one thrusting daggers into my core and shattering my misguided beliefs." She exhaled hard. "I won't lie. It made me angry at times."

"How were you able to overcome that?" asked Crimson curiously.

"His words. *'What was intended for evil, I will use for good.'* I refuse to let my past mistakes dictate my future. On the night of the warehouse attack, we were saved by an act of love, and I made it a personal cause to pass on what I had received." She gave the woman a compassionate look. "And I have to say, that practice hasn't failed me yet, no matter how dark the times."

Crimson nodded. "Thanks, Joan."

"One more thing. You'll always have a place with us."

"Even if I informed Erinys that you and your leadership team were not stepping down and about those Nephilim at that campsite?" Crimson wore an apologetic expression. "She has told the committee. I overheard it from one of your girls."

Joan smiled at her. "Even so. Actually, you did us a favor."

"First and foremost, I want to thank all the representatives of the Global Daughterhood Committee who have joined this video conference," greeted Athena. "It pleases me to say we have Daughters from all six continents: Africa, Asia, Australia, Europe, and North and South America. As you can see, joining me here are a few members of the London council, including my team's second-in-command Cherry."

The London leader opened a folder before her and took a quick glance. "Several weeks ago, this committee issued a vote of no confidence for the New York City Daughters of the Watchers Leaders after their illegitimate practices and serious infractions were discovered. A delegate, our newly elected New York leader Erinys, who is also in attendance, has recently informed us that the leadership team refuses to relinquish their authority."

"I wish to clarify that statement," someone interjected. Some of the attendees gasped.

"Excuse me, Joan, but you were not invited to this meeting. How were you even able to join if this meeting was sent to leaders only?"

"Yes, I'm aware," interrupted Joan. "My good friend and long-time companion Mist granted me access. If you will give me but a moment, I'll like to explain my actions."

Athena addressed the group. "I'm sorry, team, but we cannot continue this meeting while we have an excommunicated person on the call."

"Pardon, Athena," said the Paris leader. "But Joan helped the European groups three years ago when we were all, how you say, in discord with each other. *S'il vous plait...* Uh, please, give her the chance to speak."

Other European leaders also expressed their desire for the New York leader to speak.

"I don't consent to it, but if this is what you wish. Joan?"

"Thank you, ladies," began Joan. "I wish to clarify the delegated communication of relinquishing our authority. Actually, our council group decided to remove ourselves from the Global Daughterhood after we learned that the London team has been working under the authority of Diablos."

Gasps of horror resonated from the conference attendees.

"How dare you insinuate that!" snarled Cherry. "This is an outright lie. You're the one working for the enemy. Aren't you harboring male hybrids? You have even concocted a special formula to hide their aura!"

Joan nodded. "That's true."

"Are you not also helping those Tektonites when our bylaws clearly state that we're not to engage in civilian affairs?"

"I won't deny it. That's also true."

"We also received recent news that the Tektonites are

assisting sealed Nephilim, and your group is involved in helping them."

"You are once again correct."

Cherry slammed her fist on the wooden table. "So, how dare you make us out to be the adversary when it is clear you are the ones helping the enemy?"

Joan gave a polite smile. "The Carpenter's Son once said that we're to love our enemies, so there is a difference between our actions and yours. We're helping male hybrids and Nephilim, not pursuing an evil endeavor. On the contrary, Cherry, I've proof that is exactly what you are doing."

"Proof!" exclaimed the older woman. "What proof?"

Joan pressed a key on the laptop, and a video recording started playing. Cherry and Nyala were disputing the contents *of The Annals of the First Daughters* and the London curator who had validated its authenticity. Many faces in the video turned in astonishment on hearing Cherry validate their dealings with the enemy, ensuring the Tektonite relic was returned as requested by her superiors. Most frightening was to hear her call Psychosi the Nephilim and attack Nyala.

The New York leader stopped the video and rewound it, then paused moments before Nyala placed the phone in her pocket. It showed Cherry standing at the entrance of the temple.

"Daughters, you can now understand why we're removing ourselves from the Global Daughterhood," disclosed Joan. "It saddens me to learn that this so-called war was a means to an end and how we were all deceived."

"This is an outrage!" yelled Cherry, her face bright red. "You fabricated that recording to clear your name!"

"How can you say that with a straight face? Put a sock in it, Cherry!" Joan ended the call, but just before, she heard the Global Daughters asking slews of questions.

Nyala sat alone, enjoying the afternoon in the Tektonite garden. Her eyes were closed, arms resting on her side and legs crossed on a cherry-red yoga mat. Occasionally, she would take a deep breath, inhaling in the flowery aromas and exhaling her cares.

The young woman finally opened her eyes, and to her surprise, she saw an old friend a few feet away. "Gypsy, how long have you been sitting there?"

"Quite some time." The woman smiled from her own yoga mat. "Your silence and peacefulness inspired me to join you."

"May I join you?"

"By all means." The warrior gestured at a spot next to her. "Maybe you can teach me how to be so calm."

Nyala stood, grabbed her mat, and sat again. "Now that Apocalypse has left me, I'm learning how to center my thoughts. I still hear voices. My guess is that they are remnants of Psychosi and the medications the London team gave me."

"You look great, and taking time to meditate and focus can really help."

"Thank you." She took a look around the garden. "This place helps the most."

"Are you able to recollect everything now?"

"Only in bits and pieces. As silly as this might sound, it's like putting together a jigsaw puzzle." She let out a disappointed sigh. "I have to calm down when things aren't making sense. It can be frustrating."

"And that's OK," Gypsy comforted. "The loss of my left arm taught me that. Many frustrating moments that first year, but I eventually learned how to cope with it and adjust to my life without it."

"On that subject, I remembered our last conversation about the Residual Spiritual Projection."

Gypsy tapped the woman's arm. "That's a good thing, right? You can recall things from three years ago."

The Mozambican shot her a pearly white grin. "I also discovered how to activate it."

The warrior returned the smile. "I have all day, baby!"

Angel, Pretzel, Kitty, Cookie, and Dough sat and waited anxiously for their friend at Battery Park. Reina had sent a message to meet at six o'clock at their usual location. All the text said was **Urgent**.

Cookie looked at her smartphone and asked, "Where is she? It's five past six."

Before she could finish, her sister spotted the girl. "There she comes."

Angel blurted upon her arrival, "Everything OK, Reina?"

"Hey, guys, I'm sorry for the delay. D'Angelo and I got stuck in traffic."

"Is he here?" inquired Pretzel. "Have him join us."

"No. He thought I should meet with you alone. It's the reason for my urgent message, and since Cookie and Dough head back to Lancaster tomorrow morning, tonight was the best time to meet."

"What is it?" asked Kitty.

Reina teared up as she pulled a folded piece of paper from her back pocket. "Well, you guys remember that Tassel sent me a file with all sorts of info. I forgot about it until this morning. I was looking through it and found this letter she left us."

"What does it say?" questioned Pretzel curiously.

"I started reading it and stopped when I realized it was addressed to all of us," responded Reina. She handed the note to Pretzel. "I thought this was the perfect spot to listen. Would you mind reading it out loud?"

"Not at all." The young woman grabbed the letter and began reading.

My besties,

It's midnight, and I'm pretty sure Gypsy wanted me to sleep the night before my first field mission, but I sensed that I needed to write this letter.

For the first time in my life, the future seems obscure, as if my seer gift was shut off. Does that mean anything? Yet somehow, I feel at peace and keep thinking how blessed I am to have you six women in my life. I would love for us to have been together on my first field mission, but for one reason or another, Sovereignty had it otherwise.

I never knew my biological family, but you've been the best family a girl could ever ask for. Each of you will forever hold a special place in my heart, a love that I will carry beyond the grave.

My Latina hot pepper, Angel—since the day I met you, I saw greatness in you. Others might say you have a temerarious disposition, but I say you are simply big in heart. (Yes, girl, you'll need to look up "temerarious").

Beautiful Pretzel, your friendship is like no other. Your words and comfort were a source of inspiration more precious than gold, sweeter than honey, and yes, yummier than those New York street pretzels. All I can say is thank you.

Lovely Mello Kitty, thank you so much for your honesty and sincerity. You were that one friend that could tell me the truth whether it was raining or shining, and that I loved. I hope to be like you one day.

My favorite twins, Cookie and Dough—your strength of character and ability to love are unrivaled. Your friendship has bolstered me on my weakest days. How great to know the strongest women in the world are my friends.

Last but not least, my exuberant and rambunctious friend, Reina. You always make me smile. Thank you for spending last night on the phone with me. You are truly a friend who sticks closer than a sister. Hey, have you decided who's going to be your maid of honor? It's me, right? I'm kidding. Just know you will always be mine.

It's time to hit the sack so I can be optimal for tomorrow's ludicrous mission. Yes, it's crazy that we're rescuing a woman who has caused us so much pain, yet I sense it's the right thing to do. I have managed to make room in my heart for compassion and forgiveness. I have learned that the best weapon to use against evil is love, and even if this enemy brings harm to us *tomorrow, remember this, my besties. We always have the option to fight back with love.*

Love you guys always, and hope to see you all soon.
Your friend,
Abigail Chen Sun, AKA Tassel

No eye was dry, and all remained silent for a long time after Pretzel finished reading the letter.

Kitty finally said, "I miss her so much." She wiped the tears from her eyes. "How are we supposed to move on, given all that's happened?"

"I know what you mean," added Angel. "The future seems dim now. Nyala mentioned that Libby and her mother are still out there. Do you think they'll try to avenge Therion's death?"

Pretzel shook her head. "Libby brought me food and water when I was held at Navarro Enterprises, and she expressed that she hated Therion. I don't think that'll happen." She glanced at the group. "I know this will sound absurd, but I don't think the chick's motives were purely evil."

"What do you mean?" queried Dough. "She killed a lot of women, including our best friend Tassel."

Pretzel turned to Angel. "Do you remember what you said after Therion's death? He had all this power in the world but never received the most powerful gift, love." Her friend nodded. "Libby, in my judgment, was also misguided. Thinking about Tassel's letter, if we ever engage her again, before using the sword, let's follow our friend's advice and use love first."

"I agree," confirmed Angel. "It's time we started using the weapons our enemy will never have access to."

Kitty, who was sitting next to Angel, stood. "Hey, guys, I know I'm usually not the touchy type, but for Tassel's sake, can we bring it in? I can really use one of those weird hugs you guys do."

The group laughed and embraced each other in one accord.

EPILOGUE

A rotund man with glasses paced several rows of tables neatly arranged in a grid pattern. Each bench held a rectangular box with a metal frame and see-through acrylic sides. Attached to each were displays and dials to regulate and monitor the progress of the process occurring inside. The man systematically approached each table and meticulously wrote notes on a pad of lined yellow paper. As he continued this task, a reddish glow appeared behind him.

"Dr. Ostero, how goes the process?"

"Ah, Diablos! Come and see for yourself."

The Daimon approached one of the tables and peered through the acrylic side. A number of mechanical arms were creating a three-dimensional humanoid shape. The body was being constructed piece by piece.

"The shape looks right, I suppose."

"This biological additive printing is bleeding edge, a seamless combination of ink-jet and laser-assisted techniques to build a complete body layer by layer. Everyone else is decades away from this type of innovation. This body is about thirty percent complete. As you can see, the outer scaffolding is being constructed one layer higher than the flesh to maintain the body's structural integrity," Ostero explained, looking pleased with himself.

"So, you called me over to show me a half-baked, or more like a third-baked product?"

"No." Ostero smirked. "I wanted you to appreciate how much work this is and what the process looks like. Come this way."

The man ambled toward a table several rows away. "Take a look."

Diablos leaned in and glanced at the contents of the table. Inside lay a whole bone-white body. In the middle of the chest area was an opening in the shape of a diamond, revealing the fleshy mass inside.

"The outside material is similar to plaster. The subject will easily break out of it when infused with life."

"Will it obey?"

"Yes. Upon activation, this right here…" Ostero's voice trailed off as he reached for a triangular trinket hanging on the side of the box. "will create an imprint that will make the subject subservient to its owner."

"Is this one ready?"

Ostero handed Diablos the device. "I'll open the cradle, and you can do your woo-woo thing." He waved his hands. "Then press your thumb against the diodes on the device."

The mad doctor pressed a sequence of buttons on the display. The box opened with a loud hiss, releasing the pressurized gases inside. After the white vapor cleared, the body was exposed.

"The body is only viable for a few minutes outside the cradle's protection, so don't delay," warned Ostero.

Diablos approached the body and curled the fingers of one hand. A black mass that absorbed the light around it appeared above the center of his palm. Dark specters manifested around Diablos, drawn by his beacon. One of the shades swirled rapidly around Diablos and shooed away all others. The apparition approached the mass in Diablos' hand and was absorbed. Then, Diablos jammed the darkness into the chest cavity of the body before him.

"Was that it?" Ostero inquired.

Diablos nodded. "Now let's see if your science can handle my woo-woo."

For several seconds, nothing happened. Then the flesh inside the plaster scaffold began to pulsate. The protective covering creaked and cracked and gave way to the rising flesh. Ostero looked on as a father might during the birth of their first child.

Finally, the scaffold peeled away to reveal a man who was over seven feet tall. His eyes opened, then he stood, admired his new body, and yelled, "Akibeel, son of Azazel, is reborn!"

Diablos pressed his finger to the device in his hand, and a small red light shone for a second, then gave way to a green light.

"Welcome back to the land of the living, Akibeel."

"You're Diablos, Lord of the Fallen. Where is my father, the Lord of the Watchers?"

"Your father is no more. I rule the Fallen and the Watchers now, or what's left of them."

Akibeel stared wild-eyed at Diablos and then at Ostero.

"I want no part of you. I'll go and seek out those witches who wronged me. They will know my wrath and vengeance."

"I'm afraid not, Akibeel. You will follow Dr. Ostero here and help him finish his work."

"I-I.." Akibeel's eyes twitched. "I will follow Dr. Ostero."

Diablos grinned wickedly. "Incredible, Doctor. I'm very pleased. How is Phase Two progressing?"

Ostero adjusted his glasses. "That is going to take more time."

"Well, now you have help. He should be…" Diablos stopped in mid-sentence and stared into the distance. He reached into the pocket of his Italian suit, drew out a sigil, the hollow tree, and looked at it with a smirk.

"Is everything all right?" Ostero queried.

"Yes, more than all right. It seems a problem has resolved itself quite nicely," Diablos said as he put the sigil back into his pocket. "Continue the good work, Dr. Ostero. The world will soon witness the rise of the damned."

AUTHOR NOTES
OCTOBER 14, 2022

G.Z.

As a reader, it was simple enough to grab a book, find a comfy setting, and in a matter of minutes, critique the manuscript.

Now, on the opposite side of the spectrum, I've come to realize what a daunting process it is to be an author.

Don't misunderstand, being an author is exhilarating, but the writing process can be a challenge at times.

What took minutes to critique as a reader may have been hours, days, weeks, or even months to write. Plot points, settings, character development, research, the rewrites are just a few elements an author must face. As we complete the fourth installment of this series, I need to take the time to thank all those authors whose books I've read. Being an author has made me appreciate you more.

In addition, lots of appreciation for the excellent team at LMBPN. To Michael, Robin and Steve, thank you for believing in us and the Progeny Wars Series. Thanks to

Kelly, whose inputs and direction are like gold nuggets. To our editor, Lynn, we are very grateful for your time.

To David, Mary, and Rachel, the beta team, you guys are brutal but we don't mind at all the input – thanks.

To the home team (Wined, Levi, and Timothy), thank you so much for your patience. It's not easy being away from you guys when it's time to write, and I know you feel it as well, but how great to have your encouragement and support. Love you, guys!

Lastly, to the one and only my Perry Kletos – the biggest thank you yet. You're my comforter, supporter, and light. For those wondering who Perry Kletos is, read on – you'll find out.

D.J.

When G.Z. and I started working on the first book, we jotted down a ton of ideas that didn't make it into the first three books. We spent countless hours building out the world for ourselves, so we could connect with the motivations of the characters, but so much of that content couldn't make it into the manuscripts. We are overjoyed to be able to bring so many of these ideas to light now in this next trilogy.

Working on this series with G.Z. has been quite the journey. If you'd asked me 3 years ago if we'd even be able to publish the first book, much less be publishing the fourth, I'd say you were crazy. Yet here we are. Thank you so much to everyone who's traversed these troubled waters with us.

Our undying gratitude to the LMBPN family for

believing in us and supporting us through the creative process. Everyone has been amazing, and it's been a joy working with all of you.

To my friends and family, thank you for your patience, understanding and grace as I disappear for days when inspiration strikes. I couldn't do this without your love and support.

To the Sovereign One, Carpenter's Son and Perry, be the highest praise and honor forever and ever.

BOOKS FROM G.Z. RODRIGUEZ AND D.J. VARGAS

The Progeny Wars

Daughters of the Watchers (Book 1)
Sons of the Lords (Book 2)
Children of the Mortals (Book 3)
Daughters of the Primals (Book 4)
Sons of the Damned (Book 5 - coming soon)

CONNECT WITH THE AUTHORS

Connect with G.Z. Rodriguez and D.J. Vargas

Facebook: https://www.facebook.com/gzdjauthors

OTHER BOOKS FROM LMBPN PUBLISHING

Sign up for the LMBPN email list to be notified of new releases and special deals!

https://lmbpn.com/email/

For a complete list of books by LMBPN please visit:

https://lmbpn.com/books-by-lmbpn-publishing/

Made in the USA
Coppell, TX
23 October 2022

85151781R00194